THE SILVER LINING
THE SILVERIES
BOOK FOUR

ANGELA DANDY

This edition published in 2024 by Cottrill Publishing
Copyright © Angela Dandy 2024

ISBN 978-1-917326-00-1 (paperback 1st edition)
ISBN 978-1-917326-01-8 (ebook 1st edition)

ACKNOWLEDGEMENT

Special thanks to Phil and Jane for working their way paragraph by paragraph through my draft and providing me with invaluable feedback. And thanks to Valerie, Linda and Jan for reading through my final manuscript giving me the confidence to 'call it a wrap'. This list would not be complete without mention of the exemplary work of my copy editor, Claire Cronshaw and the wizardry, technical know-how and infinite patience of Gavin Kemp.

THE SILVERIES SERIES

Thank you for reading my Silveries series of books. Apart from aging – just a little – most of my characters remain the same throughout the series, except some come and some go! Reading the principle novels in order will enrich your experience although each novel can equally be read apart from the others. From time to time, I happen upon gaps in my series story line. It is then that I write a novella. California Dreaming, the novella, is one such, "In the beginning…"

—

The Silveries series

PROLOGUE

I t's a funny world to an old codger like me…well not that old – that's a forbidden word at Magnolia Court, according to Mrs A. "Stan," she used to say, "You are never too old and there is no such word as *can't*." Put me right in my place, she did. Always nicely, mind. Salt of the earth, if you can describe a lady that way. Sadly missed.

Stan Morrison, in case you haven't gathered. You probably know me as the builder and the man who sits up all hours with the late Henry, putting the world to rights. I'm a lucky man to have Henry's old cottage – one of twelve – and that's thanks to Mrs A as well.

We've had some real good heart-to-hearts lately, Henry and me. Everything from genders and woke, to knives and guns, to the north–south divide, immigration, and wars, not to mention politicians and their policies that are going to transform our lives, this year, next year, sometime never. Course, he doesn't answer my questions, but I know what he's thinking.

You hear about it and watch it on the box, listen to it on the radio and read about it in the papers, and then like as not, you put it out of mind and switch your thoughts to something that doesn't give you nightmares.

Until you find that it's not just happening *there*, it's happening *here* – down the road, next door, or right under your own nose.

And then you've got a decision to make. Do you step up or walk away?

MAGNOLIA COURT RETIREMENT COMPLEX

Magnolia trees line the sweeping drive up to the 19th-century Mansion House. Magnolia Court lies just a few miles outside of Stroud, Gloucestershire. The heart and soul of the community, the Mansion House is where residents congregate to laugh, chat, plan outings and events, manage the day-to-day running of the complex, and at the end of the day, enjoy a cocktail or two.

The Residents – May 2022

Max and Hetty Brightwell
Dot and Dennis Gardener
Duncan and Jennifer Gillespie
Emanuel and Dinah Levin
Sam and Jasmine Brown
Paul and Ros Gardener
Gerald Foxworthy and Thomas Littleton
Andy Finmere
Peter Smith
Stan Morrison

I

ENGLAND
2022

"Hey, you! Anyone ever taught you to drive?" Stan yelled. It hadn't been a soft landing, either. One moment, quietly going about his business, the next finding himself sitting on his backside, legs sprawled in the air. Stan was not amused. Coming out of nowhere at breakneck speed, the car, a red Hyundai Tuscon, had come to a halt no more than two feet away from where he stood. Any closer and the next conversation would have been with his maker.

A woman leapt down, quickly rounding the front of the car. "Whoa. Sorry, mate. Signpost came right up out of nowhere. Had to swing her round sharp, or I'd have gone straight past. Blind spot on that corner. Why you Poms put signposts behind trees that nobody can see beats me!"

"Pom, hey? Might have known it. Ossie," Stan said.

"Hit the nail on the head. From down under or up over, depending upon if you're here or there," she said.

"Too early," Stan said, rubbing his legs. "You could have driven on a bit further, turned around, and made a less dramatic entrance. Or didn't that cross your mind?"

"Need a hand up?" she asked.

Stan frowned. And how did this five foot nothing, skinny woman of seriously mature years think for one moment that she might help a six foot plus, sixteen stone man get to his feet? Stupid woman.

"Now, let's take a squiz at you," she said.

One minute he was down. The next on his feet. "Squiz?" Stan grimaced. "A squiz?"

"Squiz," the woman replied. "Never heard of a squiz before? Where've you been hiding all your life? Let's take a look at you. That's what a squiz is, for future reference."

Speechless, Stan stood still as the woman ran her hands down his arms, his torso, and right down his legs.

"You'll live," she said, standing back, hands on hips.

"Ma'am. I'm not at all sure that was at all proper," Stan said.

"Just checking you out the same way as I'd check out a horse. For broken bones, that is. Nothing personal. Don't go getting your hopes up. Nothing broken."

"Kind of you, ma'am. May I ask…" Stan started. The mist was starting to clear..

"Penny. Pen to my friends, by special request."

Stan chuckled. Who else? Who else would have the gall to knock a man half off his feet, demolish a gate post, dust him down, and then tell him, albeit in other words, to get on with it? "Don't tell me. You're Amy's little sister."

"Yep. Penny Reilly. How did you guess?"

"Couple of clues," Stan said. "Australian. Feisty. About the same size and build. Not backward in coming forward. The little sister, as she called you. Amy told me all about you. Need I say more?"

"Twenty years little and only an inch shorter in height, to be precise. You might find it hard to believe, but there was a time when I was a lady just like my sister. In there somewhere she is, but doesn't often surface these days. Might have got a few rough edges after spending most of my life on a ranch with a load of farmhands. You must be Stan."

"Correct," Stan replied, impressed that she knew.

"She wrote a lot about you. Good, I hasten to add. Stan, the man who worked on the original build and Stan, the man who not so long back built two new cottages and rebuilt the old stables. Right? And Stan, the man who moved into Henry's cottage when he died. And a very dear friend to my sister. Thought the world of you. Not so sure that I can see why, right at this minute, but time will tell. Know more about you than you know about yourself. Amy wrote long letters."

"Nearest thing to a real mum I ever had. Loved her to bits. Miss her. Every day."

"Guess you weren't expecting me?" Penny said.

"Wrong. We were expecting you, but as far as I know, you didn't tell anybody when."

"Didn't I? Must have slipped my mind. Guess the cremation was okay?" Penny asked. "Just like my sister. She always did do things her way."

"All fine thank you. She left it to you to decide where you want her ashes to be scattered. Right now, she's in a pot in the Mansion House."

"Thanksgiving service next Sunday. Right?"

Stan nodded. "All organised. Down to her very last wish."

"Got something right, at least," Penny said, stepping back and squinting at the gatepost. "Looks to me like I arrived in the nick of time."

"An interesting way of putting it." Stan laughed. "I'll have you know I was up to the last layer of bricks before the demolition squad showed up."

"Heard of a level?" Penny pointed at the three remaining rows of bricks that she hadn't managed to demolish. "Don't look level to me. You might think about taking it right back down and building it up again. Built a few walls in my time. Mostly dry stone, but the odd brick one too."

Stan bit his tongue. He had better choose his words carefully. She was a woman, after all. "What's that?" Stan said, pointing to the level on the grass verge. "I'll have you know I've been building walls since I was sixteen years old. Walls and houses. Plenty of them. I don't need to use a level to know when my bricks are laid level."

"Hmm. Let's see about that," Penny said, picking the level up and placing it on top of the bricks. "Am I right or am I wrong?"

Turning the level this way and that, Stan narrowed his eyes. There was no denying it. The damned woman was right. "Marginal," he muttered. "And by the way, you're blocking the drive."

"Expecting guests?" Penny asked, seeming unconcerned. "Can't see there being too many visitors at this time of the morning. What time is it, anyway?" Penny glanced at the two watches on her wrist. "One's set to Australian time. One's on your time. So, it's six forty-five your time, to answer my own question. Plane landed at one thirty – your time – two hours late. The queue at immigration – halfway down the runway. Baggage collection. Waited by that carousel for a good hour before the first case came off. Peep peep. A dozen cases and it stopped again. Peep peep, and off it went again."

Stan went to speak but it seemed that she was off on a roll.

"And, you know, the same cases went round and round a dozen times before they were claimed. Rental wasn't that bad, at least not the paperwork. Took me an hour to find the car. Not a soul in sight. Worse than the Marie Celeste. Nobody to ask. Is everyone on strike in this country, or is it always this bad?"

"Covid, Penny. Nothing's been the same since. Train drivers, nurses, doctors, teachers, you name it and they're either on strike or threatening to go on strike. How's it in Australia?" Stan asked.

"Doesn't happen often. Least not for essential services," Penny said. "Anyway, as I was saying, must have been almost five when I hit the road. Clear roads. Satnav seemed to know where it was going, but it's not great at reading signposts. Did I say sorry?"

"You did," Stan said, mulling over the fact that she probably hadn't slept for thirty-six hours but had still managed to drive from Heathrow to Stroud in less than two hours.

"Least I can do is help you rebuild that post. Two hands better than one. Let's get to it."

It was a rare occasion when Stan found himself lost for words. It was an even rarer occasion to have a near dice with death with a red Hyundai. It was unheard of for anyone, especially a woman, to criticise his building skills. Penny, like her dear departed sister, was no ordinary woman.

"I see you've still got plenty of mortar mix. Right, I'll start scraping the mortar off those bricks on the ground. You dismantle the rest of that lot. Then we'll start re-laying. And, when we've done one level, we'll both of us check it out with that level. Sound good to you?"

After carefully setting the final layer of bricks in place and checking it with the level, Stan tidied and scraped the loose mortar away and stood back. "Satisfied?" he asked.

"Good job. That'll last for the next fifty years, provided someone like me doesn't cut that corner." Penny raised her eyebrows and looked up at Stan. "And while we're about it, why don't we—"

"Shift the sign?

"Mind-reader as well as a brick layer, hey, Stan? You need that sign for Magnolia fifty yards up the road. Not inside the gatepost where no one can see it."

"Tried that. Planning said no," Stan replied.

"What's new? Same problem back home. Jobsworths. You want a lift with all that stuff back up the track to the village?"

"Don't mind if I do," Stan said. "And it's not a village. A village is…No, but I won't confuse you with that, for the moment."

They headed for the car, loaded up, and got in.

"We're going to get along just fine, Stan," Penny said, crunching the gears. "First time I've reversed this thing. Didn't think to ask for an automatic."

Stan squeezed his eyes tight shut, leant well back in the passenger seat, and pulled the seatbelt tight around him.

"Don't tell me. Those are magnolia trees. Hence the name of this place," Penny said, gazing left and right, everywhere but on the track ahead. "I miss the show this year?"

"Yes, and yes. Flower in March and April, long over by May. Stick around long enough and you'll see them next year," Stan replied. There was no harm in a bit of fishing, but she didn't rise to the bait.

"Who's that?" Penny pointed to the left. "Nice bit of kit. Got a couple like that for riding around on the ranch. Used to be horses once. Now it's horsepower. Know what I prefer."

"That's Dennis. One of the residents. He's an early bird too. Not too fussy about waking everyone up with the ride-on. We're used to it. He and Dot look after the grounds. That's his pride and joy. Once he's got his earmuffs on and his head down, he's in a world of his own. Car park dead ahead on the right."

"Well, get an eyeful of that," Penny exclaimed. "She told me it was something, but that…"

"That's the Mansion House. Not bad, hey?" Stan grinned as he looked at it with fresh eyes.

"Pretty damned impressive," Penny said. "Hmm. Still, pretty early to go waking folks up to get the key to Amy's cottage."

"Duncan's got the key, and for an unexpected guest, yes, it's way too early," Stan said. "You've caught them all napping. If they'd known you were turning up today, the girls would have been in there cleaning and polishing…I hope you like cake."

"I hate cake. Pet hate of mine. Never made one in my life and spent my whole life trying to avoid eating it. Mind you, I'm a pretty good cook on most else."

Stan chuckled. Everyone at Magnolia ate cake. It was the go-to for every possible occasion.

"Guess it's not the famous cocktail hour, either. Amy told me about that. I'd kill for a beer," Penny said, cutting the corner into the car park, leaving tyre tracks across the edge of the lawn.

"Six o'clock. Ten hours' time," Stan replied.

"Back home it's five, maybe six in the afternoon. Sun's always somewhere over the yardarm. Guess I'll have to kick my heels right here for a couple of hours. Not a bad car park as they go. Nice view," Penny said, leaning back in the driver's seat.

"Or kick your heels in my cottage. You're welcome, and it just so happens I've got a few beers in the fridge. How does that sound? Don't mind if I don't join you, do you?" Stan said. "I'll carry your bags for you, and I'll ring Duncan later."

"Oh, my, a gentleman as well," Penny said, leaping out before opening the car boot. "Just the two cases. Prefer to travel light."

"Not planning on staying for long then?" Stan asked.

Penny shrugged her shoulders.

Picking up the heavy case, leaving the smaller one for Stan to carry, Penny stopped and looked down at the tyre tracks in the grass. "Strewth! Did I do that?"

Stan nodded.

"I'll apologise to – what did you say his name was?" Penny asked.

"Dennis." Stan smiled.

2

ENGLAND

2022

"Don't ask me. It wasn't here last night. Maybe somebody's dumped it. Andy, can you check it out, please?" Max said, pointing under the car.

"Check it out? You mean for bombs, that sort of thing? I've done most things in my time, but bomb disposal isn't one of them. But since you ask…Nothing to beat a bit of morning Zumba," Andy said, lowering himself to the ground and gradually easing his head and half of his body under the van. "Looks oddly like a car to me. Engine. Drive shaft. Exhaust. Four wheels. Not many miles on the clock. Nothing here that shouldn't be. Can I come out now?"

"I'm on it, Max," Duncan called, keeping his distance. "Checking the number plate right now. A few seconds, please… Genuine plate. Rental vehicle. Red Hyundai Tuscon." Duncan tapped away at the keyboard.

"Who's the renter?" Max asked.

"One job at a time, Max," Duncan said.

"Picked up from Heathrow at four-thirty this morning. Renter's name…Wait for this"—Duncan took a deep breath, a half-smile crossing his face—"Penny Reilly. Mrs Penny Reilly. Surprise, surprise."

"Do we know this Penny Reilly?" Thomas whispered to Gerald. "Am I missing something here? Why has Duncan got a grin like a Cheshire cat?"

"Oh, Thomas, don't you take anything in?" Gerald laughed. "It's Amy's sister. This'll put the cat among the pigeons, you mark my words. Don't you remember Amy telling us she qualified as a barrister or was it a solicitor and then upped sticks to Australia to marry a sheep farmer?"

"Really?" Thomas frowned. "Better watch your step, Gerald. None of your old tricks!"

"Not Penny Reilly." Hetty looked at Max. "After all these years, and now she just turns up here out of the blue, unannounced," Hetty said indignantly. If there was one thing Hetty was not keen on, it was people dropping in, unless of course they were Magnolia Court residents, and then only at a reasonable time of day. Given plenty of notice, nothing fazed her, but this was unacceptable. "All the way from Australia. Ridiculous, Max. And where's she going to sleep? We haven't even changed the bed yet. Did you know about this, Duncan? If you did, I wish you'd let the rest of us in on the secret. It's too bad."

"Steady, Hetty," Max said, resting his hand on his wife's shoulder. "We can't be surprised that she's come over, what with Amy's memorial service coming up. A little notice would have helped, I must agree."

"Clearly not, Hetty," Duncan said. "But I am looking forward to meeting her. I know about as much as you. The last time I spoke to her was when I rang her to tell her about the will and that Amy had left the cottage to her. Haven't heard a dicky bird from her since."

"Look at me," Jennifer said. "Old jeans, a tatty sweater, and my roots growing out. If I'd known, I'd have made more of an effort...I look a mess."

"You look beautiful, my love – as always," Duncan said. It was little less than a week since they'd made their wedding vows. Duncan was besotted. Always had been. Never in his wildest dreams had he thought she would say yes. "Now, before you all get too het up, think about it. Isn't this just the sort of thing that Amy would do? Turn up out of the blue? I've got a feeling in my water..."

"I want to know who's going to repair this corner of the lawn," Dennis said. "That green was nigh on perfect. Ready for the summer. Ready for croquet, and now look at it."

"Stop fussing, Dennis. It's a bit of old grass. With all the rain we're having, it'll be green again in a couple of days," Dot said.

"Hey, we missing out on something?" Sam shouted, marching up towards the car park, hand in hand with Jas. "Heard the racket from the cottage. What gives, guys?"

"Penny. Penny Reilly. That's what gives, Sam. It appears she has turned up all the way from down under," Max explained. "But we seem to have lost her."

"Wow. That's something alright," Jas said. "Hiding inside that car, is she?"

"Not that I can see," Andy replied. "And, what's more, she's not under it, either."

"So where is she?" Hetty asked. It was exasperating, to say the least.

"On her way." Jennifer shielded her eyes from the morning sun. "That's got to be her, and she's with Stan."

"David and Goliath," Thomas whispered. "They make an odd couple."

"A little pre-emptive, Thomas, old chap." Gerald grinned. "But you never know."

Max cleared his throat and waved to everybody to gather around. "Right, everybody. All hands to the pump. Let's give Penny Reilly a proper Magnolia welcome. Time now is fifteen forty hours. Rendezvous sixteen hundred hours in the Mansion House. Sam, you go and tell Paul and Ros. Jennifer, you alert Peter. Duncan, can you ring Dinah and see if Emanuel's up to an outing this afternoon? Hetty, Dot, you open up the Mansion House, put the heating on if it's cold in there, and get the kettle boiling. The rest of us – Thomas, Gerald, Andy, Dot, Dennis, Jas and I will form a reception committee and keep her here until you've had time to set up."

"Red Leader speaks," Gerald said. "Stand to attention!"

"I didn't wake you, did I?" Stan asked, setting a cup of tea down beside Penny.

"Wake me? From what? Don't I know you?" Penny mumbled, half awake, half asleep.

"You knocked down my gatepost just over eight hours ago. Ring a bell?" Stan grinned. "Take sugar?"

"Hell, no. Bad for your teeth. Not good for your weight, either. Thanks." Raising the mug to her lips, Penny grimaced. "Tea! You English."

"Sorry about the state of the bathroom. Did you find the clean towels?" Stan asked.

"Yep. Best shower I've had in days. Only shower as it happens. Nice shower gel. Mint and cucumber. How long have I been out?"

"Seven hours, give or take. It's just after three fifteen, and if I'm not mistaken, there'll be a party of residents surrounding that car right now, wondering what it's doing in Magnolia's car park.

Leave it much longer and someone will be calling the police to have it removed. How about we go and put them out of their misery?" Stan grinned. Now, this he was looking forward to.

"Thought you were going to call that Duncan?" Penny said.

"I decided to wait until you woke up. When I looked in on you a couple of hours ago, you were spark out. How about we just stroll over there?"

"Bet I look like I've been dragged through a hedge backwards. You can be honest with me, Stan," Penny said, dragging her fingers through her greying, wispy hair.

Stan raised his eyebrows.

Penny grimaced. "That look says it all."

"Earl grey or English breakfast, Penny?" Hetty asked, one pot in each hand.

"A slice of cake, Penny?" Dot handed her a plate.

"Bad for your teeth and bad for your weight too," Stan whispered in her ear.

"Don't mind if I do. Thanks." Penny grinned, glancing sideways at Stan and whispering in his ear, "Wouldn't have a beer, would they?"

"Tea and cake first. Drinks later. That's the way it works here." Stan winked at her.

"English, please, Hetty. When in Rome, do as the Romans do, isn't that right?" Penny held her cup up under the teapot and watched as the dark liquid flowed from the spout into her cup, followed by a dash of milk.

Max waited patiently until everyone had been served tea and cake before tapping his spoon on his cup. "Ladies and gentlemen. If I may have your attention, I'd like to say a few words." The room quietened, all eyes turned to Max. "I'd like us all to extend a warm welcome to Penny Reilly, who you all know is our dear Amy's younger sister." Max smiled at Penny and organized his thoughts. "From the few brief words that I've exchanged with her, I understand she left her home in Australia almost two days ago to come here. Quite a feat for somebody – what shall I say – for someone not so young?"

Penny narrowed her eyes – not so young indeed!

"We all know how much Amy loved her sister and how much she looked forward to being reunited with her one day. To be able to visit her in Australia was one of her dearest wishes. Sadly, it was not to be. More than anything, we know that Amy would want us to make Penny welcome among us. Let's put our hands together for Penny."

In true Magnolia style, the residents put their hands together and clapped loudly, Peter less enthusiastically than the rest. Patience was not his middle name. It was all very well, but was nobody going to ask the burning question? Peter stood up. "Of course, you're most welcome here, Penny. I, like all my friends, am delighted to meet you at last. But would you mind if I asked you a question? The question I have is, what brings you here?"

"Peter!" Ros exclaimed. "Don't you think that's being just a little insensitive? We know why Penny's here. To pay respect to her sister. And to come to her memorial service, of course. Wouldn't all sisters do the same?"

Peter flushed crimson. Maybe he could have phrased it slightly better. He was no diplomat, either. "No offence intended, dear lady. What I meant to ask is, have you given any thoughts as to how and when you will be selling Amy's cottage? Maybe the question is a little premature. If so, forgive me for raising the subject."

"None taken," Penny said. "Hell, no. Give me straight-talking any day. I'm all for it."

Stan grinned. So much alike, the two of them – Amy and Penny, Penny and Amy – made in the same mould.

"Ask whatever you like. Spent the last forty years beating around the bush – literally – and like my sister before me, I believe that an honest question deserves an honest answer."

Penny drew in her breath. She'd had plenty of time to think about it on the plane, but if she were honest, she still wasn't at all sure. Maybe she'd stay for a while, maybe she'd stay for longer, maybe she'd stay forever. It depended. The only certainty in her mind was that she'd had to make the journey to England, not just to pay her respects to Amy, but because of what Amy had said in her last letter. Something that Amy wanted her to do, which she couldn't do from the other side of the world. Reading between the lines, it had occurred to Penny that there was nothing Amy would have liked more than for her to take up residence at Magnolia.

Peter had asked a straight question, and she'd said that he would have a straight answer. On balance, she might stay. If she changed her mind later, then so be it. That would be her prerogative.

"If you will have me, then I plan to stay in England, live in my sister's cottage, and be a part of this wonderful community that my sister has told me so much about." There, she'd said it. Not without a twinge of conscience and not without noticing the sideways glance from Stan.

"Well, that's clear enough," Duncan said, breaking the silence. "That makes the matter a whole lot clearer. Wouldn't you agree, Peter?"

"I would indeed. Less money in solicitors' pockets, no bloody estate agents, no viewers wandering around Magnolia…Neat and tidy," Peter said, nodding his head in approval. She'd do. A woman after his own heart.

"But what about your family in Australia? Won't you miss them?" Jennifer asked.

"Lost Bluey ten years ago now. Died young – younger than he should. The boys are grown up – men. Grandchildren won't be long before they fly the nest. The ranch is in safe hands," Penny said, wondering what other disasters had occurred since she'd left. "My time now. Time to do what I please and when I please and not what they all think is best for me. Mean well, they do, but over-protective. Have been since Bluey died," Penny said. At least that part of the story was true.

"They can be," Jennifer replied, remembering how Jamie had sat her down and given her the fifth degree when she'd told him that she and Duncan planned to get married.

"Bought me a rocking chair and put it on the deck. That's where I'm supposed to sit and read. Never have been a reader. Books have never been my thing. Don't get me wrong. The boys have my best interests at heart. Forget that I'd been herding sheep and chasing roos for forty years or more…"

"Sounds idyllic to me. Not the herding sheep or the roos, mind you," Jennifer said.

"Not my style, Jennifer. Can't sit still for five minutes. Can't watch other people doing things I know I can do myself. Used to envy Amy. Wrote regularly telling me all about what you folks were up to. There's me rocking backwards and forwards in the back end of beyond, and there's Amy, twenty years older, having the time of her life."

"And how did they take it? The family, I mean," Jennifer persisted.

"Didn't believe me at first. Did believe me when I showed them the air ticket. We talked it out and they came round.

Wouldn't be surprised to see one or more of them turn up on the doorstep in the not-so-distant future to see if I'm taking it easy – which, let me tell you, is not part of my plan. Amy said that you all muck in to keep this place together, and that's precisely what I plan to do if you'll let me."

Max stood up and squared his shoulders. "Thank you, Penny. It seems to me that, since we are all here, we should take a vote on Penny coming to live with us at Magnolia. Are there any dissenters?"

There were none.

"Excuse me." Gerald raised his arm. "Isn't it traditional to break open the bar when we have a new resident? What will it be, Penny?"

"A beer would hit the spot, and, my apologies, I've forgotten your name already." Penny's face lit up.

"Gerald. Gerald Foxworthy, at your service. We happen to have a local brewery just down the road. Stroud Brewery. Organic. How does a Tom Long Amber Bitter sound to you?"

"Painful, but is it cold?"

"I can put some ice in it, if you like." Gerald grinned.

3

BUCHAREST

E lena glanced across at her sister, her blonde hair splaying across the pillow and spilling down to the floor. Her eyelids flickered, her long lashes brushing the soft, pale skin beneath her eyes; she muttered contentedly in her sleep. Irina was beautiful, inside and out, a stranger to unkind thoughts – a girl who smiled her way through the day and the night, a girl who never coveted her neighbour, a girl who was totally comfortable in her own skin and wanted nothing. Unlike herself.

Elena could not settle. The sheet she lay on was of a course cotton that irritated her skin. The stuffing in the ancient synthetic pillow had long since coagulated into hard uneven lumps and dug into her cheek as she tried every which way to get comfortable. A frayed, almost threadbare blanket barely reached from her feet to her shoulders, but she was not cold.

Glancing once more at the sleeping figure in the bed alongside her, Elena felt a moment of envy tinged with anger. Was this all there was to look forward to in the future? Living in a ninth-floor apartment of a twenty-storey block in what was probably still the most neglected part of Bucharest. Ferentari, a neighbourhood that had not long since been described as one of the most dangerous places to visit in the world. A no-go area. Thankfully, that was no longer the case. It had become an embarrassment to the government, an embarrassment to the country. It had been improved. Apartments had been renovated, attracting more and more families and working-class people to move in. There were supermarkets, restaurants, and bars but the residents still lived cheek to jowl, their apartments divided one from the other by paper-thin walls, sharing the same odorous concrete staircases, the only access in the absence of well-maintained lifts. The crime rate had fallen, but it was still Ferentari. Once it had frightened her, the walk to school fraught with danger. Now it didn't. The way to survive was to walk with a purpose, head held high, looking neither left nor right.

Elena's plans for her future did not include Ferentari. Neither did they include Irina. The reason that she could not sleep.

Elena reached for the mobile phone that lay on the wooden floor beside her bed and stroked it fondly. Given to her by her late grandmother, it was her lifeline and her window on the world. A lifeline that had opened her eyes to the endless opportunities beyond Ferentari, beyond Bucharest – opportunities to which she, like anybody else, was entitled. All she had to do was make that first move.

Irina had been given a phone too. It had been of little or no interest to her. Uncharged and untouched, it lay buried in a drawer.

Elena cherished her phone. Working for a pittance on Saturdays and Sundays in a nearby café, she handed her wage to her mother each week, pocketing the tips she made. The more tips she made, the more data she could afford to buy. There was nothing more important in her life, and nothing she wouldn't sacrifice to stay in touch with the world. Going out to cafés to meet friends or going to the cinema were luxuries she'd never been able to afford and didn't miss. Her wardrobe comprised two

sets of school wear, a couple of pairs of jeans and T-shirts, a few
sweaters for when the days were cold, an anorak, one pair of
synthetic, brown leather shoes, and one pair of well-worn
trainers.

There were moments when she resented handing over her
hard-earned cash, but she understood. Money was tight. Tata was
the only breadwinner in the family. Working all hours God sent on
building sites and grabbing every opportunity of overtime that
came his way, it still wasn't sufficient to keep a family of eight,
soon to be nine, clothed and fed.

Serghei, one of four boys, fast approaching five years old, was
the latest addition to the family. Alexandru, twelve, Luca, ten, and
Danut, eight, had been born two years apart. Elena and Irina were
the oldest of the siblings. The apartment was small and claustro-
phobic. Too small for such a sizeable family. The four boys slept
in the second bedroom in bunk beds separated by no more than a
few feet of floor space. Tata and Mama occupied what was
euphemistically called the master bedroom, while Elena and Irina
occupied the box room at the back of the apartment. The kitchen
was the hub and the only room in the house that was permanently
warm. It was there that Mama and Irina cooked, the family ate
together, they watched television, and Elena tried to do her
homework.

Yes, Elena understood the economics of the situation, but she
would never, ever understand how they could deny her the opportunity to improve herself. What had once been gratitude for food
on the table, a roof over her head, and clothes on her back had
long since turned to resentment, albeit silent resentment.

Elena had a thirst for learning, and she was bright, very bright.
Consistently excelling in exams, she had a brilliant career ahead of
her – so her teachers repeatedly reminded her. The school had
rarely had such a mathematician in their midst. Baccalaureate was

a certainty with the strong probability of a scholarship to a top-class university to follow.

It both hurt and angered her that Tata and Mama were seemingly so unimpressed with her achievements. Her school reports were barely scanned, never discussed, and within days – at times, hours – to be found in the recycling. Routinely, Elena rescued them and boxed them away for the future.

Elena would soon be packing her satchel for the last time. Her education would be at an end. Her fate had been cast by Mama and Tata. She would be starting in full-time employment within weeks.

Unusually, there had been tantrums, stand-up rows, and one occasion when her mother, known for her volatility, had lost her temper with her completely. Elena was called a selfish, spoilt brat who had no respect for either her mother or her father, who both knew, far better than she, what was good for her and, moreover, good for the family. It was time she earned a real wage – paid her way. She'd responded by saying it was shortsighted. If she completed her education, then she could bring some real money into the family. In time, they'd said, when she had a family of her own, she would understand. Elena hoped and prayed that day would never come. From time to time, she thought she'd caught a soulful look from Tata. Maybe Tata Albescu understood, but it was Mama who wore the trousers in the family.

Elena's resentment doubled by the minute, by the hour, by the day.

And there was her sister, slumbering happily after a day of school – albeit a vocational one – followed by working side by side with her mother in the kitchen from the moment she'd got home until the moment the lights had been turned out and all the family had gone to bed. All without a murmur of dissatisfaction.

Irina was a natural homemaker, a domestic goddess, happy to

wash, iron, mend, clean, cook, and look after her brothers. What little schoolwork she brought home lay untouched. Like the phone, it was of no interest to her. Instinctively, she knew that this was where her future lay. Meeting a man she loved, she would get married, bear a family, and happily pass the rest of her days in their service. It was from this that she drew her contentment.

Elena was soon to reach her sixteenth birthday and had been blessed with good looks. She had inherited her father's genes. Tata was six foot three in his stockinged feet and towered over Mama, who was portly. Elena, at five foot seven, could easily have been mistaken for being older – seventeen, eighteen, or even nineteen. She was well-endowed, with long blonde hair reaching down to her waist. She had a perfect complexion; there was no need for expensive make-up. With perfect teeth, she never needed to visit a dentist, and she had never stepped foot into a doctor's surgery or a hospital, other than for routine vaccinations. Elena had no time for vanity.

Resting the side of her head on the lumpy pillow, Elena turned to face the wall, switched her phone on, and opened the browser to the same page – the page that had drawn her back time and again for the past three days.

4
BUCHAREST
2021

E lena chose a small table outside the café, tucked away in a corner under a parasol. The café was buzzing, waitresses scurrying back and forward between the kitchen and the tables. Hoping she might not be spotted and asked to place an order, Elena buried her head in her phone. What little money she had in her pocket would not cover the cost of a glass of water let alone a cup of coffee at such an establishment. It had been Miriana's choice of café.

"*Draga mea.* You must be Elena."

Elena looked up. Walking towards her was a smartly dressed woman wearing the highest stilettos she had ever seen. She was stunning. Dressed in a red tailored blazer, white roll neck top, and white cropped trousers, her shoes were red patent, a perfect match with the blazer. She might easily have walked straight out of a magazine. Make-up immaculate, her dark hair was cropped short, framing a perfectly oval face. Elena hardly recognised her – so much more elegant and beautiful than the photograph on her webpage. Her head held high, her shoulders back, she exuded confidence. Elena glanced down at her own appearance and momentarily considered taking flight.

"Miriana?" Elena asked.

"How did you guess?" Miriana said, stepping back and taking Elena in at a glance. "Beautiful. Quite beautiful, young lady. Clever, ambitious and beautiful as well. My, that's a winning combination. I'm delighted to meet you, my dear Elena. Thank you for coming to meet me today."

"No, no, no," Elena stuttered shyly. "It's me who should be thanking you."

"You're sweet," Miriana said.

Not used to such compliments, Elena felt herself colour crimson and bit her lip. "And you're very kind."

"Just honest, Elena. No need to be shy. Now, thank you for speaking English today as requested. That's your first test. We can only help those candidates who are fluent in English."

Elena nodded. "It's one of my best subjects. Nine point five. And nine point five in all other subjects as well. I finished grade nine a couple of weeks ago and then left school."

"No ten out of tens! Maybe I'll have to reconsider." Miriana laughed. Elena's face fell. "I'm joking, Elena. Those results are more than impressive. Let's start from the beginning. Tell me about yourself. But first let's order. Coffee and pastries okay with you?"

"Tap water would do fine, thank you very much." Elena jangled the few tiny coins she had in her pocket. "I really can't stop long. I'm on my lunch break and I'll lose an hour's pay if I'm late back."

"Lunch, hey? Well, a glass of water isn't lunch in my book. Neither is a pastry and coffee, but it's better than nothing. That's what we'll both have," Miriana said, waving her hand in the direction of a waitress before turning back to Elena. "Now where were we? Ah yes, you were going to start from the beginning and tell me all about yourself and why you wanted to meet up with me today."

"Your website. It said that education could be organised for me and that I could earn fifty thousand pounds a year with the right qualifications. If I was earning that sort of money, then Mama and Tata would never have to worry again. I could support the whole family," Elena started, almost falling over her words with excitement.

"Wow, cut to the chase, don't you!" Miriana said.

"I'm sorry, I don't know that one. Can you explain it to me, please?" Elena asked.

"It means that you go straight to the point. You don't go around the houses…In England they use so many clichés you fall over them. You'll get used to them." Miriana laughed. "You know what you want, which is very commendable, and you are ambitious. That is good too."

"Beat around the bush. That's another one, isn't it?" Elena grinned.

"And smart too," Miriana said. "You mentioned a family? You have a big family?"

"Mama and Tata of course. Then there's Irina, my sister, four brothers and another baby on the way. There'll be nine of us before long."

"A sister as well? How old is she?"

"Just a little younger than me," Elena said. A few minutes younger, if the truth were told but Miriana wouldn't be interested in such detail. "She's just finished at the vocational school and now she helps Mama at home."

"And does she have your good looks?"

Elena nodded. "We're very alike."

Miriana's face lit up. "But not quite so clever as you. That's not always a problem in this world, is it?"

"School was never her thing, but she's lovely and very good with the boys. I don't know what we'd do without her."

"And how old would they be?" Miriana raised her eyebrows.

"Alexandru, the eldest, is twelve. He's on the school football team. Plays in goal. Then there's Luca. He's ten and a bit of a tearaway. Danut is eight and much more serious than Luca, loves reading. Serghei, the baby as we call him, is almost five. He's not long since started school. And, of course, there's another baby on the way. We don't know whether it'll be a girl or a boy. Mama prefers not to know."

"My, that is a big family."

"It costs such a lot to bring up a big family. There's the rent, the heating, the food, Tata's travelling costs, not to mention all the things that growing boys need."

"And money is a bit tight? Is that why you've left school so soon? They need you to help bring in some money to help pay the bills."

Eyes glazing over, Elena nodded. "I so wanted to get my baccalaureate and go on to uni. My teachers all said that I was capable. Instead, I've just started working in a grubby office. I answer the phone. I stand over the photocopier. I file the papers. I email the bills and have to ring people up when they don't pay on time. I make the tea and coffee, I wash up. I sweep the floors. I empty the bins. I run back and forward to the sandwich shop. I might as well not have a brain at all."

"Go on," Miriana said, giving her a smile.

"I tried, I tried so hard to talk them around. Mama and Tata that is. Even Irina tried. To try and make them understand that if I stayed at school, then in five years' time, I would have a good job.

One with prospects. And bring home real money. I knew it was unrealistic. How could they ever afford to keep me at school and then at university?"

"And then my message popped up on your Facebook? You must have been googling education," Miriana said.

Elena nodded.

"Some things are meant to happen, Elena," Miriana said reassuringly. "It's not often but sometimes dreams can come true – even pipedreams. Mine did."

"You had dreams too?" Elena said.

"Just like you. Our stories are so similar it's almost uncanny. I, too, had to leave school early. Get a job. Help the family out. I worked in a call centre right here in the city, dealing with packages that hadn't arrived on the day they were supposed to, or returned to the depot because nobody was in to receive them. Insulted eight hours a day. I handed over my wages to my mother – all except a few measly leu, which I kept for myself for fares and essentials. No coffee shops for me in those days, either. And certainly, no pastries. I remember it well."

"So, how did you—?"

"How did I find a career? A friend told me about opportunities in England. I was sixteen, just the same as you. I didn't believe him at first, but as it turned out it was all true," Miriana said. "I went back to school in England, worked hard for my A levels – that's what they call the higher-grade exams in England – and from there I went on to university. Then they found me a job in a recruitment firm, and I worked my way right up to the top and then started my own company. Here I am now, over thirty years later, with a good career and a very handsome income. Set up for life, one might say."

"But I can't afford it. I can't afford to go to school or university. Not here and not in England," Elena said.

Miriana linked her fingers together and rested them on the table. Elena couldn't help but notice the beautifully manicured nails and the huge diamond ring hugging the third finger of her left hand.

"Cast your mind back to what you read on my website. Think, now, what did it say?" Miriana asked.

"No costs. But that can't be true," Elena said.

"No *upfront* costs. That's the operative word and an entirely different matter. In the end it would be you paying for it. It's like taking out a loan. The deal is that once you've completed your education, my company finds you a good job, and then you pay back the upfront costs of your education out of your earnings over a period of years – and still have plenty of money in your pocket to live a good life. Once your debt is paid off, then your earnings are all your own."

"And that's what you did?"

"I did," Miriana said. "And I was lucky that the firm found me a job with such good prospects. I've never looked back. England is my home now. I've lived there for the past thirty-two years, since I was sixteen, and other than to visit my family, I rarely come back here. And I most certainly don't plan to come back here to live. But that is my choice. I'm visiting family now – here in Bucharest. And I have to tell you that the family has a whole lot better standard of living now that I am earning so well. They have a beautiful house, good food on the table, holidays. Luxuries they could never have afforded in the past."

"Will your company find me a job?" Elena asked.

"With your brains, I can't see any problem at all. Every company needs girls with brains. We're in recruitment, as I mentioned. We recruit people from all over the world. We help them re-establish themselves in a new country and match them to our client database. If they need financial help, we give it to them, and then they repay it to us when they are able. It's a very simple model, Elena. It is a business. There are no free lunches."

"So, you left home. And went to England," Elena said, her spirits lifting higher and higher with every word she heard. It was almost too good to be true, heaven sent.

"I did, and what's more I didn't even tell my parents that I planned to leave. I'm far from heartless, Elena, but I knew even at sixteen that my parents would object and that they'd have found a way to stop me, had I told them."

Miriana pulled out a twenty leu note and placed it on the waitress's tray. "Keep the change."

It was a great deal of change. Enough to feed a family, Elena thought as she watched the waitress placing the cups and saucers and the plates carefully on the table. She did not want to spend her life in a grubby office or waiting on tables.

Her head spinning, Elena took a sip of the dark rich coffee and eyed the pastry, thinking all the while about how her own parents would react if she packed up and left without a word. They'd be hurt and angry and they'd most certainly not understand. "My parents would kill me. They'd never forgive me if I did this."

"I hear what you say, and I struggled with my conscience too," Miriana said, leaning forward and taking Elena's hand. "But I'd strongly advise you to do the same – that's if you decide that what I can offer you is right for you.

"I just packed up my belongings and left. I'll not tell you that it wasn't tough at first. Tough on me and tough on them. But believe me, it all came good. Now I'm the prodigal daughter. They never stop boasting about me to their friends. The first in the family to get a degree and the first to land a good career. I send money to them each month. It's made all the difference to their lives.

"Tuck in. Too much information. Let's eat and drink our

coffee. If there's one thing you don't need to worry about it's your figure. There's a lot to think about, isn't there? And what about boyfriends, Elena? Is there someone special in your life?"

Elena laughed. "I don't have time for boyfriends. I never have."

"So, would I be right in thinking you're a virgin?"

Elena blushed and nodded.

"I'm so sorry, I didn't mean to embarrass you. It's just that you're one of a rare breed in this day and age. It's a perfectly ordinary question and I only ask because I need to know that, if you come to England, then you'll dedicate your time to your studies and not go running off with the first boy you meet."

"I wouldn't do that," Elena whispered. "I promise."

"It's a massive decision to make. A life changer," Miriana continued, swallowing the last of the pastry and delicately brushing the crumbs from her jacket. "You'd need to think very carefully about it all before you make any decisions. I can give you some references if you'd like to check out how well it has worked for others. Now I'm sure you've got questions for me…"

Nibbling the ends of her nails, Elena took a deep breath. "Where would I live in England?"

"I lived in a house share with five other girls. Nothing too posh but quite adequate. We each had our own rooms for study with our own bathrooms—"

"My own bathroom?" Elena exclaimed. Her own room and her own bathroom. Yes, she'd miss Irina enormously but to have her very own space…

"We were given a weekly allowance by the firm for food and other essentials – travel to and from school, books, stationery, and girlie things. Again, not huge but more than enough to get by on. I lived there for two years, and then I lived in halls at uni for the first year, and then another house share. School fees, rent, and living expenses were all covered by the firm. Does that answer your question? Next?"

"Would I have time to take a part-time job? You know something after school and at weekends?" Elena asked, thinking ahead. "I'd like to be able to send some money back to Mama and Tata while I'm at school. I know it wouldn't be as much as I give them now, but it would help."

"Dear Elena, you've such a lot to learn. In England, you could earn more money within an hour each evening and a couple of hours at weekends than you'd ever earn in a full-time job in Romania. But, overall, we prefer for our girls to concentrate on their studies. I'm sure we can send a little regular money to your mother and father, without you having to work for it. As with your education, you'd have to repay that money when you start earning. But…if you were to insist, I'm sure we could find you a small part-time job."

"You'd do that for me? If I could tell them that I'd be sending money home, then maybe I could leave with their blessing…"

"Remember what I just said, Elena. It would be so much easier if you said nothing about this until you've made the move. Best take it step by step. Let's get you to England and then you or we can start sending money back to your family. Plenty of time to tell your family once you're settled in. It would be silly to risk them stopping you," Miriana suggested. "It's your choice, but if you take my advice…"

"I do. I do," Elena said. "I trust you, Miriana, and I can't find the words to tell you how grateful I am."

"Then I take it you'd like me to go ahead with getting things moving. The next step is for you to meet up with our local rep to make the necessary arrangements. I'll pass on your mobile number. You don't need to worry about any of the paperwork, and if you don't have a passport, then he'll deal with that as well."

"I don't have a passport. I've never been out of Romania," Elena said.

"That's no problem. The man you will meet is called Flaviu. He's the most suitably named man I have ever met. The name means yellow or golden-haired, and that's him. You'll spot him a mile away. A mop of golden curly hair that's the envy of every woman. We've known each other and worked together for quite a while. You can trust him. I'll ask him to text you and arrange a place for you both to meet up and go through the detail. You'll need to take your birth certificate when you meet him. And your school certificates as well."

Elena grinned. "Flaviu. He sounds nice."

"Oh, he is. Very nice indeed," Miriana said.

"When would I have to leave for England?"

"As soon as Flaviu can make the arrangements. A week, maybe two at most."

"And when do you think I might be able to start school in England?"

"I'd guess that we might be able to get you in for the autumn term – September time, probably late September. If we get things moving quickly, then that should work. We need to get you to England as soon as possible. There'll be a lot of paperwork to do."

"So soon?" Elena said.

Miriana nodded. "Not having second thoughts, are we?"

Elena shook her head. This was her one and only opportunity to make a life for herself. She couldn't afford to pass up on it.

"Then, you'd better run along now. By my watch, you've just lost an hour's pay! And, Elena…Not a word. Not to anybody, not even your sister. And I'll see you in England. *Ne vedem curând,* sweet Elena."

· · ·

Miriana watched until Elena was out of sight then pulled her mobile out of her bag and scrolled down to *F*.

"A job for you, Flaviu, and believe me you're going to love it. She's a real looker and innocent as a baby. And what's more, she's got a sister. A double whammy, hey?"

5

AUSTRALIA
2022

A blistering hot day, Penny chose a booth alongside the window and picked up a dog-eared menu. The same café she had frequented for the past forty years; little had changed. The once red plastic bench seats, now well past their sell-by date, were faded to orange and held together with Gorilla tape. The specials menu chalked up on a blackboard hung from a string on the wall and listed the same limited range of breakfasts as back in the day. If it was choice that one wanted, then the Halo Café was the wrong place to go. The coffee was more than acceptable. It was filtered. It was coffee. Americano, espresso, cappuccino, latte, macchiato, or mocha were unheard of. The pancakes, the house speciality, were to die for. More important, it was not a café that would be frequented by members of her family. This was going to be a private conversation – not for their ears.

Close by the highway, on the outskirts of Wodonga, the Halo Café was a popular stop off point for truck drivers taking the M31 between Melbourne and Sydney, and locals alike. With a huge lot out front and to the side of the café, parking was never a problem. Inside the café, the air conditioning, clattering and banging – a noise familiar to all regulars – maintained a steady seventy degrees.

Checking her watch, Penny nodded in satisfaction. She'd made good time. Fifty kilometres in forty minutes wasn't bad going at all, especially with twenty-five kilometres over dirt roads. Eleven o'clock in the morning and eighty degrees, it was building up to be a scorcher.

Day dreaming, she recalled the many times she and Bluey had sat opposite each other at this very same booth. They'd talked about everything. Children, sheep, horses, friends, expansion, land purchases, buildings, parties, Christmas, birthdays, anniversaries. No secrets. Ever. And they'd dreamed. Dreamed about what they might do together when eventually they were able to step back a little from the day-to-day running of the ranch. They'd even discussed a trip to England. Theirs had been the perfect marriage. Neither of them could have foreseen what happened. When Bluey's tumour was diagnosed and he'd died six weeks later, he took a part of her heart with him.

Penny started as a firm hand squeezed her shoulder. She knew that hand. The same hand that had squeezed her shoulder on so many occasions over the years. In good times and in bad. A dear, dear friend of the family and her saviour when Bluey had died.

"Well, if it's not my favourite lady," he whispered in her ear. "Fancy meeting you here. And looking as pretty as ever."

"You old rogue!" Turning, Penny looked up into the rugged old face criss-crossed by lines from the relentless Australian sun. Tall and broad, he and Bluey had stood shoulder to shoulder. His once black and then silver mop of hair was now reduced to a few grey wisps that defied gravity, but he still cut an imposing figure. As close to one another as they could have been, Bluey had loved Ronnie as a brother and trusted him implicitly. Well placed trust. A highly qualified accountant, later in life a financial advisor, he was family. Always had been. Now in his early eighties, there were no flies on Ronnie.

"Past time I chased you down, Ronnie. Talking on the phone's one thing, but…" Penny said, "we should do this more often. Creeping up on me like that. One of these days you'll give me a heart attack."

Ronnie grinned. She didn't change. He'd laughed when Bluey had introduced them all those years ago. All five foot two of her and skinny as a rake. Looked like a puff of wind would blow her away. An incongruous couple, she hardly came up to Bluey's elbow. Six foot four, if an inch; he was a big man, a powerhouse, and fit. A gentle giant. And Penny – a petite English rose who he had thought would never stay the course. How wrong he had been. Beneath the pretty exterior was a determined woman who had never been afraid of hard work.

Ronnie sidled into the bench seat opposite, slid across to the window side, and leaning across the table, kissed Penny on the cheek. "You were miles away. Didn't you hear me knocking on the window? Where were you? I'm sorry about Amy, Pen. Just wish I'd got to meet her."

"She'd have liked you, Ronnie. The number of times I promised her that I'd go to England. Next year. Next year. The path to hell, as they say," Penny said, her eyes glazing over. "Just two days ago. April 14th. Can't get my head around it somehow."

"She made it to a ripe old age. Had a great life from what you told me about her." Reaching out, he took Penny's hand in his. He knew that, although the sisters had spent almost the past fifty years on opposite sides of the world and had been born twenty years apart, they were as close as two sisters could be. Amy had been like a second mother to Penny. "How old was she?"

"Old? Wash your mouth out, Ronnie. Amy was never old. Liked to defy nature did my sister. Almost ninety-five and nothing ever fazed her. She knew, you know? That she didn't have long left."

"Some people do," Ronnie replied.

"She wrote, you know? The letter was postmarked 7th April, seven days before she died. It arrived at the collection point on the 14th," Penny said.

Ronnie raised his eyebrows. "Sixth sense?" If Penny wanted to share the contents of the letter, then she would. All in good time.

"Shall we order? Same old blackboard. I'm going for the coffee and pancakes – the large stack with extra syrup. The boys wouldn't approve, but what the eyes don't see, the heart doesn't grieve over, at least for the time being. Ah well," Penny said.

"Make it two. Don't think my doctor would be over impressed either, but I won't tell if you don't. It's not often I get to sit in a posh café with a pretty woman these days. Coffee, pancakes, and the pleasure of your company – what more could a man ask for? You're right, we should do this more often."

"I should make the effort to get into town more often, but you know how it is. It's Bobby's birthday in a couple of days. Thought I'd make the effort and buy something personally. Socks probably. Then, hell, I thought – going all that way, what about ringing Ronnie?"

"You hate shopping. Always did," Ronnie replied, waving to the waitress. "Now tell me why you're really here other than to pass a couple of hours with the most eligible old man in town."

"Strewth, am I that transparent?" Penny said.

"Coffee, pancakes, large stack, extra syrup. Twice, please," Ronnie said, turning back to Penny. "We've known each other too long, Pen. I know you've just lost Amy and it must be hurting one helluva lot, but you look like you've got the worries of the world on your shoulders. Is it the boys?"

Shrugging, Penny took a deep breath. "Guess so. When isn't

it? Spending money like it's going out of fashion. Gary's just bought himself a new 4x4. Bobby's talking about taking up flying and even getting his own plane when he gets a licence, which is going to cost a fortune. Julia and Natalie spend most of the week either in shopping malls or in beauty parlours. If it's not Botox, it's nails, eyebrows, or lashes. Kenny and Will are partying their way through university. They do keep in touch. I'll give them that. Not a week goes by without a phone call asking for a few extra dollars. All three girls are at private schools. Won't be so many years before they're off to uni as well…They all seem to think that money grows on trees."

Pouring copious amounts of maple syrup onto his pancakes, Ronnie listened. The biggest mistake Penny had ever made after Bluey had passed was signing over the farm to Gary and Bobby. He'd warned her it was too soon. Born and brought up on the sheep farm, they were fine boys with the same build as their father. But unlike their parents, neither of them had a head for business. Either that or they never bothered to apply themselves. Or – maybe they'd had it too good, too soon. Life on a silver plate. When Bluey died, Penny had insisted that it was time they took responsibility. It would make men of them. So, she had signed it away. Now, ten years on, little more than a lodger in her own home, she was reaping the rewards. Or, more precisely, suffering the consequences of that decision.

Penny hadn't come into town to do shopping. He could read her like a book. Always had. She needed to know what was going on in the business – the one thing that he couldn't share with her. Long-term family friend or not, Gary and Bobby were his clients now. She was not. Had been for the past ten years. If the boys had listened to him from time to time, then they wouldn't be in a mess. He'd done his best for both Bluey and Penny's sake, but it had been like pushing water uphill. Now it was a matter of client confidentiality.

"And what about Tara? Prettiest filly I ever did see. Sweet as candy that one," Ronnie changed the subject.

"She's the one good thing in my life, Ronnie. We ride out every day. Unconditional love," Penny replied. "Come and take a squiz at her sometime and make it soon. Maybe we can ride out together. Dude's still going strong. Twelve now. As headstrong as ever. A one-man horse, Bluey always used to say, but I think he'd let you ride him."

"I'd like that," Ronnie said.

"But you know what my question is, Ronnie."

"What question?"

"You know full well what I'm talking about. I don't need protecting. Never have. The ranch, Ronnie."

"Anything in particular?" he asked.

"It's going to rack and ruin. Fences broken. Dingoes dropping in for breakfast, lunch, and dinner. You know as well as I do that if security isn't maintained then the losses are huge. Farm machinery lying in the yard that needs fixing. Looks more like a scrapyard than anything else. Bluey and me drummed it into them enough. Been going downhill for a long time now." Penny frowned.

"I guess you've reminded them," Ronnie said.

"Until I'm blue in the face. Soon as I mention anything, they go crook on me. Big time. And then it's, 'We got it all in hand, Mum – not your problem.' Nothing gets fixed. Cotton wool in their ears. When I see fences down, I fix them. Even now. When they see fences down, they ride right on by in their big fancy four-by-fours. *Mañana,* as they say in Spain."

"Do you want me to have a word?" Ronnie sighed, shaking his head. If it might make her happy, then he'd have another go at them, stony ground or not.

"Save your breath, Ronnie," Penny said. "And they've sacked two of the farmhands. A whole bunch of lambs went wandering a couple of months back. Never did find them. Some cock-and-bull story about the hands leaving gates open. I didn't believe a word of it. Still don't. I spoke to the men. Said they didn't do it. Those two worked on the farm for thirty odd years, and in all that time, me and Bluey never had cause to pull them up. They got more sheep farming experience in their little fingers than Gary and Bobby put together."

Ronnie concentrated on the ever-dwindling stack of pancakes on his plate. There was little she was telling him that he didn't already know. Word got around in the farming community. And the monthly accounts he prepared for them spoke for themselves. The business was teetering on the edge. He, too, had tried to tell them, but they always knew better. They had a plan. Always a plan. It wouldn't be long before the bank pulled the plug on the loans.

"And then the fire," Penny continued. "Just finished shearing. Barn stacked high with fleeces waiting to be collected. Burnt to the ground. I know that it's not a big earner, but it's income. Good income. But not this year. Maybe not next year either, unless that barn gets rebuilt in time."

"Fire? I didn't hear about that." Ronnie frowned.

"Last week. In the early hours."

"Lightning strike?"

"No storms that night. Fire forensics are in. Insurance isn't playing ball."

"And you think—?"

"Nothing. Just crossed my mind, the way things might look," Penny said. "Feed bills are stacking up. Vet's bills not paid. Idiots leave stuff sitting around. Do they really think that I'm not going to check them out?"

"And no insurance payout," Ronnie mumbled to himself, turning over the possibilities in his mind. An insurance payout would help subsidise the ranch for a while, but surely the numbskulls wouldn't be that stupid.

"So how bad is it, Ronnie? I've been in this business too long not to know that the ranch is in trouble. You can tell me," Penny said.

"You know you can't ask me that question, Pen. Client confidentiality. I know they're your sons and it was your business, but you signed it over to them," Ronnie said glumly. The whole thing was a disaster waiting to happen.

"I'm asking as a friend – and for a reason," Penny said.

"No can do." Ronnie sighed and shook his head.

"I think you've just answered my question. Am I right?" Penny sighed.

Ronnie shrugged his shoulders and looked deep into her eyes. He couldn't tell her, but neither could he lie to her. "It's not looking great, Pen."

"You'll keep an eye on things when I'm gone," Penny said, knowing full well that if anybody could talk sense into her two sons, it would be Ronnie. If it wasn't too late already.

"Gone? Going where?" Ronnie sat bolt upright. "You're not telling me…"

"No, I'm not dying or anything like that, you silly old codger. Hey – put that smile back on your face! Going over to England. To say goodbye to Amy properly. And there's her dying wishes to be seen to. She's left the cottage to me, you know, and money. God only knows I don't deserve it."

"Guess she would. You're her only living relative. Have you told the boys?"

Penny gazed out of the window. When the call had come in from a Mr Duncan Gillespie, she had been devastated about the news of Amy's death, and at the same time, completely over-whelmed by her sister's generosity. She'd blurted it out in front of the whole family. Had they taken time out to comfort her in her loss or say how much they wished that they'd known their aunt better, then she might not have regretted her words. Instead, they had simply asked her how much the cottage might be worth. They hadn't been able to get her on a plane soon enough.

"I told them, Ronnie." Her expression said it all.

"When are you going?" Ronnie asked.

"On the 26th. She's being cremated Tuesday, straight after Easter. A private cremation. No service. That's what she asked for in her will. Then a thanksgiving service on the 1st May. Thought I'd fly out the week before. Give me time to settle in and get to know the natives a bit. Sydney to London Heathrow via Perth. Hired a car from one of the rentals at the airport and I'll drive from there. Stroud. It's in Gloucestershire."

"At least they drive on the left-hand side of the road," Ronnie said. "The break will do you good. You deserve it. Take your time. Forget about the ranch for a couple of weeks…And don't forget that this is your inheritance from your sister. Yours and yours alone." It wasn't difficult to read between the lines, but if he had to string those two boys up one by one, he'd make damn sure that Penny was not the one left with nothing. "A retirement commu-nity, I remember you telling me," Ronnie said.

"Not just any retirement community, Ronnie. Magnolia Court. Twelve cottages and eighteen residents at the last count. Seventeen now that Amy's not with them anymore. Not all old fogies, either. There's at least four of them in their sixties. You wouldn't believe some of the stories Amy's told me over the years. You could write a book about them. With a bit of luck, and if I time it right, I'll be there in time for the cocktail hour. Hope the beer's good and cold."

Ronnie laughed. The last time he had visited England, albeit thirty years ago, the beer had been both brown and warm. "When are you coming back?"

Penny shrugged her shoulders. "Tell you the truth, Ronnie, I really don't know."

Throwing his arms around her shoulders, Ronnie hugged her tight. "You're still a fine woman, Pen. Enjoy life." Second only to his own departed wife, she was indeed the finest woman he had ever met. There had been times after he'd lost his wife and Penny had lost Bluey that he'd been tempted to ask her to marry him. Now he'd left it too late. "Take care, Pen. I'll look after things at this end – best I can. Stay as long as you need to."

After walking hand in hand with her to the parking lot, Ronnie opened the driver door to the old truck, the same that she had driven for the past twenty-five years, to his knowledge. He leant in and kissed her on her cheek. "I'll miss you. Keep in touch," he said.

6

ENGLAND

2022

"**M**orning, Penny," Dot said.

Still in her dressing gown and slippers, Penny opened the door. "G'day, Dot."

"I'm another of those early birds around here," Dot said, wiping her feet on the mat as she followed Penny into Amy's living room. "You know birds and worms and all that. Best part of the day, if you ask me, which of course you haven't. But had the feeling you might be up and about. How about I put the kettle on? Nice cup of tea. That's what we need."

"Help yourself," Penny replied, somewhat bemused that anybody should knock on her door at seven thirty on a Thursday morning. "You'll find—"

"No problem. I know where everything is, unless you've had a move around," Dot called from the kitchen.

Penny carried on where she had left off and left Dot to it. Upstairs, her suitcases were unpacked, and her clothes stacked in several piles on the floor. A quick examination of the wardrobe and the chest of drawers confirmed that until she had cleared out some of Amy's clothes there would be no room for her own. There was no hurry.

"Tea break," Dot called up the stairs.

"Going to have to cull down Amy's clothes a bit. Been trying to find a bit of cupboard and drawer space for my own. There isn't any. Plenty of room in the spare bedroom but no wardrobe or cupboards. So, right now, I'm hanging everything on the floor," Penny called from upstairs. "You know, some of these clothes hanging in the wardrobe, I remember her wearing back in the seventies before I took off with Bluey. That girl certainly knew how to make clothes last," Penny said. "Tea, you said? Just for the record, Dot, I don't do tea, not unless it's forced down my throat. Next time make it coffee for me, will you? No offence intended."

"None taken and noted." Dot laughed. "Do you want me to make you one now?"

"No, one last cup of tea won't kill me." Penny came downstairs and found the drink Dot had made her. She lifted the cup to her lips. "Dreadful stuff. Smells as bad as it tastes."

"Just as well you didn't bring much with you – just that big suitcase and the smaller one."

"No good hiking a load of stuff halfway around the world if you're never going to use it," Penny said. "How many clothes can you wear, anyway?"

"That's one way of looking at it," Dot mumbled.

"Have you decided what you're going to do with all her things?"

"No. Right now, it's still Amy's cottage. Get around to it, sometime. Its fine for the moment."

"Upstairs probably isn't so bad, but I think you'll find it's a different matter down here. Amy kept everything, especially paperwork. There are piles of it, and probably another four or five boxes stuffed full in the storeroom at the back of the Mansion House. Happy to help you sort through it, if you like."

"No," Penny said a little more sharply than she had intended. "It's kind of you to offer, but that's one job I have to do myself." It was one of Amy's dying wishes and she had been very precise about it.

"You'll have your work cut out there," Dot said. "The offer stands, if you change your mind. What about the books? I'm sure if you wanted to make a bit more space, we could find you some room to store her books. You did say that you're not a reader, didn't you?" Dot asked.

"That's right. I'm not, but Amy had a habit of writing in books. If there was something she didn't like when she read a book, she'd always make a note of it in the margin. Did it from the time she was knee high to a grasshopper. Library wasn't so keen on her habit, but that's life. If something sparked a memory of a place or a person, another note. And words of wisdom galore. She was a thinker, was our Amy. Maybe I'll learn something from them."

"You wouldn't have to worry about them. They'd be safe and dry in the store. Lucky you weren't here eight years ago. Couldn't store anything in that old place. Leaky sieve it was. I don't suppose Amy told you about that?" Dot asked.

"Heard all about it, chapter and verse. That was some coup you all pulled off." Penny laughed, glancing at the box under the tea tray. In it were all the letters that Amy had sent her over the years.

"Well, keep it under your hat. Even the new residents don't know the half of it. Those of us who were here at the time decided it was best to keep schtum about it. Right, what can I do to help?"

"Only thing I am planning is to put some of Amy's photographs away and replace them with a couple of my own,"

Penny said, reaching for a small carrier bag and passing a small, framed photograph to Dot. "That's the family."

"Beautiful house. Sunshine. Lovely family."

"Hmm. They are. Like most families. That's Gary and Bobby with Julia and Natalie." Penny pointed to her two strapping sons standing side by side with their two immaculately coiffured and dressed wives. "And that's the five grandchildren – the two boys are at uni and the girls heading the same way. All bright. Expensive things, kids these days. Taken not so many weeks ago. And me in the middle. I was going to send one to Amy but…"

"You weren't to know." Dot finished the sentence. "Two children, and grandchildren as well. Lucky woman."

"Could have been three, but some things just aren't meant to be."

"I'm sorry, I didn't mean to pry," Dot said.

"A very, very long time ago, Dot." Penny swallowed hard.

"And that's the other love of my life," Penny said passing the second photograph frame to Dot. "Tara. The last present that Bluey ever bought for me. She's a real hybrid. Part Arab, part Brit, and a lot of thoroughbred." Penny stroked the photograph and carefully placed it on top of the bookcase. "Pride of place. Reckon I'm going to miss that one even more than family. If anything were to change my mind…"

"I guess everyone rides in Australia. At least according to the films, they do," Dot said.

"You won't find many that don't. There was a time – and not so long ago – when we did all the rounding up on horseback. Now it's off-roaders. Times don't change for the better."

"She's a beauty," Dot said.

"And uncomplicated. They give you all their love and ask for nothing in return. We used to ride out every day for miles."

"She's pretty, alright," Dot said. "Haven't ridden a horse for donkey's years. Not sure I could get my leg over anymore…I'm not sure that came out the way it should!"

"You wouldn't have any problem with Tara. Big softie. Goes down on her haunches. Waits for me to mount her – and don't you get me wrong either – and then up she gets and off we go. Thirteen hands. Not a sweeter-natured mare in the world, and she loves kids. Taught the grandchildren to ride on her, and half the local kids as well. Gary's going to look after her for me while I'm away."

Dot frowned. "I must have been twenty-five, maybe thirty. My best friend persuaded me to give riding a go. Saturday mornings. Riding stables. Snowball, he was called. Don't know why. He was a dirty grey. Well, if he'd laid down for me to get on, I'd have been very pleased. But no, not Snowball. I would get on, hanging on to the saddle and using the stirrups just as they showed me and then…He'd lay down and wouldn't budge an inch. Really quite funny when I look back on it. Bit embarrassing at the time," Dot recounted.

"You should have shown him who was the boss." Penny laughed. "So you gave up?"

"I'm not often beaten by anything, Penny, but old Snowball had my number," Dot said. "Too old now…"

"Never too old. Wasn't that what Amy always used to say?" Penny said.

"So, I can't help you unpack or anything?" Dot asked.

"Nothing to do, but thanks all the same."

"Time that I left you in peace and checked up on Dennis. We're on brambles duty today. Thanks for the tea. You don't need to show me to the door. Doubt that's moved, either. Keep the kettle on. By the end of the day, you'll be swimming in tea and never want to look a piece of cake in the face again. But we all mean well. Cocktails at six?"

"Wouldn't miss it for the world," Penny said.

"Dennis. What do you think about horses?" Dot asked.

"They lose more often than they win, old gal. Right answer?" Dennis replied, folding up his newspaper.

"No, what I meant to ask is, do you like them?" Dot persisted.

"Do you?" Dennis turned the question around.

"Well, not especially, but I don't dislike them. I'm not sure."

Dennis raised his bushy grey eyebrows and looked up at Dot. "I'd be right in thinking that there is a purpose in this conversation?"

"Remember my bucket list. Well, I've been thinking about it, and I think I might like to add another one to it."

"Like climbing the mast on cruise ships?" Dennis reminded her. "So, we've got Cheltenham Festival on the list now, have we? You're out of luck, Dot. Threw my top hat away right after our wedding. And don't remind me about that penguin suit. I looked a right Charlie, and don't say I didn't."

"That's Ascot, Dennis. Not Cheltenham, and no, I have no interest whatsoever in going to the races or backing horses."

"Aren't we meant to be going brambling?" Dennis changed the subject.

"We are. That's what got me thinking. If we clear the brambles and tidy it up, that area behind the 19th hole would make a perfect paddock."

"For a horse…"

"For a horse," Dot confirmed. "Or a pony. You are following me then?"

"We haven't got a horse or a pony, Dot."

"No, we haven't, but I may know one that needs a home. Think of it as free manure for life."

"What's this got to do with your bucket list?" Dennis grinned, raising one bushy eyebrow.

"I knew you wouldn't mind," Dot said. "And be a dear. Can you get the door, please? I need to get changed."

"Is Dot back?"

Dot listened from upstairs. It was unusual for Duncan to be up and out so early. She headed down.

"Dot, you've got a visitor. There's an aged Hell's Angel down here in a tatty old wheelchair. Saying he needs to speak to you." Dennis side-stepped just in time to avoid a straight right in the stomach from Duncan. "I was just about to put the kettle on. You're a godsend, pal. Just saved me from a morning of brambling with her ladyship."

"Morning, Duncan," Dot said, entering the room. "To what do we owe this honour?"

"A word with Dot," Duncan said. "Am I right in thinking that I just saw you leaving Amy's cottage, or should I say, Penny's cottage? It's about her. Did she say anything to you?" Duncan asked.

"Like what? She showed me some photographs and told me that she had no immediate plans to change anything in Amy's house. I think that was all…"

"She didn't say anything about the family back home?"

"Yes, she did, and showed me a lovely photograph. Why do you ask, Duncan?"

"Because I just had the most peculiar phone call from Australia. Checking to see if she'd arrived safely. Not picking up her calls apparently," Duncan said, shaking his head.

"Oh, it's not about Tara is it?" Dot frowned. "That would break her heart. She's wedded to that horse. I was even going to ask you to find out how much it might cost to have a horse shipped over here – as a nice surprise! Dennis and I are off down to clear the brambles away from behind the 19th. It will make the perfect paddock."

"It's not about the horse…" Duncan started. "What would you say if I told you that Penny has an open return ticket?"

7
ENGLAND
2022

"If I could have a little quiet for a moment, please." Max stood up and did a quick headcount. Seventeen. Including Dinah. No Emanuel, but that was only to be expected. Racked with arthritis, he rarely managed to get out. "Thank you all for coming. This matter affects us all. I'm going to hand straight over to Peter so that we don't keep you any longer than necessary."

"Thank you, Max." Picking up his notes, Peter stood and straightened his already perfectly knotted tie, a habit he had acquired during his early years as a bank manager and never since lost. "Now I don't have to tell any of you that the cost of just about everything has skyrocketed in the past year. Not only the price of gas and electricity but insurance premiums, labour, and materials. The list goes on…There's no need to panic, but no place for complacency, either."

"Can we turn the heating up a bit?" Thomas asked. "I've already got two layers on. Maybe I should pop back to the cottage and find another."

"It's the end of April, Thomas," Peter said. "Almost summer."

"You can have my jacket over your shoulders," Gerald whis-

"That's settled. For the moment, anyway," Peter said. "Next?"

"Well, I have noticed that it's only Sam and I and Ros who make use of the swimming pool, and it must cost a lot to heat, especially in the winter," Jas said. "How about we made it available to non-residents for, say, a couple of days a week? There's a good changing room. I'm not thinking of a free-for-all. A membership arrangement. I don't know, maybe £20 a month. And for that they'd get a half day a week usage of the pool – they'd choose the day they prefer – with a guarantee that there would never be more than six people using the pool. I've done some figures. If we managed to fill all the slots, then we might be able to put an extra five hundred pounds into the kitty each month."

"It would need managing carefully, Jas," Max said. The idea of unknowns wandering around Magnolia Court didn't have a great appeal.

"Or there's swimming lessons for children..." Jas added. "That's a money-spinner, if ever there was one."

"Definitely worth exploring further. Jas, can you work up some detailed proposals, please? And then we'll discuss it again at the next meeting," Peter said, scribbling in his notepad. "Next?"

Thomas glanced sideways at Gerald with a shall-I-or-shall-I-not look. Gerald nodded. "Gerald and I have had a few thoughts. Well, as you all know, we do a lot of buying and selling of antiques and collectibles. We've picked up quite a few gems from the Stroud and Stonehouse car boots—"

"Thomas, I flatly refuse to have a load of cars and vans driving over my lawns. Don't even think about it," Dennis cut in.

"No, no, no. Not a car boot sale, but an antique and collectors' fair. A far more discerning group of sellers and buyers. No boots open, no blankets strewn over the lawns, no junk. Gerald and I know of several people that might find it of interest. And we might even be able to attract some of those TV people. But if you think its fanciful, then we won't be offended, will we?" Thomas turned to Gerald.

"Not at all." Fingers crossed beneath the table, Gerald smiled. It had been their way of contributing to the discussion, but neither of them had any great enthusiasm for the prospect.

"So long as it's on the car park and not the gardens," Dennis reminded them.

"Excellent idea, Thomas," Peter said. "If you and Gerald could do some more research, then we'll put that on the agenda for the next meeting."

Gerald grimaced.

"Peter," Hetty said. "The girls have come up with what we think might be a money-spinning winner. Cookery classes. Masterclasses in the art of cake making. Both Dot and I have pages of our own recipes – tried and tested on you all. Ros, as we all know, is an absolute master at making wedding cakes…"

"And I think it's got legs as well," Max said. "Duncan and I have been googling in the last few days, and from what we've found, it's a good earner and a huge market. And if we could throw in overnight accommodation, then we could be looking at a package price of up to two hundred per person. Small events – no more than, say, four couples – or singles – at a time…We wouldn't have to run many to put a tidy sum in the pot. And the kitchen upstairs is already there, and we've already passed the health and safety inspection."

"Maybe I could run bus tours for them as well. Scenic tours of Stroud." Andy shrugged his shoulders. "Or maybe not, but we can use the bus for the taxi service between here and Stroud station."

"Paul and I have a nice spare bedroom. Never been slept in," Ros said.

"Likewise," Jas added.

"And we've got the suite in the Old Forge. It's only been used a couple of times by Gabby and Greg. I'm sure they wouldn't mind," Hetty said.

"That's three couples with a bed to sleep in. Any more offers?" Peter asked, having already decided that he valued his privacy too much to offer strangers a bed for the night, however nice they may be. Glancing around the room, he saw he wasn't the only one.

"That dirty old Portakabin sitting doing nothing," Penny said.

"The 19th hole, you mean?" Jennifer said indignantly.

First mistake. Hit a sore spot there, Penny thought to herself, but what the hell. "If that's what you call that run-down thing on stilts down at the bottom of the garden, then yes. That's precisely what I am referring to. I may only have been here for a few days, but no one – no one to my knowledge – has been anywhere near it. Rusting away and an eyesore." Frosty looks all round. What was it with Poms? Too bloody sensitive.

If looks could have killed, then they would have done. A few days at Magnolia and already this woman from down under thought she owned the place and knew better than any of them – that's the message she was getting. It was only later that she was reminded by Stan that for many years it had been the residents' community meeting place when the Mansion House had been unusable. It had been the ladies sewing room, the men's games room, the café, the bar and even the war room, way back when they were fighting Harry Trumper. She should have remembered. Amy had often referred to it with fond memories. Better tread softly.

"It could do with a coat of paint, I wouldn't disagree…" Jennifer said.

"Looked in the window recently?" Penny retorted. "Not that you can see much. Half the spiders in the county have taken up residence. All I can see is boxes of rubbish that no one's found any better place to store." Whoops, Penny thought to herself. Not softly enough.

"So what precisely, dear lady, are you suggesting we do with it?" Peter asked, his interest piqued. Penny was quite right. He'd had the same thoughts.

"Do it up and let it out to paying guests," she said. "Wouldn't take much work and it doesn't need to cost much, either. You're saying that you need another source of income for this place, and it's there right under your noses. Solves your problem with accommodation for your masterclasses as well. Had three units just like that back on the farm. Bought them for next to nothing, kitted them out, and put the farm workers in them."

The mention of farm workers did little to further her cause. "A Portakabin may be suitable for farm workers but not paying guests," Hetty said indignantly.

"Don't mind telling you we looked after our farm workers. They were good homes. Can't remember any of the boys ever complaining. So, we spend a few extra dollars on the inside. Could still work," she said. "Look, it's just an idea. No skin off my nose. What have you got to lose? How about I check it out?"

"She's got a point, Peter," Stan said. "We shouldn't dismiss it out of hand. I'll give you a fair and honest appraisal from a builder's viewpoint. We'll both take a look."

"Mmm. I'll take your word for it," Penny whispered in Stan's ear…She'd never let him forget that crooked gatepost, but it was a personal joke between the two of them. She hadn't shared it with anyone and neither had Stan.

"And what do you three ladies think about Penny's idea?" Peter asked. "Bear in mind what I said earlier – we can't afford paying out without a good return on our investment."

"I say we let Penny and Stan look into it. If it's not a goer, then maybe we back-pedal, cut the master course numbers down to three, or consider day courses instead. We've got options," Hetty said.

"She's right," Dot said reluctantly, making a mental note to keep an even closer eye on Penny. All very well to make suggestions, but if you didn't plan on sticking around…

"What's the harm?" Ros said. "And, at the risk of putting my foot in it as well, Paul and I have been here for a couple of years now, and I could count the number of times we've been inside the 19th hole on one hand."

Jennifer raised her hand in the air. "If it turns out that we do convert the 19th into living accommodation, then I should very much like to have a say in the décor."

"Welcome, Jenn," Penny said. "Not my forte."

"We done?" Penny asked, turning to Stan. "No time like the present."

8

BUCHAREST

2021

"The third time this week, Irina," Daciana said, attacking the herbs on the chopping board with a sharp knife, narrowly missing her fingers. "She should be here, helping us at the end of the day. You work your fingers to the bone. Your sister…Blah!"

"I like being here, Mama. Helping you and the boys. Elena's working and bringing in the money we need. She needs time to herself as well."

"Who is it this time?"

"The girls from school. She's hardly seen them since she left," Irina replied, turning the gas on under a pan of potatoes.

"She's left school. She's a new life now. It does not do to look back." Daciana scraped the finely chopped herbs noisily from the board, adding them to the bean casserole. "Who are these girls?"

"Juliani, and I don't know the other two. There's no harm in it, Mama. Nothing to worry about," Irina said, anxious to placate her mother before another scene ensued.

"Harm? She's sixteen. That's where the harm is. She should be at home with us, not gallivanting out every night. Tata will not be pleased."

"She's not gallivanting, Mama. She's meeting friends for a coffee, and then going back to Juliani's house. And she's not out every night."

"Spending money that could be put to better use here, in her home. Coffee. Next, it'll be drinks in the bars. Then clubs. Then the Lord only knows what. What is wrong with bringing her friends to our house? Is she ashamed of us? I shall speak to her."

"Spending her money, Mama? She hardly keeps anything for herself. You need to cut her some slack, Mama. You and Tata. She needs to have a life of her own."

"Now, my own daughter, telling me what I should do and what I shouldn't do. Not you as well, Irina. Your sister has a life. Here with us. She has a good family, a roof over her head, food on the table, and a job. What more could she want? One day she will meet—"

A good man. Irina silently finished the sentence for her mother. There was no arguing with her. It wasn't her mother's fault. It went way back through the generations. Women were homemakers. Women got married. Women had children. Women looked after their men and children. It was the way it had always been since time immemorial. "But you won't stop her going out, will you, Mama?"

"How can I stop her? Tie her to the bed? Lock the door?" Daciana slammed the oven door shut. "One hour."

"You could be happy for her," Irina muttered under her breath. "If we're finished here, Mama, I'll go and check on the boys." Irina took off her apron and hung it on the peg on the back of the kitchen door.

"*La naiba!* Those boys. Now. Go right now, Irina. One of these days…" Daciana shouted, throwing open the door. "Out. Out the lot of you. No ball in here. How many times do I have to tell you? You do that one more time and there'll be no supper for any of you. Break the glass in my window and there'll be no supper for you for the rest of the week, for a month. Irina, sort them out."

Herding her brothers in front of her, Irina tripped lightly down the nine steep flights of steps and out into a shared concrete backyard that served as a ball and skateboard park as well as a meeting place for the less desirable of the area. At the bottom end of the yard were two small bushes looking very much worse for wear, familiarly known as the goal posts. "You kick the ball between the goal posts. See how many goals you can score. You, Alexandru, you stand in goal, and don't be mean to your brothers. And Alexandru, you are the eldest and responsible for their safety. Keep a close eye on Serghei. No one leaves the yard. One hour, Mama said, and then straight back up the steps."

Peace had been temporarily restored.

"Is that a new T-shirt?" Irina asked, watching Elena pull it on over her head.

"Not new. Nearly new. The charity shop in Smârdan. They have some nice stuff. All freshly washed and pressed. Do you like it?" Elena asked, checking her appearance in the mirror.

"You look lovely. You're wearing make-up. You never wear make-up." Irina studied her sister's face. She had drawn a fine blue line – almost imperceptible – along the length of her eyelids before brushing her eyelashes with a light coating of blue mascara. A touch of blusher and a pale pink lipstick completed the transformation. "You look lovely. Different. Grown-up."

"Juliani showed me how to do it. Tomorrow, when everyone has gone to bed, I'll show you how it's done."

"That's kind of you," Irina said. "I have some cologne in the cupboard. It's not expensive, but it smells nice. You'll be the envy of your friends."

"The lavender? Not the same lavender that you were given for Christmas?" Elena exclaimed. "I'd love that. It'll remind me of you all evening."

"The same." Irina reached up to the shelf at the top of their shared wardrobe and picked out a small white and lilac box and handed it to her sister. "Will Juliani's father be picking you up again? And bringing you back?"

"Of course." Elena turned her head away. "He'll be here soon. We're meeting at the end of the road as always."

"Mama would like you to invite your friends to come over here one evening," Irina said. It wasn't quite what Mama had said, but near enough, and Irina knew that if her sister were to do so, then it might take the heat out of the situation. "For supper. You know how Mama loves people around her table. There's always enough for a few more mouths."

"I'll mention it tonight. I promise. Wish you were coming with me," Elena said, picking up her handbag.

"Thanks, but they're your friends. I'll meet them when they come round here. Take care, Elena. Love you."

"Love you too."

Irina sat in the kitchen listening for the door. If it hadn't been for her, there would have been all hell let loose the following day. Curfew was nine thirty. Working through from six in the morning until seven that evening, her father had arrived home shortly after Elena left. By seven thirty, supper was over and the boys were tucked up in bed, leaving her mother and father and herself time to watch the news and catch up on the day's events.

Daciana yawned, struggling to keep her eyes open. It was 9.00 p.m.

"You should go to bed, Mama. You have been on your feet all day. It's not good for the little one," Irina said, kissing her mother on the cheek. "And you, Tata. It's been a long day for you too."

"You are wise beyond your years, my darling." Daciana smiled at her daughter. "And thank you for everything you do. I don't say thank you often enough. I forget. But I mean what I say. You are a good girl."

"I'll wait up for Elena. She will be in soon," Irina said.

Irina listened as the clock chimed nine fifteen and then nine thirty. As the last of the chimes faded away, Irina quietly padded out to the front door in her slippers, opened it, and closed it noisily before walking heavy-footed along the hallway. The floorboards creaked. Nobody could miss the sound of footsteps on the bare floorboards. She knew her mother would not sleep until she had heard that sound. Opening and closing their own bedroom door, Irina picked her way carefully back along the hall, avoiding the telltale floorboards.

The clock chimed eleven. Irina walked to the front door, opened it, and left it very slightly ajar. When Elena returned, no one would hear her come in.

"Irina."

Catching a faint waft of lavender and feeling a light tap on her shoulder, Irina lifted her head from the table. "Elena, you're home. I was beginning to worry about you. What time is it?"

"Midnight. I'm sorry I'm so late," Elena whispered. "Thanks for the door. Bedtime."

Removing slippers and shoes, Elena and Irina carefully tiptoed along the hallway and made their way back to their bedroom, silently opening and closing the door behind them.

"Did you have a good time?" Irina asked as she slipped under the covers.

"The best." Eyes shining, Elena lay down on the bed, her hands clasped together behind her head and resting on the pillow.

"You can tell me, you know," Irina said.

"There's nothing to tell. We talked. We listened to music. We danced. I forgot the time."

"You know, Elena, at times you think I'm stupid. I'm your sister. I know you almost better than you know yourself. I know every one of your expressions. I know when you are happy and when you are sad. I can see it in your eyes. I can hear it in your voice. I know when there is something that you are not telling me."

"I promise you, Irina—" Elena started.

"No, don't do that. Is it a boy?"

Elena took a deep breath and slowly exhaled. "I'm in love, Irina."

"How old is he?"

"Twenty-five. You'd love him. He's the most gorgeous boy that ever walked this earth. He's kind. He's generous. He treats me like a princess. He is so handsome. He has golden hair that curls down onto his collar, the brightest blue eyes, and a smile that would melt any girl's heart. He's clever as well. He travels the world. There's not a moment when I tire of listening to his voice. We go out for pizza when we meet up. To a real restaurant. A real restaurant, Irina. Can you imagine? The tables are laid with pretty serviettes, knives and forks, glasses, and always a red rose in a vase. It's so romantic. Tonight, we went back to his flat for coffee. That's why I'm so late."

"He is not a boy, Elena. At twenty-five, he is a man, and you are still a girl," Irina replied sharply, wishing that she had not been quite so abrupt. "Maybe he is just a little too old for you?" But who was she to spoil her sister's fun? "I'm pleased for you. You should ask him home to meet Mama and Tata. It would be so much better than deceiving them. Tell them tomorrow that you met a man while you were out with Juliani and your friends. Tell them he wants to meet your family. It would make them happy."

"I will. Soon. I promise."

"Does he have a name?"

Elena hesitated. "Flaviu."

"Where did you meet him?"

"You sound like my inquisitor. So many questions." Elena paused and gathered her thoughts. "He came into the office a week ago to pay a bill. We started talking and he asked me out."

"Does he ask you to do things that you shouldn't? I care for you."

"He lifts my chin so that I am looking deep into his eyes, and he kisses me. Lifts my hair from my shoulders and brushes his lips across my neck and my shoulders. So gently I can hardly feel it. Tenderly. I can feel his heart beating when he holds me close. I can see it in his eyes. He loves me too. He gave me this tonight." Elena reached into her jacket pocket and pulled out a small box. "Isn't it beautiful? This is how much he loves me." Stroking the bracelet, Elena passed it across to her sister.

"It is pretty. And expensive. He must be very rich. He must care for you very much." Irina's heart sank. It was not the sort of present that a boy or even man would give somebody after a few dates. "Have you had sex with him?"

"No. What sort of a question is that to ask, Irina?"

"A normal question," Irina said, passing the bracelet back to her sister. It was a gold band engraved with Elena's initials, *EA*,

Elena Albescu. Whoever this Flaviu was, he had gone to a lot of trouble.

"Have you?" she asked again, knowing full well that her sister had just lied to her and was about to do so again. A musky smell pervaded the room. It was the same as that in her parents' bedroom, the same odour that she smelt each time she changed the sheets.

"Not yet, but soon maybe," Elena said.

"When you do, be sure to make it safe sex, my love," Irina said, switching off her bedside light and pulling the bedclothes up over her shoulder. A cold shiver ran down her spine. The rift had begun.

Elena tucked the bracelet under her pillow and turned off her own bedside light. It was too late for the warnings. Maybe he had taken precautions, but she had had her eyes closed. It had happened in a moment of passion. It had not been planned – for either of them. The sensation of him inside her lingered on. She did not regret one single second of it. Her only regret was that she had lied to her sister.

9

ENGLAND

2022

Reaching out for the paracetamol beside the bed, Penny made a promise to herself. Stick to the beer. Give the gin and tonics a miss, especially the way that Gerald poured them. And maybe give her liver a rest for a couple of days too. Amy had had her day, or afternoon and evening to be more precise, and it had been perfect in every way. Just as she had wanted it to be. A short service, her ashes in a pot centre-stage on a white-clothed table at the front of the Mansion House, bedecked with roses from the magnolia garden. Amy wasn't going to miss her own thanksgiving service. A few hymns, and readings that Amy had penned herself to be read by Stan, Hetty, and Ros, deputizing for Gabby who, much as she had tried to change her schedule, had been unable to be there. And then her ashes had been scattered under the magnolia trees that lined the drive before the small, gathered assembly returned to the Mansion House to toast Amy's eternal happiness. It wasn't often that Penny shed a tear, but she had on that occasion.

The cottage looked as though a bomb had hit it. In her head, she had it all mapped out. Exactly how she was going to tackle the problem. One drawer at a time. One cupboard at a time. Sort everything into neat piles. Those papers that could go straight in the recycling. Those that looked official but that had probably not been looked at for years, ergo, non-urgent. Piles and piles of them in fine print. Penny made a mental note to sweet talk Peter into working his way through those. Personal papers like marriage certificates that she would probably keep, letters, cards, brochures, valuation certificates, warranties, and receipts – hundreds and thousands of them. And not forgetting the two boxes filled with God only knew what gathering dust in the store at the Mansion House. Dustbin bags – plenty of them. She was going to need them.

The best laid plans, Penny thought, surveilling the carnage as she caught sight of herself in the small mirror above the mantelpiece. Still in pyjamas and dressing gown, she hadn't so much as washed her face or run a comb through her hair. A sight for sore eyes. Fortunately, it was still only nine o'clock in the morning. Visiting hours didn't start until ten – an unwritten but golden rule. Where once it might have been seven or eight, like it or not, oldies needed a bit more time in the mornings to get their heads together. And she was no exception. Particularly on days like this.

And then the phone rang.

"Penny," Stan said. "Hope I didn't get you up."

"You didn't," Penny replied, fetching the phone from the kitchen back into the lounge. She stepped carefully around the debris. There was a chair somewhere. "But you're damn lucky I found the phone. Don't ask. If you're thinking about dropping in for a cup of tea then the answer's no. Not personal, but no."

"I wasn't," Stan said. "Peter's agreed our estimate for the 19th. It's on. Andy and I are just making a list of all the materials we need and then Peter's going to place the order with the builders' merchant. How about popping down and making sure we haven't missed anything?"

"Love to, Stan," Penny replied, almost falling over one of the piles. "But right now I'm knee-deep in papers. Decided it was time I got stuck into sorting out Amy's papers. Wonder she didn't ask you to build on extension on this cottage. Never seen so many papers in my life. Every nook and cranny," Penny said, glancing around.

"Can't it wait? It'll still be there tomorrow," Stan asked.

"Can't wait, Stan. Gotta be done. Days of work here and then maybe I can sleep with a clear conscience," Penny said. Fact. She hadn't slept for more than an hour at a time since she'd arrived. Adjusting to the time zone hadn't helped. The only way to work out if it was day or night was to look out of the window. If it was light, then it was day. If it was dark, then it was night. High time her body clock got the message. And then there was Amy's cryptic letter. Bless her heart…but right at that moment she could happily have wrung her neck. What was wrong with plain speaking? If you have something to say, then say it. Don't wrap it up in riddles. But Amy had always been good at that.

"Happy to come up and give you a hand."

"Need to do this myself, but thanks for asking. About to put a 'gone fishing' note on the door. Believe me, I don't need visitors today. See you later." Penny cut the call.

I need you, Penny, to go through all of my papers. No one else. I know you'll do this for me. When you find what you are looking for, then I will leave it to you to decide what to do.

. . .

She'd read that paragraph in Amy's letter so many times that she could recite it backwards. It was ingrained in her memory. Somewhere in among this pile, there was something waiting to be found that Amy had not shared with her during her lifetime.

Penny took a deep breath. Where the hell to start? The biggest pile. Cards, she decided. Then at least she'd be able to use the coffee table again.

There were cards going back sixty or more years. Birthday cards, Christmas cards, anniversary cards, and Easter cards. Cards from Gerard, cards that she had sent from Australia over the years still in their original envelopes with original postage stamps, cards from Amy's Magnolia family going back to 2001, and cards from other friends going back years.

Sitting cross-legged on the floor, Penny started with Gerard. His words swam before her eyes and conjured visions of their life together, a wonderful life albeit cut short by his death. Somehow it didn't seem right. The cards weren't hers to read.

"Amy," Penny said. "These are all your personal memories. I've only looked at a couple of them so far and already I feel like an interloper. I'm going to take a punt that whatever it is I'm looking for, it isn't in a card from Gerard. If it were me, I'd want them gone. So, if it's okay with you, I'm going to put them all in the dustbin bag. Sorry, sis, but you did say that you were leaving the decisions to me."

Not without a little remorse and sadness, Penny opened the dustbin bag and dropped Gerard's cards in it.

And then the same with the cards that she had written to Amy from Australia. They certainly contained nothing of interest. At least she knew that for a fact.

Cards received from persons unknown, Penny placed on a separate pile. It was always possible that they didn't know of Amy's passing and might need to be informed. A job for later.

Finally, a box of Christmas cards probably purchased in the January sales and waiting for Amy to get her calligraphy pens out. It made her smile. The annual ritual of writing cards normally started in June or July and often didn't finish until September or October. Penny opened the box and grinned. Wrong. This year, the cards were all written and awaiting postage or hand delivery – as if she'd known. A pile of envelopes with the names of the recipients most beautifully written on each. No doubt the greetings within would be equally as beautifully penned.

Hetty and Max, Duncan and Jennifer, Dot and Dennis, Emanuel and Dinah, Gerald and Thomas, Paul and Ros, Sam and Jas, Peter, Andy, and Stan. All her Magnolia friends.

And then Gabby and Greg, and one to herself and the family in Australia. And finally, four cards at the bottom of the box addressed to persons unknown: Herbert Lodge, Adrian Grzeskowiak, Gwen Makepeace, and Fiona Underwood.

Returning all the cards to the box, Penny made a mental note to check out those names. Come Christmas, she'd make sure that the intended recipients received them, under cover of a small note that she would write to accompany them.

One pile down, or at least a whole lot smaller than it had been an hour ago. Time for a well-earned cup of coffee. Ten o'clock and still no visitors.

Letters next. Letters from Gerard to Amy, and letters that Amy had written to him – Penny deposited these in the dustbin bag. And then there were the hundreds of letters that she had written to Amy over all the years. Unable to resist the temptation, Penny sat down and started scanning them one by one, right back to the first one she had posted after she'd arrived in Australia. It was their history, their memories. Most poignant of all was the letter she'd written to Amy when Amelia had died, just three months old. It had broken her heart. And Bluey's as well. The tears she had shed at the time still marked the paper on which she'd written the letter. Amelia had been diagnosed with a rare form of leukaemia shortly after birth and had been given a month to live. In the days long before the likes of Cancer Research were pioneering new treatments, Amelia hadn't stood a chance. Now it might be a whole different story. Always in her heart. And then along came Gary and Bobby to help ease her pain...

It was history. A long time ago. One couldn't change the past; only the here and now. And one could maybe influence the future. Penny's letters to Amy joined those from Gerard in the dustbin bag.

Next on the pile, a small bundle of letters held together with a bulldog clip. Written by Gary. Her Gary. Two letters each year, one sent after his birthday, and one after Christmas, dating back to when he would have been sixteen years of age. Brief and to the point, they were thank-you letters for the small gifts of money that Amy sent him on those occasions. Letters she had never known he'd written. At the end of each, he had written: *Maybe we'll get to meet soon. You come over here or I'll come and see you. Xx. Gary.* There were no such letters from Bobby.

Penny frowned. Maybe she'd been too hasty in thinking that Gary hadn't cared about Amy's passing. He'd always been the quiet one.

And then a small bundle of letters tied together in a red ribbon. Faded with age, they were on notepaper headed 'The Foreign Office' and personally signed by 'Edward Frederick Lindley Wood, Viscount Halifax'. 1940 and 1941. They were letters commending her sister for bravery. They were part of history. The unsung heroes. Penny stroked the letters and made a mental note that they should be kept for posterity somewhere like the Imperial War Museum. And that's where she would send them.

By eleven, the pile of letters was one-eighth of the size it had been.

Receipts next. Rolled into neat balls and held together with elastic bands, none were less than two years old. They took a dive. A quick glance through a pile of warranties confirmed her suspicion that they were all well out of date. To her sure knowledge, Amy hadn't bought anything new in the past decade, especially clothes.

So far, she had found nothing that fitted the bill. Nothing that moved her any further forward in understanding Amy's message. *When you find what you are looking for, then I will leave it to you to decide what to do.*

It was five o'clock and still she was in her pyjamas. After getting dressed in jeans and a check shirt, Penny washed her face and her hands, reorganised her hair, dusted her face with powder, and applied some lipstick. It was going on cocktail hour. The resolution she had made not more than eight hours since flew out of the window. And perhaps the other residents might be able to shed light on a few names. As good an excuse as any.

By seven thirty, a little squiffy after two Tom Long amber ales, Penny was a little wiser. Herbert Lodge was Dr Bertie Lodge, Amy's GP. Adrian Grzeskowiak was a gentleman that Amy had met within the last year, and Fiona Underwood was her hairdresser. The name Gwen Makepeace rang no bells with anyone.

Bidding goodnight to her friends, Penny set off back to her cottage, Duncan keeping pace in his wheelchair.

"If you've got a moment to spare tomorrow, Penny, I might be able to help you. Didn't want to say anything in front of the others."

It was settled. They'd meet up at Duncan's cottage at five thirty the following evening.

10

ENGLAND
2022

The three cardboard boxes that she had asked to be brought up from the Mansion House were waiting for her on the doorstep. Each fifteen inches square and twelve inches deep, they were sealed up with copious amounts of packing tape. Somebody had been up early. Day two of the massive clear-out, and Penny was ready to begin work again.

Having manhandled the boxes one by one into the lounge, Penny reached for the scissors. The first box was labelled 'Poetry'. That was something she certainly hadn't expected. To her knowledge, Amy had neither read nor written poetry in her whole life. Resisting the temptation to assign the contents of the box directly to yet another dustbin bag, Penny lifted the six thick files out of the first box and placed them on the floor. Taking the first file, she opened it up and flicked through. Page upon page of lined foolscap sheets held in place by two long since rusted clips. Pages faded by age, almost illegible in places. Purple ink. Finely crafted words filling the pages. Verse. Simple verse. Poignant. Written from the heart.

Yard upon yard of verse about religion, belief, love, values, and the politics of ages past. A diary in verse. A very personal perspective on life. Poems that had not been written to be read by anyone other than the writer, but to express the writer's private thoughts – regrets, dreams, and desires.

Printed on the front of each file was the writer's name: 'Mary Philips'. It was their mother's name. Penny ran her hands over her face. Now she remembered. Their mother sitting up in bed late into the night, screwed up pages littering the floor of a morning, other pages neatly stacked on her bedside table. Penny smiled. Their mother, a poet!

And Amy had kept their mother's poetry all these years…

Penny opened the first file again and selected a page at random. The poem was titled *Do You Remember?* Written alongside a note: 'Our wedding, June 1925 and the birth of our beautiful Amy, September 1927.'

It was a love poem. Mary and Charles, their mother and father.

Do you remember – My dearest, dear
The things we used to do
When we were young and full of fun
And troubles so very few?

We met at a dance on a festive night
Dressed as Pierrot and Pierette.
We fell in love at first sight,
Oh – I remember it yet.

Our love was great that summer morn,
When the bells of the church did chime,

For that was the day our marriage born,
And a wedding ring was mine.

Do you remember our honeymoon
And the lovely time we had?
How it passed so fast, too soon—
How sorry we felt, yet glad.

Do you remember that certain day
Before the break of dawn?
Sweet were the words you did say
The day our Amy was born.

Do you remember, can we forget
Those wonderful days of yore?
Never a day do I regret
As I love you more and more.

Ripping a tissue out of the tissue box, Penny wiped her eyes. It was never going to win the poetry prize, nor would she ever have achieved fame as Poet Laureate. But it spoke of the love between two people. Words that would otherwise have remained unspoken and lost in time. Feelings that their mother had never shared with her children, as had so often been the case in those days.

In true Amy style, in the margin, Amy had written her own little comment. 'And we were both lucky too, me with Gerard and Penny with Bluey. Blessed by God.'

Penny locked the front door, then after making herself a cup of coffee, sat down to read more, checking Amy's comments as she went. Those that spoke about politics and war, she scanned briefly – the 1982 invasion of the Falkland Islands, the Bloody Sunday massacre of 1972, the strikes of the eighties under the government of Margaret Thatcher. By far her greater interest was in learning more about their mother, a loving but remote woman.

Raised herself in the Victorian era, their mother had maintained Victorian standards in raising her own children. Rarely could Penny remember having a real conversation with her mother. The poems in the file were a revelation. For the first time perhaps ever, she felt close to the woman who had raised both her and Amy.

An instinct that she couldn't describe told her that somewhere in these books of poetry lay the secret, if that was what it was. *When you find what you are looking for, then I will leave it to you to decide what to do.*

The phone rang. Penny ignored it. The doorbell sounded. Penny ignored it. She was on a mission. Cocktail hour came and cocktail hour went. The one concession that she did make was a quick call to Stan to let him know that she was fine and that with luck she might emerge from her mission the following day.

Not so very long ago, Amy had sat in the same room and probably in the very same chair that she sat in now, looking through the same poems, pen in hand.

The very last poem stopped her in her tracks. The title was *My Very Own Dolly,* and the date alongside, 'June 1924'. Next to this were two words penned in Amy's hand: 'A conundrum.'

II

ENGLAND

2022

Stretching her back, Penny shook her head. It was swimming, her eyes bleary. The history of their family in words and pictures – photographs, hundreds and thousands of them, dating back to the year dot when the only form of transport on the streets was the horse and carriage. Tiny little sepia photographs, faded with time, a history of a bygone past.

Tidying the last of the papers into neat piles, Penny put on her coat. Five thirty. Time to drop in on Duncan.

A tray with a blue-and-white china teapot, cups and saucers, milk jug, and sugar bowl lay on the dining table, together with the ubiquitous cake. Penny took one look and grimaced. While in Rome and all that…Before long she'd have to find a different expression.

"Coffee for you, Penny," Jennifer said, coming in from the kitchen with a mug in her hand. "Tea for Duncan and me, and I have some cake if you fancy it."

"You're an angel, Jennifer. I didn't even have to ask," Penny said, taking the mug.

"Cake?" Jennifer asked.

Penny planted a smile on her face. "Thank you. Coffee cake?"

Jennifer laughed. "We do make other cakes, you know. This one's carrot cake. Carrots out of our own vegetable garden."

"You won't mind if Jennifer stays, will you? She and I have no secrets, and we both know how to be discreet," Duncan said. "It's about Gwen Makepeace."

"Gwen?" Penny's interest piqued. What was it that couldn't be said in front of the other residents, that Duncan wanted to share with her now?

"Mind me asking why you are interested in Gwen?" Duncan asked.

"No secret there, Duncan. You'll probably not be surprised to know that Amy had written her Christmas cards before she died. In her bureau. All boxed up and ready to post or deliver by hand. Card for each of you here at Magnolia, one for me, one for Gabby and Greg, and four others. Three we've identified, leaving just the one. Gwen Makepeace. She didn't write that many cards, so I'm just guessing that there might be a special reason her writing one to this Gwen woman. Maybe she doesn't even know that Amy has died."

Duncan nodded sagely. "Never did leave anything to the last moment, our Amy."

"Not like her sister. Last minute dot com. Hands up. First to admit. Didn't even have the courtesy to tell you that I was on a plane and on my way here."

"A month maybe six weeks before she died," Duncan started, "Amy asked for the boxes from the store to be taken up to her cottage. I had the feeling that it was part of her putting her house in order, but I didn't want to think that way. Anyway, a few days later she came down to see me and asked if I would do something for her." Duncan hesitated.

"She asked me if I could help her trace a baby that had been born in 1924. Her name was Dolly…"

"Dolly?" Penny narrowed her eyes. The poem. Amy's written note alongside the poem. A conundrum.

"Dolly Marilyn Philips was the child's birth name. Amy thought that the child might either have died at birth or been adopted. Amy asked me if I could establish which it was."

"Philips was our mother's maiden name," Penny said.

"I know. Amy told me," Duncan said. "With the help of Ancestry.com, and records from Kew that date back to 1837, I managed to trace the registered birth of the child. The mother, seventeen years old at the time, was a girl by the name of Mary Philips…"

"Our mother," Penny said. "Strewth. Mum and dad were married in 1925, and yes, I remember her saying that she had been twenty at the time. Strewth. That means she had a baby before she married our father. Hell's bells, bet that caused trouble in the family." Penny drew breath and hesitated. "That mean what I think it means? Amy and I had an older sister or a half-sister…"

"That would appear to be the case," Duncan said. "And then, after much going around the houses, I managed to trace Dolly Marilyn. She was adopted at birth. She died in 1992. Married with one child, Gwen Makepeace, now in her mid-fifties, I believe."

"Did Dolly Marilyn know she had been adopted?" Penny asked.

"I don't know, but it's always possible that her adoptive parents told her. 1926 was the year that the Adoption of Children Act was enacted. There was no provision for access, by a child, to its birth records before that. It was more about placing unwanted children, removing the burden from society, and papering over the cracks. But there are still records if you know where to look."

"Does Gwen know that her mother was adopted?"

"Same answer. Don't know."

"So did Amy tell you what she planned to do?" Penny asked. It was a huge deal. To find out too late that they'd had a sister they had never met in life. And to find out that their mother had a hidden past – one which, if the poem were anything to go by, had haunted her throughout her life.

"She didn't. I simply remember her saying that there was a great deal to think about. The following day the boxes of files were returned to the Mansion House. Amy never mentioned it again, and neither did I. Neither of us have mentioned it to anyone. The secret might have died with her had you not spent time going through all her papers."

"Can we trace this Gwen?" Penny asked hopefully.

"There's only one Gwen Makepeace that I could find in her fifties. I didn't mention it sooner, partly because it was Amy's secret, and if I'm honest, partly because I wondered if it might be a kindness to let it drop. It's a long time ago."

"Do you have an address or a phone number?"

Duncan hesitated. "No, but I have got an email address you could try."

"What would you do, Jennifer?"

"Not so very long ago, I found that I had two grandchildren that I hadn't even known existed. It's a long story, but it worked out well for me. Perhaps I was lucky, but now I can't imagine them not being in my life – our life."

Duncan nodded.

"Then, I have my answer. Be forever wondering whether I had done the right thing or not. Clearly Amy was in two minds, otherwise she wouldn't have written that Christmas card. Can't ignore it. If this Gwen wants to leave the past in the past, then of course I will respect her wishes. If I draft an email, will you send it for me, Duncan? Not so hot on computers."

"Happily," Duncan said. "And good luck."

Extracting the blue file from the box, Penny opened it to the final page. The clue was in the last verse.

A little scrap
> *Once here, then gone*
> *Not on the map*
> *My first newborn*

The title, *My Very Own Dolly,* and alongside it, 'June 1924'. Three years before Amy was born. Amy's comment couldn't have been more appropriate. A conundrum.

Sally Roberts knocked on the door and walked straight in. It didn't surprise her in the least that Gwen didn't so much as look up. A new thriller series about to go into production and the first production meeting in half an hour; no doubt she was rereading the script for the ninety-ninth time, making notes, and checking she had everything listed that needed to be covered. Guarding against complacency and always keeping an open mind, Gwen treated each new series as though it was her first.

Sally knew Gwen inside out. PA for the past twenty years – where Gwen went Sally followed, from London to Birmingham.

"Giles Sharp. Do we know him?" Gwen said without looking up. "I haven't come across him before."

"The sound designer?" Sally said. "Brilliant. Team player. Creative. A ton of credits."

"Hmm. Good. The rest I know. Any apologies?"

"No." Sally laughed. "Not when the great Gwen Makepeace calls a meeting. They wouldn't dare! Spare a minute?"

It was one of the many things Sally loved about Gwen. With no airs and graces, she was a true people person. She treated everyone the same, from the big wigs in head office to the tea lad; she always made time for them, and that included her public. It was fairly unusual for a director to have a fan club, but Gwen's was the biggest she had ever come across, bigger than most of the superstars. Petite, softly spoken, and one of the older directors in the BBC, Gwen was a force to be reckoned with. Wearing clothes that she had worn, to Sally's knowledge, for the past ten years at least, comfortable in her own skin, and confident in her own abilities, Gwen wore a coat of many colours.

"All yours," Gwen said, closing the script before putting it, together with a pile of papers, into her briefcase.

"Just a few queries from today's inbox. A dozen messages from new fans to which you'll no doubt want to reply in person. I'll forward them to you. A whole load of wannabe new script writers. I've referred them all back through the online submission process. Meetings that I've added to your calendar. Several from the producer about finance…you'd think that it was coming out of his own pocket. You might like to check these out before the meeting. The casting director confirming the final cast. Information only. Oh, and the writers copying you in on endless emails to the showrunner. Not happy with some of the interpretations."

"Nothing new there," Gwen said. "Anything else?"

"Just one. It's an odd one. It's just come in. An email. It's not fan mail, that's for sure, and it doesn't seem to have anything to do with work. It's a she. Probably a crank. She says that she'd like to meet up with you to talk about family. She says that she might be your aunt. Correct me if I'm wrong, but you haven't got any. Family that is. Not since you lost your dad. So, she's got to be a crank."

"Did she give a name?"

"Yes. Penny Reilly. And a phone number. Do you want me to ring her to find out more about it?"

Gwen frowned. "Thanks, Sally. Leave the message on my desk and I'll make the call myself."

It was just one more job in an ever-increasing list of jobs. One more job that her conscience reminded her about day after day but that somehow always managed to get pushed down the priority list. Two weeks later, Gwen retrieved the note with the telephone number for Penny Reilly from her handbag and made the call.

12

ENGLAND

2022

I t was time for the final inspection. Standing back from the Portakabin, now renamed No. 19, Stan and Penny admired their handiwork. Work had started immediately following Amy's thanksgiving service, and the transformation was completed within two weeks. What had once been a builder's Portakabin, a temporary meeting place for the residents and an eyesore for several years, was now the highly desirable No. 19, Magnolia Court. Shell painted willow-green with the steel frame picked out in a darker green, it melded perfectly with the trees and the pasture land beyond. A bistro set, comprising two ornate wrought-iron chairs and a small table, sat outside the front door. A pot of yellow chrysanthemums had been carefully centred on the table as a finishing touch.

"You know she's got an eye for colour, that Jennifer," Penny said. "I'd have painted that front door willow like the rest but that sunshine-yellow looks pretty darned good. Specially with the chrysanths."

"And Andy's done a pretty fine good job on that ship's bell

and the number." Stan pulled his handkerchief out of his pocket and ran it over the brass.

"Think Amy would approve?" Penny asked. "Personally, I'd have liked to call it Wilsonville, in memory of Amy, but I have to agree that it doesn't have quite the same ring about it. Key, Stan," Penny said.

Stan pulled the key out of his pocket and slid it into the lock. "That's strange. It's not locked. No worries…I remember now. Jennifer mentioned she was coming up to check out the inside – make sure that everything worked and the beds were comfortable. She must have beaten us to it this morning. After you, ma'am."

"Not going to carry me over the threshold?" Penny joked.

Stan blushed. "You should be so lucky." He laughed, waving Penny in ahead.

Stepping inside the door, Penny stopped and roared with laughter, turning back to Stan. "Well, will you look at that? Now that's what I call dedication. Looks like she slept here. That's one way of testing the bed. Curled up under the blanket. Fast asleep. Had a row with Duncan, maybe?"

Stan peered over Penny's shoulder and narrowed his eyes. "See those dirty old trainers by the bed?" he whispered. "Never once seen Jennifer in trainers. She wouldn't be seen dead in them. And if, by any remote chance, she's decided to do so, they wouldn't be that colour. They'd be white."

"They're not hers you mean. And that's not Jennifer," Penny whispered as she crept a few steps closer to the bed.

"Goldilocks, maybe," Stan said.

"As in the nursery rhyme…"

"And the three bears, yes. Who's been sleeping in my bed, and all that…"

"Not going to get three bears in that bed, but Goldilocks, well, she might be a different matter. After you, Stan," Penny said taking a step backwards.

"Bloody cheek, road-testing No. 19. Let the fox see the rabbit. Stand back," Stan said squaring his shoulders. "Whoever it is, I reckon they're out for the count under that blanket. I'll deal with this. Might turn nasty."

Gingerly Stan pulled the corner of the blanket back one inch then two and then six. "Holy Moses. It's a woman."

"Bed, no breakfast for this one, and she'll have to pay for the privilege," Penny said, stepping forward alongside Stan. "Best if I wake her up. Good looking bloke you may be, but this woman might not have the same taste."

"Wakey, wakey, love. Time to wake up. Much as I hate to tell you, if you wanted a hotel, you've come to the wrong place," Penny whispered in her ear.

"Nothing?" Stan asked anxiously.

Penny shook her head. "Dead to the world. Or out of her head. Drugs, maybe…"

"But not dead, dead?"

Lifting the girl's arm, Penny felt for a pulse. "Don't worry, Stan, done this plenty of times back on the farm. Accidents happen everywhere…Pulse fairly normal. Head's half buried in that pillow. That can't help with her breathing. I reckon it's pretty shallow. Let's try rolling her from her side over on to her back. Then we can see what's what. Slowly now."

"Christ Almighty!" Stan gasped. "A baby, too."

"Strewth, what have we got here?" Penny stepped back in shock. "She's no more than a kid herself, either. Didn't see that coming, Stan. Amy always said that there was never a dull moment at Magnolia Court. Guess she got that about right."

Penny gently lifted the sleeping baby off the girl's chest and laid her down at the foot of the bed. "It's a little girl. She stinks,"

Penny said, screwing up her nose as she unpinned the nappy. "Poor kiddy. Reckon she's been in this state for a while. Wonder she's not screaming her head off. Come on, babe, Auntie Penny's here."

"How old do you think she might be?" Stan said.

"Maybe a week. Possibly two," Penny replied. "With a young mum who looks completely worn out. Poor kid."

In that moment the baby opened her eyes and smiled. Penny grinned. It took her back. A baby girl, just like her Amelia. "She's hot, Stan. Wonder she didn't suffocate under those blankets…Do you see that?" Penny pointed to the sheets, at the same time lifting the baby gently into her arms.

Stan leant in over the bed. "Blood. The girl's been bleeding."

"No need to panic. Not entirely unusual so soon after giving birth, but we shouldn't take any chances," Penny replied.

"I'll get Sam," Stan said. "Thank God for a doctor in the house. Can you hold the fort for five minutes?"

"We'll be okay. By the look of it, this one isn't going anywhere. I'll keep an eye on the both of them." Penny pulled up a chair and sat beside the bed. "Pretty soul, you are. Where've you come from? Sixteen, seventeen, eighteen at a push. The baby's okay if that's what you're worried about. We'll soon have you both sorted." Penny chattered on. Deep in sleep, the girl seemed unaware that she had company or that her baby was in another's arms.

Walking straight into No. 19, Jennifer threw her hands up in horror as she took in the scene. "Oh my God, what's happened? Who is she? Penny…a baby? I-I just came up to check out that everything was ready for our guests as I said I would…" Open-mouthed, Jennifer stared down at the bed and the lifeless soul that occupied it. "This can't be happening. Not here."

"It's okay, Jennifer, she's not dead. We don't know who she is or how she got here. Stan's just gone to fetch Sam." Babe in one arm, Penny rested her other arm on Jennifer's shoulder reassuringly.

"She's no more than a child," Jennifer said.

"At least she's alive. And this little one too. That's two things to be thankful for. We'll get those dirty old clothes off the both of them and clean her up as soon as we can. Poor as a church mouse, by the look of her."

Jennifer leant over the sleeping body and examined the girl's jacket and T-shirt beneath. "A church mouse maybe, but not poor, Penny," she muttered. "Those are, or were, expensive clothes she's wearing."

"What makes you say that?"

"A dedicated follower of fashion, Penny. That's me. Maybe from afar these days, but I know designer clothes when I see them. And these are top of the range."

"I think we can move her. Probably won't even know we're doing it," Sam said. "We need to get her and the baby somewhere warm, where they can be cleaned up and looked after."

"My place," Penny said, without hesitation. "I think this little one's taken a liking to me. There's the spare bedroom and the bed's made up."

"Are you sure you're up to it?" Stan asked, looking concerned.

"I know what I'm doing, Stan. I've had a few of my own in my time," Penny replied.

"If you need anything, just ask. I'll do it," Jennifer said.

. . .

Leaning over the bed, Sam ground his teeth. "Look at this, Jas. Episiotomy."

"In layman's language please, Doctor," Jas said.

"Episiotomy. Makes the opening of the vagina a bit wider. Let's the baby come through more easily."

"Thank God I never needed one," Jas said.

"Yes, well this one is pretty extreme. That's a long cut. And the stitches. Looks like a four-year-old put them in. This poor kid."

"Horrendous."

"Look, we need to get evidence of this," Sam said. "Will you take my phone and get stills and video – just in case we need it later?"

Jas took the phone and walked slowly around the bed, zooming in and zooming out again. "In the can…And those are blood clots coming out?" Jas asked.

"Mostly. Not unusual. She'll need sanitary towels for the next few days. I know that it's all tampons these days, but don't suppose you've got any?" Sam grinned. It was a long shot, but worth asking.

"As it happens, Mr Brown, I do keep a stock for emergency purposes."

"Too much information, wife." Sam laughed. "She's lucky so far – this one. I can't see any infection, but you never can be sure. Whoever did this should be locked up and the key thrown away. Even that would be generous." Sam shook his head in disbelief and stepped back. "Thankfully her heart rate is okay and blood pressure there or thereabouts. My guess is that she's just physically and mentally exhausted. I've cleaned her up as best I can."

"She'll wake up soon?" Jas asked.

"When her body tells her that it's good and ready and not until. You can't tell."

"Drugs?"

"No outward sign, which is good, but who can tell what concoction's inside her. We'll have our answers when she wakes up. Some we might like, most we probably won't."

"But she'll pull through, won't she?" Jas asked.

"Yes. She's skinny as a rake, even after giving birth. With a frame like hers, it wouldn't have been an easy birth, one way or the other. Frightened, exhausted, hungry, out of her depth…she'll need help when she comes around – and kindness."

"Should we take her to the hospital?"

"Five maybe ten hours waiting in A&E. Then no beds. If they had the resources, I'd say yes, we'd be on our way right now, but we both know, it's not like that anymore. They're better off here. At the first sign of trouble, we'll call an ambulance," Sam said. Jas nodded. Sam was a damned fine doctor. If anyone could see them through it, then it was him.

"Second patient?" Jas said, pointing to the door and the stairs beyond.

"Second patient. But judging from those lungs, that little one down there is faring better than her mother. It's a long time since we had one that size, Jas. You forget what noisy little blighters they can be. Don't happen to have any earplugs at home, do you?"

"No, I don't! Sanitary towels, yes. Earplugs, no!"

"And there was me thinking that you had everything." Sam laughed. "You're a wonder, you know that?"

Jas grinned. She might even put earplugs on her next shopping list. "Penny was feeding the baby last time I popped down. Some formula she's made up. Said it used to work wonders with the lambs."

"God help us." Sam raised his eyebrows. "I'm not asking."

"And Stan's there sitting right by her, cooing at the baby like a lovesick pigeon. If it weren't so tragic, it would be laughable," Jas said, trying to lighten the mood.

"If anything's going to bring her out of that sleep, it'll be the sound of her own baby," Sam said.

"In a cot beside the bed, you mean? Got you. Is that a hint? Job for Mr Fix It? I'm on my way. Pity about the launch party, but there's always another day," Jas said.

"The 19th hole, you mean?"

"Get it right, Sam. No. 19."

"And while you're going, stick those clothes in a bag," Sam said, pointing to the pile of clothes on the floor. "And make sure you wash your hands after."

"Twenty seconds and with soap," Jas replied.

Andy heard a knock on his door – once, twice, and three times to be sure.

"Morning, Jas. To what do I owe this pleasure? Come on in. Caught me out. Place is in a bit of a mess. Few jobs to do on the old bus. Carburettor today. All happens here in Andy's surgery, otherwise known as the kitchen. Better close your eyes," Andy said.

"High priority, Andy. We need a cot – that will stand on a frame," Jas said.

"That's a good one, Jas. You've found Moses down by the stream, or should I be congratulating you? Which one is it?"

"Neither. Actually we've found a baby, and it needs somewhere warm and comfortable to sleep alongside its mother."

"You serious?"

Jas nodded. "Deadly."

"Lordie, Lordie! Where?"

"No. 19. Penny and Stan found them when they went up there an hour ago. Mother and baby are now down at Penny's cottage."

Andy scratched his head. A cot. Okay. A wooden crate for a starter. Okay. He'd seen one kicking about recently. It would come back to him in a moment. The timber left over from making the bedframes up at No. 19. Hmm. Not too much of an ask. "Leave it with me. I'll get the frame made, and then I'll pop down and see Dot and ask her to see what she can find to line it and make it nice and cosy. Might take an hour or so. How big?"

"Baby size," Jas said, planting a kiss on his cheek.

"No problem." Andy grinned and cleared the kitchen table. A kiss from Jas – there was a first time for everything. The Post Its, Andy's never-ending to-do maintenance jobs for the residents, stuck up on the kitchen cupboard, would have to wait for another day. As would the bus.

"Let yourself out."

Jas opened the front door and Andy continued muttering to himself. "Lordie, Lordie. One day a dagger and the hunt for Red October. The next a girl and a baby. Repair workshop, my boy! Let's go." There was nothing he liked better than a challenge, and to come up with a cosy, lined cot in one hour would be the ultimate test.

13

ENGLAND

2022

Feeling drowsy, Stan undid the top two buttons of his shirt and leaned back contentedly. Nothing to beat a good steak and kidney pie with lashings of mash and gravy. A good cook was Penny. A very good cook. First, Mrs A's steak and kidney and now Penny's. Mrs A was what he had always called her when they had first spoken together, and the name had stuck. Always Mrs A. Stan, she had called him, but Stanley when he stepped out of line, which hadn't been often. Not with Mrs A.

And now here he was in Mrs A's cottage, now Penny's. It was almost like old times. Poetry. Penny had hardly changed a thing. As comfortable, cosy, and friendly as it had ever been, nothing had changed, other than two new photographs. One of which resided on Amy's old bookcase – the family photograph. The other – of Tara, Penny's beloved horse – was in pride of place on the mantelpiece.

There'd been rumours. Tittle-tattle. That Penny had an open return ticket. Who would buy an expensive ticket if they hadn't planned to go back? Duncan had learnt about the ticket from an unexpected phone call from Australia and had mentioned it to Dot and Dennis. One or other had mentioned it to Andy, and it had quickly made its way back to Stan. He preferred to believe that she had no such plans. That was what she had said, loud and clear, the very first evening they'd all been together in the Mansion House. She planned to stay for good – her words. It wasn't for him to ask questions, although…If there was something that she wanted to tell him, then she would, but in her own good time.

Always busy. Just like Amy. Hands never still. Amy, when she wanted help, always said that she would ask for it. Penny had said the same. Not in an unkind way, but making herself clear. No room for misunderstanding. Piling plates and dishes high on top of one another, balancing them on one arm while picking up more with her spare hand, Penny cleared the table before waltzing back out to the kitchen. It was the sort of thing that waiters and waitresses did in posh restaurants. Maybe in an earlier life? No, not Penny. Probably an art form learnt from feeding and clearing up after a big family, Stan thought.

Eyes heavy, he drifted off.

"Will you get that, Stan? I'm up to my elbows…The phone."

Awoken abruptly, Stan reran the words in his head. *The phone.* A phone was ringing, and he was supposed to answer it. Reaching for the landline, he picked up the handset. No one was there. Just the calling signal. Out of the corner of his eye he spotted her mobile, fast wriggling its way towards the edge of the dining table. Catching it just in time, Stan took his glasses out of the top pocket of his shirt and perched them on his nose – crooked, but that didn't matter. He pressed the green button.

"Hello," Stan said politely.

"Who's that?" the caller replied. Stan held the phone away from his ear. Not in the least bit sure that he liked the caller's tone, he was sorely tempted to press the red button. But it was Penny's phone and Penny's caller.

"Stan," he said.

"Stan who?" the caller asked.

It was a conversation fast turning into a farce. One that he could well do without. "Stan Morrison."

"Maybe I've got the wrong number. Is this 07977 8146923?"

"Pen," Stan called. "There's a man on the phone asking if this number is 07977 something, I think he said."

"Depends who's asking. If it's one of those calls from India, then the answer's no."

"Did you hear that?" Stan said, returning the mobile to his ear.

"Who did you say you are?" the caller asked again.

Even more tempted to hit the red button, Stan took a deep breath. "Stan. S T A N. Morrison. M O R R I S O N."

"Did I hear my mum's voice in the background?"

"That depends on who your mum is, wouldn't you say?"

"Penny. Penny Reilly."

"I'll hand you over…And who did you say you were?" Stan asked.

"Gary."

"Gary Reilly?"

"That's right."

"Pen, there's a fellow on the line who says he's your son. Name of Gary. Do you want to take it?"

"Tell him to wait while I dry my hands," Penny shouted.

"You'll have to wait while…"

"I heard. Thank you!"

Putting the phone on loudspeaker, Penny grinned. It appeared she'd enjoyed that little interchange immeasurably. Stan at his most mischievous.

"Good evening, Gary. Nice to hear from you," she said, turning to Stan. "Sit down, Stan. You don't need to go hide in the kitchen."

"Who's the guy? Whoever he is, he's not the brightest in the cabbage patch," Gary said.

Penny winked at Stan. "Oh, that's Stan. He's my new boyfriend. Well, toy boy really. Pretty good looking and got all his faculties. Know what I mean?"

Stan stifled a laugh. Bring it on. Cabbage patch indeed.

"Don't you think you're a bit old for that, Mum?"

"Old? Never too old as your aunt always used to say, and by jingo, she was right," Penny said.

"When are you coming back? We're missing you. We all miss you. The place isn't the same without you."

Stan's ears pricked up. The sixty-four thousand dollar question. Penny raised her eyebrows and looked at Stan. "Well, Gary, the fact of the matter is that I'm kind of enjoying being back here. Great company. Lovely little cottage. Got a lot going for it…"

Stan sat back and listened. She still hadn't answered the question. Cleverly side-tracked it.

"You've got friends and family here, Mum. Tara's missing you."

Penny pursed her lips. It seemed Gary knew which buttons to press.

"Pleased to hear it. You made a promise to look after her."

"You'll soon get bored there. Nothing to do all day," Gary said.

"Like I had something to do back home? Just finished refurbing a Portakabin. Like the ones back home. The ones that the hands used to live in before you sacked them…"

"For a good reason, Mum. Be fair."

"Huh. Well, the Portakabin looks ace now. Remember when I did that back home. You were no more than ten or twelve. Helped me paint it."

"How was Amy's thanksgiving?"

"Oh, so you did remember? Sad and happy at the same time. The sun shone. It was a good day. We scattered her ashes under the magnolia trees."

"So, that's done and the Portakabin's fixed. You'll be coming home now?"

"Ah, not quite so easy, Gary. You see, I've got a baby now... Are you still there?"

"You're not serious."

"Deadly. She's called Flossie."

Stan grimaced. Where in hell did that come from?

"Remember that sheep of ours that used to go wandering off on her own for months on end. She was a bugger to find, wasn't she? Called her Flossie, I did. Pretty little mite, she is...No, not the sheep. The baby. Just a couple of weeks old. We're getting on a treat."

"Look, Mum, I really think you need to get back here – to your family."

"Uh oh! I can hear her crying. Time for her next feed and a nappy change. Babies don't have watches. Internal clocks. Stomachs and bums. Sorry, son, got to go."

"We need you here, not halfway around the world. Remember Nanny Cats?"

"Sure," Penny said. "Thanks for reminding me."

"I mean it, Mum."

"Good of you to ring, but I really do have a baby to see to. Send my love to the family," Penny said, cutting the call before turning back to Stan. "That told him, wouldn't you say?"

Remembering the old adage 'He who speaks first loses,' and still no wiser about Penny's intentions, Stan kept his mouth firmly closed.

After putting the phone down on the table, Penny stood with her hands on her hips. "I'm a mind-reader, Stan, and it doesn't take much to read your mind. First, Nanny Cats was our mother – mine and Amy's. She had dozens of cats…and she did have dementia at the end. And I don't need to tell you that Amy had a mild form as well. That's what Gary was getting at. Sometimes I forget things. Goes in one ear and out of the other. Thinks I'm well on the way. So, I was winding him up about the baby and, maybe, the toyboy, but I didn't see you objecting. Second, as of right now, I have no inclination whatsoever to go back to Australia. This is my time and I'm going to pass it where and how I want. Lastly, I know he's my son and it's my family out there, but they don't need me. Not since Bluey passed on. Not since the day I handed over the running of the ranch to them. The fact that they've messed up is no longer my concern. When Gary rings, he wants something. Believe me. And most of the time it's not my welfare he's got in mind."

"Maybe you should tell him that you're planning on staying," Stan said as Penny's phone rang again. "Don't answer it. Let him stew."

"If that's you again, Gary, I've just told you in no uncertain terms that I have a baby to sort out, and now's not a convenient time…" Penny snapped.

"Not Gary. Gwen. I'm so sorry. Been a helluva day."

"I must have the wrong number. I was trying to contact Penny Reilly."

"No, no, you haven't, Gwen. I'm so, so sorry. Just been having a barny with my son in Australia. Thought it was him again. Can you just hold a mo?" Penny stuttered, turning to Stan. "It's a private call, Stan. Would you mind?"

Stan shook his head and shrugged his shoulders. Something else she wasn't being straight with him about. That had put him well and truly in his place. "See you tomorrow," he said, slamming the door behind him.

Gritting his teeth, Gary slammed the phone down on the kitchen counter.

"How did it go? When's she coming back?" Bobby asked. "Couldn't help but overhear bits of it. If we had her money, we could all get back to normal."

"You little shit," Gary said, walking away before he let fly.

"So, what are you going to do about it, big brother?" Bobby called after him.

"I'm going to buy an air ticket and go on holiday. Objections?"

14

ENGLAND

2022

S tan licked his lips, immediately dismissing the advice of his doctor. There was nothing to beat a good bacon sandwich to get the day off to a good start. So, he had to watch his weight and his cholesterol, but just now and again…Eight rashers of bacon sizzled away in the frying pan; the empty packet lay on the work surface next to the cooker. Two thick slices of bread, made by Hetty's fair hand, sliced and ready for the final part of the ceremony. Stan spread a liberal amount of ketchup over one slice and carefully layered all eight rashers of the crispy bacon across the bread, added the second slice, and reached for the carving knife. Perfect. And no one except Henry around to chastise him.

"Look, Henry, it's no good you looking at me like that," he said out loud to the invisible presence. "It's done, and in a few minutes, you'll never see this sandwich again. Close your eyes!"

Stan carefully carried the plate and a cold cup of coffee – timing wasn't his best suit – and sat down in front of the TV, selecting, as always, the armchair next to Henry's. It was a few years since his old friend and the former owner of the cottage had passed, but he was always there when Stan needed him.

"Morning, Henry," Stan said, attempting but failing to ignore the news report that yet another politician had stood down after being accused of improper behaviour with a member of the opposite sex. "In our time, Henry, you didn't get hauled up in front of the beak for putting your arm around a woman's shoulder or giving her a friendly peck on the cheek, or even tickling a woman to make her laugh. Now it's called sexual harassment. A hanging offence. I ask you. In our day it was harmless flirting or even showing a kindness. The world is not a better place, Henry. You're better off out of it."

As usual Henry didn't answer. It was, and would always be, Henry's cottage – a real old gentleman, if ever there was one. At opposite ends of the social structure, they'd hit it off right from the start. Henry, a well-respected orchestral conductor, had welcomed Stan into his world, sharing with him his love of classical music. If anybody had ever told Stan that in years to come, he would be sitting down and listening to Mozart and Vivaldi, he'd have thought that they'd lost their marbles. In return, Stan had tried to explain the intricacies of laying foundations, building walls, and roofing. It had fallen on deaf ears.

The news was depressing. Always depressing. Stan switched the TV off, reached for a CD, and slotted it into Henry's precious Bose player. The room filled with Vivaldi's *Four Seasons*.

Biting into his sandwich, Stan savoured the moment. "You'd enjoy this, Henry. Take my word for it. Cheers…So, what do you think about the latest shenanigans? It's a sign of the times – kids out on the streets, kids having babies, drugs and alcohol, knives, and even guns. Don't worry, Henry, I'm not going to launch into another 'in my day', but you know what I mean. It's out there, but somehow you don't expect it to land on your own doorstep. Amy would know what to do, wouldn't she? Remember what she always used to ask? 'What would you do, if…?' Clever that was.

Made us think for ourselves. We could do with her here right now, but we've got Penny instead. Nice woman. Down to earth. Quite fond of her, not that I'd admit that to anyone but you. No, nothing like that, Henry. A friend, that's all…Winds Andy up something rotten – reckon he's got an eye on her too."

Stan looked at his plate. It was empty. A greasy layer of fat and the odd blob of ketchup stood testament to the fact that once there had been a bacon sandwich on that plate. He'd done it again. Started a conversation with Henry and hadn't even tasted one mouthful of the sandwich. It was a sin and the end of the bacon. "Washing up, Henry? And then housework? I agree with you mate, not the best way to spend the day."

Up to the elbow in soap suds, Stan stood by the sink pondering the rest of the day. No. 19 was complete, other than that Jennifer would have to go up there to change the bedding and check out the mattress. No. 19 launch event was on hold. Only three days since they had found the girl, it didn't seem right to have a celebration. Perhaps when the girl had recovered enough. Maybe she and the babe might even join them.

Blow the housework. There was the picnic table that needed fixing before somebody broke their neck. It was a fine day and not one to spend indoors. Stan wiped his hands on his apron, noting that it was well overdue for the wash, and hung it up on the peg behind the kitchen door – the very same moment that the front door started to shake.

"For God's sake," he yelled. "Leave a bit for another day, will you? I'm coming. On my way."

"Stan, I need your help," Penny shouted through the letterbox.

"Sorry, wasn't expecting you, Pen," Stan said, opening the door. "Everything alright, love? Come on in."

"Can't stop. Got to get back. Can you come, please? Right now."

Before Stan had a moment to ask what the emergency was, Penny turned tail, dressing gown flying out behind her, and was running hell for leather back towards Amy's cottage. It had to be the girl. Had she died in the night? Please God, no. Stan pulled on his work boots, slammed the door behind him, and ran.

Amy's door was on the latch. Without a single moment of thought to the fact that he would likely leave a trail of mud throughout the house, Stan strode straight on in and through to the kitchen. Penny leant over the sink, her body heaving as tears ran down her face.

"Come here." Holding her shoulders, he turned her around to face him and took her in a bear hug. Sod sexual harassment. This wasn't Pen. "Shush," he whispered. "What was it your sister always used to say at times like this?"

"Don't know, and right at this moment, don't care," Penny howled.

"Let me remind you. It was 'Nothing matters half so much as you think it does.' Now dry those tears, calm down, and I'll make us a nice cup of tea."

"I hate tea," Penny whined.

"That's my girl. Welcome back, Pen. Coffee then, and you can tell me all about it."

"The girl, Stan…"

"She's not…"

"Dead? No, she's not dead. Far from dead, that's for sure," Penny said. "I draw the line at killing someone, but right now I could swing for her."

"She's managed to upset you alright." Stan frowned. "Giving you a hard time, is she?"

"She's gone. Buggered off, if you'll excuse the language." Penny paced the kitchen. "Just like that."

"Where?"

"If I knew that, I'd have gone after her."

"When?"

"I must have crashed out just after two this morning after feeding the baby. Or was it? Don't rightly know, lost track of time these last couple of days. Every three hours it is, Stan. Feeding and changing. Should have been up again at five. I couldn't help it. So, anytime between two and seven this morning when I went in to take her a cup of tea and start the changing and feeding process all over again. The bed was empty. I was bushed. Forty-eight hours on the trot. My head didn't touch the pillow."

"So, she woke up, then," Stan said, recalling that Sam had said she'd wake up when her body was ready.

"Yes, late afternoon, it would have been. Er, must have been about six. I'd just stuck my head around the door, and there she was, sitting on the edge of the bed, cradling the baby in her arms."

"Did she say anything? About what had happened to her?"

"Nothing. Couldn't even get a name out of her. Either she didn't understand what I was saying, or she wasn't telling. She looked haunted, Stan. I made her a cup of tea – strong – just the way you like it – and a sandwich and sat with her while she ate it. Didn't touch the sides. She was starving. So, I made her another one and showed her the bathroom. She was wobbly, but she got there.

"She wasn't afraid of me. Seemed to understand that I was looking after them both. Kept saying something that I think might have been 'Thank you'. I went downstairs and made up the baby's bottle and handed it to her. Not a moment's hesitation, Stan. I'll tell you that baby downed that bottle in double quick time, so I left them to it – to get to know each other again. Stood on the other side of the closed door and listened. Didn't want to take any chances. Chattering away to the baby, she was, happy as Larry, as far as I could make out. One thing for sure, that girl's foreign."

"I rather gathered that, Pen," Stan said.

"Next time I looked in she was fast asleep and the babe back in her cot. I fed and changed the babe, put her back in her cot, closed the door, and went for a lie down.

"Don't know what time it was, but I shot out of bed. Screaming and shouting and yelling. Sounded like a herd of roos stampeding through the house. She was having one helluva nightmare. By the time I'd hoisted myself off the bed, it was quiet again. So, I just lay on the bed listening out for her. Then I crashed. A pack of howling wild dogs wouldn't have woken me up."

"So, she's gone," Stan said with a growing feeling of relief.

"Helped herself to a pair of Amy's old jeans and a blouse from the wardrobe, took one of her jackets, and an old pair of slip-ons, and left without a by-your-leave. If she doesn't take size six shoes, then she's going to have very sore feet before long. And she took some cash…out of my handbag. I had three hundred pounds in there and now there's only one hundred. I counted it yesterday, so I know I'm right. And my mobile."

Stan said, "Not the way to behave, hey? Not when someone's doing their best to help you. Not your fault. We – you – did your best. You've been a trooper. No less. Nothing to beat yourself up about. I hate to say it, but if she's gone, she's not our problem anymore. You can get some sleep tonight."

"That's where you're wrong, Stan. She is our problem." Penny frowned and pointed towards the ceiling. "She left the baby. So, what do we do now?"

Slapping his head, Stan winced. "Can I say 'Shit' in front of a lady?"

"I'm no lady. I've already told you that," Penny replied.

"Then shit, shit, shit, shit." Stan bit his lip, deep in thought. "There's only one thing to do."

"Care to share that?"

"We go and see Max," Stan said, nodding his head.

Penny shrugged her shoulders. "Why would we do that?"

"Because, Pen, that's what we do around here. When there's trouble, Max steps up. A solid bloke, a calming influence, a bloody good organiser, and – most of the time – buckets of common sense."

"Take your word for it," Penny said. "I haven't got the energy to argue. Guess I'd better put some clothes on and do something with this bird's nest on my head. And talking about clothes, I checked the girl's pockets before I put everything in the wash this morning and found these."

Stan scanned the note. "Foreign," he said, running his hand over yesterday's stubble. "Change of plan," he said. "Duncan first. Maybe it's a thank-you note."

15

ENGLAND

2022

Pulling her cardigan over her shoulders, Hetty tut-tutted as she opened the front door. 9.00 a.m. It was never actually said and certainly not written in the rules – not that there were any – that social calling before ten was generally considered inconsiderate, except in an emergency.

"Good morning, Stan," Hetty said, pointedly checking her watch. It did not go unnoticed. "And Penny. And good Lord, is that you, Duncan? To what do we owe this honour?"

"The girl," Penny said, pushing forward in front of Stan. "We've got a problem."

Hetty frowned. Another problem? Wasn't one enough? It wasn't that she didn't feel every sympathy for the girl and the baby for that matter, but deep down it had worried her right from the start that however kind an act it had been to keep them both at Magnolia, it may not have been a wise decision.

"She's gone," Penny said.

"Well, maybe that's for the best." Hetty was still at a loss as to what might have brought the three of them to her doorstep at such an unearthly hour.

"And left us holding the baby," Penny said. "Literally and figuratively, Hetty."

"She's gone alright," Stan added.

"You mean she's gone and left the baby behind?" Hetty looked askance. "I don't believe it. Why ever would she do that?"

"You tell me," Penny replied.

"Fact," Stan said, towering over Penny. "Pen came racing up to tell me not more than an hour ago. And we dragged Duncan out of bed."

"I'm sure the connection will become clear," Hetty said, shaking her head. "You'd better all come in. I'll call Max. I think he's in the bathroom shaving and then I'll put the kettle on. Go through." Hetty opened the door to the lounge.

"Bit early in the morning, Pen," Stan whispered. "Take no notice. She can be a bit tetchy until she's had her first cuppa. She'll come around."

"Bit early in the morning for all of us," Penny snapped. "Some of us hardly got any sleep at all."

Penny and Stan followed Duncan into the lounge.

"Morning, Max. Sorry to disturb you both this early. Bit of a problem," Duncan said.

"Morning, Duncan, Stan, Penny. Hetty tells me that the girl has gone and left us with a guest," Max said. "A non-paying guest."

"That's the gist of it," Stan replied.

Max frowned and shook his head. He should have put his foot down right at the start. Right from the moment he'd heard about the girl and the baby. But Sam had been insistent. She was better off with them than in a hospital.

"What I don't understand is why she came here in the first place. How on earth would a young girl like that even know that Magnolia existed? And why choose to make it home?" Max said.

"I think I can answer that question," Penny said. "Yesterday, went to see Ros to ask if she could take the baby for the odd hour. It was then she mentioned it. Completely slipped my mind to mention it to anyone else. What with looking after the girl and the baby, and not much sleep...

"Ros said she'd come across the girl in Stroud the day before we found her here – last Sunday. She was sitting at a table in the same café that Ros happened to be in. You know what Ros is like. She'll chat to anybody. Apparently, the girl had a glass of milk in front of her and was drip feeding the milk to the baby with her finger. They got into a conversation – well, exchanged a few words. Ros said there was no doubt that the girl understood her and that she spoke English. With a foreign accent but reasonably fluent. Somehow the conversation moved onto where Ros lived. And Ros told her about Magnolia Court. She can't remember exactly what she said, but she does remember waxing lyrical about it. That it was a retirement complex. That it was full of lovely, kind people. That it was a safe place. Not far from Stroud. And then the girl thanked her and left. Ros said that she had felt genuinely sorry for her. She looked scared, worn out, and ill."

"So, you think that she might have been looking for a safe place? A refuge?" Hetty asked.

"Can't think of any other reason she might have turned up," Penny said.

"Well, that answers one question," Max said grumpily. "You'd better start from the beginning. Gone where and when?" Max asked.

Penny filled them in and sipped her tea – now was not the time to remind Hetty how much she hated the bloody stuff.

"...And that just about summarises my last twenty-four hours. Maybe I should also just mention the two hundred pounds she borrowed from my purse, and that my mobile phone has gone walkabouts—"

"So, she's a thief as well. It gets better and better. Nothing like biting the hand that feeds you. That's gratitude for you." Exasperated, Max shook his head and rubbed his forehead. Unbelievable.

"That girl was desperate. I'd put money on it that when the time comes, she'll pay every penny back," Penny said before changing tack. "By the way, Ros is at the cottage keeping an eye on the little one right now. She's been fed and changed. I told Ros that if she wakes up, then to count sheep on her little fingers. Works every time."

"The question is, Max"—Stan scratched his head—"do we ring the police like we probably should have done in the first place or"—he hesitated—"is there another way?"

"Another way?" Max said.

"That's right, Max. Another way," Penny interrupted. "Don't know how it works over here, but back home if this situation arose, the police would be round asking questions and five minutes later they'd be off to social services with the babe strapped in the back of the car. Might be the best thing. Not saying it isn't. But one thing for sure is that it'd be the last the girl saw of her child, unless she was very, very lucky."

"The child's welfare comes first, as it should," Max said.

"That would be a tragedy." Hetty frowned and picked up her knitting.

"There's one person who agrees with me," Penny cut in, seizing the opportunity. "Thanks, Hetty. Two women of like minds. It would be a tragedy. Like I told you all a few minutes ago, that girl loves that babe. No doubt in my mind. I've seen bad mothers and I've seen good mothers. She's got the makings of one of the good ones. She's young now. Hardly more than a child herself, but she's got what it takes."

"I'm not quite sure where this conversation is going." Max frowned. Listening carefully to every word that Penny had said, so far nothing had persuaded him that there was any option other than to make the authorities aware of the child's existence and the mother's disappearance. The girl had gone. There was no place for a baby at Magnolia.

"What Pen is saying, Max…Sorry, Pen, do you mind if I come in here?" Stan started.

"Be my guest." Penny grimaced as she took another sip of tea. Only one thing worse than hot tea – cold tea.

"What Pen is saying is what if the girl came back – today or tomorrow or even in an hour's time – and found that we'd palmed her baby off to a bunch of strangers? What sort of people would that make us?"

"Law-abiding," Max said sternly. "It's crossing the line, in my opinion. Not reporting the girl and looking after her for a couple of days is one thing. But it's a completely different matter when the baby's been abandoned. And that's the way it looks to me. If, as may well be the case, she loses the baby because of her own actions, then she has nobody to blame but herself. I'm sorry, Stan, but that's the way I see it."

"And it's also crossed my mind to ask myself what Amy would be saying right now," Stan interrupted. "And I'll tell you what…she'd say that we'd be doing a kindness to look after the kiddie until the mum came back. So, I suggest that we keep the baby here for the moment and see what happens. Provided, of course, Penny is happy to do the honours."

Penny nodded. "She's no trouble really. I can manage."

"Not even a starter," Max said.

Glancing sideways at Hetty, Max couldn't help but notice the stitches that were flying off one knitting needle and on to the next. It was a sign. Hetty was putting her thoughts in order.

"Max, don't you think that you are being a little callous? This is a child's future we are playing with. No one should be allowed to separate a child from her mother without a very strong reason. I know social services do their best but they're just like every other organisation these days. They don't have the resources to check everything out. It will be the easiest solution. A foster home, and if the child's one of the lucky ones, adoption at some point. She'll probably never know who her real mother was. It's happening far too often for my liking." Hetty put down her knitting. "You mentioned another way, Stan. And so did you, Penny. What did you have in mind?"

"That's why Duncan's here," Stan said.

"Instead of sitting here on our backsides debating the rights and wrongs of it all, we could try and find her." Duncan let the statement hang in the air.

"You've got my attention, Duncan. How might we do that?" Hetty said, brushing a few stray hairs away from her forehead.

Max shrugged his shoulders and sat back in his armchair. There were times when you did not argue with Hetty Brightwell.

"Allow me," Penny said. "It doesn't take me to tell you that something bad's happened in that girl's life, otherwise she wouldn't have ended up here in that state. This morning I decided to get all her clothes in the wash so that when she was ready to get up, she'd have something nice and fresh to put on. I always check pockets. The boys were the worst – stones, old nails, sticky sweets, worms – you name it, even a toad once. In the back pocket of her jeans, I found a short, handwritten note. Torn out of a note-book by the look of it. Worse for wear, but still legible. Written in a foreign language. That's where Duncan comes in."

"Ah! Excellent. I was wondering where you came into this," Max said, re-entering the conversation.

Duncan pulled a sheet of A4 out of his pocket. "The original note is written in Romanian. I've only been able to do a quick Google Translate job, but you'll get the gist of it."

Our friend tells me that you will be leaving soon. I want you to know that I will never blame you for anything. You followed your heart, and I followed you. It was my choice alone.

The baby must come first. Maybe one day I will meet him or her.

Alexandru and the boys are safe. I make sure of that. Miriana seems pleased with my performance and keeps me updated on the news from Romania.

I wonder if Flaviu – golden boy – is still part of your life?

Don't worry about me. I am not alone.

God be with you both.

"And where exactly does that get us," Max asked impatiently.

"Probably not that far. It tells us that the note was written by somebody close to the girl and it also tells us that whoever that person is knows about the baby. And it gives us three names: Alexandru, Flaviu, and Miriana. All Romanian, I'd guess," Duncan said. "Not much to go on, but we do have one lead that might be more promising. Penny…"

"A card. A small business card in the same pocket. It's the name of a B&B – would you believe – not so very far away. Called The Towers. On the other side of Stroud. Maybe that's where she's come from and where she is right now."

"It can't hurt to make a couple of enquiries," Duncan said. "It's worth a shot."

"I should go," Penny said. "She knows me. She trusts me. Maybe she'll listen to me."

"I'll go with Penny," Stan said. "And we'll get Andy to drive us there. Should be pretty straightforward. Either she's there or she's not. Then, if Penny gets to talk to her, it's up to the girl. She can come back with us. If she's not there, then we report the whole incident to the authorities."

"You do know that Gabby's coming down this afternoon?" Hetty said, apparently changing the subject. "Collecting the calligraphy set that Amy left her in the will."

"All packed up, Hetty. Ready for her to collect," Penny said.

"Maybe Gabby will have a few ideas," Hetty said, turning to Max. "Romania. Gabby spent quite a lot of time out there last year. Isn't that right, Max?"

Max grunted. "She did."

"Then maybe I should just give her a ring in a moment. Give her something to think about in the car as she's driving. And I'll get the Old Forge aired and ready for her just in case she decides to stay on."

"Perfect timing." Duncan grinned.

"I'm still not happy about any of this." Max glowered. "If the girl is not at this B&B, then we report to the authorities and hand over the baby."

"How about we all talk again when Stan and Penny have been to the B&B and Gabby has given us the benefit of her wisdom? I suggest that tomorrow at close of play we make the decision," Duncan suggested. "One day isn't going to make a lot of difference."

"I agree," Hetty said.

Penny and Stan nodded.

Max ground his teeth.

16

BUCHAREST

2021

Thursday 5th August 2021. It was a date indelibly printed in his brain. The very first time that he had met Elena. It was in the Ferentari area of Bucharest, an area he frequented on very rare occasions and an area that he preferred to avoid even when driving. An area in which he most certainly would not choose to walk.

A girl had sat perched on a low brick wall, once part of a building that had long since been demolished. He drove past her cautiously in case his presence might be misinterpreted as soliciting. In his rear-view mirror, he watched as a man stopped and spoke to her and put his arm around her shoulder. Maybe she was one of the hundreds of prostitutes that frequented the area, or maybe he was a dealer. She brushed his hand away, turned her head away, and pulled her thin jacket tight around her chest. The man moved on, turned back, tried his luck again, without success.

Flaviu drove on past and rounded the block. The next time he saw her, he was certain. She was anxiously watching the passing traffic and looked up as their eyes locked. Miriana had described her as slim, five foot seven or eight, with long blonde hair, and had said she was reasonably attractive.

Winding down the window, he called out to her. "I'm Flaviu, Miriana's friend. And you are Elena?"

Attractive did not begin to describe her. She was stunning. The photograph on his phone did her no justice at all.

Opening the passenger door for her, he watched as she gracefully sidled in. Better dressed, she might well have been a model. Her complexion was perfect, she wore no make-up. Her hair, soft and silky as though it had been freshly washed, hung down to her waist.

There was a certain shyness about her, signs that she had been brought up to understand the meaning of respect, to speak when she was spoken to. He tried to put her at ease. Turning her head towards him, she listened as he spoke, but said little other than that she was grateful, very grateful, and so pleased to meet him.

You should not be grateful. You will not be grateful for long, he vividly remembered thinking.

He had booked a table at a small pizza restaurant, on the other side of Bucharest and far enough away from Ferentari that nobody might see or recognize them. It was a restaurant not far from his apartment. One that he frequented often for business and occasionally for pleasure.

The proprietor had welcomed them both. He took her jacket, hung it up, and returned with the menus. It was a small booth – his regular table, at the back of the restaurant away from other diners, of which there were rarely many. She drank water. He drank Fetească Neagră, a full-bodied fruity wine from the Banat region – a wine which Miriana had introduced him to. He ordered Pizza Neapolitan for both of them.

Beneath the denim jacket, she wore a simple T-shirt, almost white, with the outline of a cat picked out in tiny blue diamantés, and jeans, blue, faded and with cuts across the knee, as was the fashion. On her feet she wore trainers with no socks. An outfit that was plain and simple.

They said little as they ate. He was content to study her face, watch her lips opening and closing, the pretty tongue within, as she slowly ate her meal. She was shy and intent on her food. He ordered coffee for them. Black and strong – before remembering that he was there for a purpose. To win the heart and mind of this girl. To take her to England.

She had clung to his every word, her eyes sparkling with excitement.

He was captivated by her. Captivated by her innocence. Captivated by her voice. Captivated by her charm. Captivated by everything about her. There was nothing that he could find fault with. All too soon the evening was over. It would soon be curfew, she said. Too soon, it was time to drive her back to Ferentari.

Usually, he had all the business concluded within an hour. By that time, he would have checked the papers Miriana would have told the girl she must bring to the meeting, and he'd have made all the necessary arrangements for the final pickup, checking and rechecking that the girl had understood everything that he had said. But he had hardly begun. Instead, he found himself asking if they could meet up the following evening.

Dropping her in the same spot, he watched as she strode away and out of sight, wishing, wishing…

On the second evening, he took her back to the same pizza restaurant, the proprietor hiding his surprise to see him back with the same girl in tow.

On the third evening, he took her to his studio apartment, cooked dinner for her, and shared a bottle of wine with her. On a whim, he had bought her a bracelet and had it engraved in the hope that in the future she might remember him with more fondness than he deserved. That night Elena had missed curfew. Nothing had been further from his mind, and he had not been prepared. It was midnight before he checked her papers and made the final arrangements before driving her home, the scent of lavender lingering in the car long after she had gone.

Sunday 8th August. The rendezvous point, the brick wall at 8.00 a.m.

Just another job.

17
ENGLAND
2022

"Nice name," Andy said. "The Towers. Bet there won't be a tower in sight. Never is. *Fawlty Towers*. You remember *Fawlty Towers?* Now that was comedy. Proper comedy. Not like the rubbish these days. Manuel – he was my favourite. 'Mr Fawlty, I no know that word. It rude?' Had me splitting my sides, rolling around the floor, it did. And what about that classic episode? Old Bas out in the street beating hell out of that Austin with those branches. They don't make them like that anymore."

"Eyes on the road, mate," Stan said, gripping the seatbelt.

"Well, Penny, what's the plan?" Andy said, turning to look at Penny in the back seat, and then quickly back to Stan. "Don't panic. I've got eyes out of the back of my head."

"Do we need a plan?" Penny asked, thoughtfully.

"Not necessarily, but if it was that sister of yours sitting in the back of this car, she'd have one – just in case," Andy said. "Not sure that marching up to the door asking whoever owns that B&B if they happen to remember a young girl with long blonde hair who might have dropped in for a night or two counts as a plan."

"I do have a plan, as it happens…" Penny said. "Stan, will you marry me?"

"What!" Stan exclaimed. "You're not serious."

Penny grinned. One day maybe but unlikely. He wouldn't be such a bad catch at all. "For the next couple of hours or at least the duration of this visit, you're going to be my husband, and we're thinking about booking family into the B&B. You can propose to me properly on another occasion when you've got a three-carat diamond ring. I'll probably say no."

Letting out a long sigh of relief, Stan screwed up his face. He wasn't quite ready for wedding bells yet and so far, he'd managed to avoid landing a part in one of Jennifer's theatrical productions.

"I'm not a great thespian, Penny. Ask Jennifer," Stan said. "Behind the scenes work. That's what suits me best. Why not marry Andy?"

"Andy's driving. You're not."

"But, Pen…I won't know what to say," Stan whined.

"You don't have to say anything, well, not much. I'll do the talking. You just nod and shake your head at the right time, smile, and make the odd appropriate remarks," Penny said.

Andy laughed. Wait until he told Jennifer. Stan wouldn't know what had hit him. Lead role in the next production.

"Nearly there, Bonnie and Clyde. Past the church – St Mark's – and then next turn on the left if this map is right," Andy said, running his finger over the map on his lap. "Haven't been over this way for a while. Not bad around here. What number did you say?"

"Number 14, St Mark's Road," Stan replied. "That's it."

"Anyone see a tower?" Andy laughed. "Not even one of those

mobile masts. What did I tell you? Where would sir and madam like me to park the limo?"

"Around the corner. We'll walk from there," Penny replied. "No point in drawing too much attention to ourselves."

Linking her arm in Stan's, Penny set a brisk pace back around the corner, stopped outside the gate to No. 14, and looked up at the sign. Leaning at an angle not dissimilar to the Leaning Tower of Pisa and planted in the garden alongside the brick wall, the wood was rotten, the lettering fading.

"All rooms ensuite. Colour TVs in rooms. Hot and cold running water. No vacancies." Penny shook her head. "Not keen on spending money on signage. If I came here looking for bed and breakfast, one look at that sign and I'd walk in the opposite direction."

"Run more like," Stan said. "Looks a bit grim, doesn't it? Looks like she's good at growing weeds." Stan pointed to the front garden.

"Best foot forward, Stanley. We haven't come all this way to check up on her DIY skills nor her gardening skills," Penny said, marching up the short garden path. "No bell, either. You'd have thought…Oh, well…Each to their own." Penny lifted the rusted brass door knocker and rapped twice, and then again.

"No one in?" Stan said.

"You know, Stanley, at times you do have a tendency to state the obvious," Penny said, knocking again. "Perhaps she's in the bathroom or hard of hearing…Or perhaps you might be right."

"Home then?" Stan turned and started back down towards the gate. "Wild goose chase."

Penny stood by the gate, glancing up and down the road. "See what I see? Three more B&B signs in the road. I'll bet my bottom dollar that whoever owns those knows what goes on in these parts. Let's go. We'll take the last one in the road. Take my arm."

"The last one?" Stan asked.

"Yes." Penny grinned. "A woman's instinct. Trust me."

Detached, built in the late sixties or early seventies, the similarity between The Towers and La Bonne Maison ended there. A freshly painted sign – 'Bed and Breakfast. Dinner optional. Ensuite. Communal lounge for guest use. Vacancies' – welcomed guests and was firmly attached to the gatepost top and bottom. No amount of wind would shift it. Blindingly white, ruched, net curtains hung from each of the windows. Marigolds, lobelia, and multi-coloured begonias bedecked either side of the garden path leading up to the front door. The grass was freshly mown.

"Now smile, Stan. You're a happily married man. You have a beautiful wife on your arm and a lovely family," Penny said as she rang the doorbell.

"Can I help you?" The woman who answered was smartly dressed and wearing a flowery blouse with blue slacks mostly covered up by an apron. "Oh dear! You've caught me out," she said wiping her hands on the apron. "It always happens when I'm cooking. What can I do for you?"

"G'day to you," Penny said, exaggerating her Australian accent. "We're looking for a nice little place for my daughter and son-in-law and their family to stay for a couple of days. They're coming all the way from Australia for a family wedding, and we haven't got room to put them up. The happy couple are getting married just up the road at St Mark's, so we thought we'd just take a walk around the area and see what we could find within easy walking distance. This looks nice. A hundred percent nicer than all the rest of them in the road."

The woman smiled. Compliments were always welcome no

matter from whom they came. "A family?" the woman said. "With children? I don't normally take children in."

"Two kids. Teenagers. Best behaved kids you'd ever meet," Penny replied. "Couldn't be a better location. Reckon they'd love it here."

"And you are?" she asked.

"Penny, and this is my husband, Stanley. Penny and Stanley Morrison. He's not an Aussie, you'll be pleased to know. Picked him up on a cruise. Took one look at him and said, 'That's my man.'"

"You'd best come in. Please, do call me Daphne," she said, before hanging her apron on a coat hook in the porch. "Do you mind coming through to the kitchen? I've got scones in the oven. I'd hate them to burn."

"Very kind of you. Don't mind if we do," Penny said, following Daphne into the kitchen. "Nice place. We did start at the other end of the road. Didn't like the look of that B&B up there. Blessing in disguise. No one in."

"The Towers, you mean? Tonya's house. Dreadful, the whole thing," Daphne replied, taking the scones out of the oven before turning to Stan. "I don't suppose you'd like one of these with some homemade jam. I've made far too many for myself. And a cup of tea, perhaps?"

"That's very civil of you, Daphne." Stan brightened up visibly. "We do love a nice cup of tea, don't we, Penny dear?"

Penny narrowed her eyes. He was pushing his luck and loving every minute of it.

"And would I be right in saying that the gentleman likes cream with his scones? I can tell, you know. I just so happen to have some Cornish clotted cream in the fridge." Daphne smiled, a glint in her eye.

Stan winked at Daphne. "You know the way to a man's heart, don't you, Daphne?"

Penny grimaced, returning to the matter of The Towers. "Dreadful thing, you said. Do you mind me asking what might have happened up the road?"

"We've none of us got over it. It was last Sunday night. The 21st, if I'm not mistaken. I've a good head for dates. It's very important when you're running an establishment like this. Yes, Saturday night sometime. Haven't been myself since. She died, you know…"

"That's terrible." Penny sympathised. "A friend of yours?"

"Tonya? I wouldn't exactly say that, but I'd like to think we were close. In the same business obviously, you have to stick together. Such a sweet warm person, she couldn't do enough for people. An absolute lifesaver during Covid. Shopping for the elderly folk. Baking night and day, leaving little parcels on doorsteps. Of course, we couldn't have guests at the time. Prisoners in our own homes. Every day at eleven we'd see her. Out walking. Just for an hour, of course. We'd all stand outside our front doors and have a little chat with her. It made such a difference. So considerate for one so young."

"Well, with a track record like that, God probably gave her the best seat in the house," Penny said. "Young, you said?"

"Yes. In her mid-thirties would be my guess. Not early thirties. Not late thirties. You know."

"Best scones I've ever tasted," Stan said, licking his lips.

"I must be honest with you. I wasn't at all sure of her when she first moved in. Must be about five years ago. It was during that time when you couldn't go to supermarkets without being surrounded by foreigners – mostly eastern Europeans, you know. Cosmo. That was her surname. And she was from Romania. Never judge a book by its cover, I learnt. Tonya was quite exceptional in many ways. A kind but private person, in her own way."

"Sounds like the perfect neighbour," Stan said.

"I'm not entirely sure why she decided to go into the B&B business, other than for the money, of course. They're quite pricey these houses. Good location. Not too far from the town centre. A good bus service. Quiet area. I think she might have had a windfall. You'd need a tidy sum to buy one of these houses. Especially an end one on a bigger plot like Tonya's. And you'd need a good income to live comfortably. With the price of everything these days. Council tax, heating, food. Skyrocketed. And there's the strange thing…"

Penny's ears pricked up. "Strange?"

"Yes, strange. She rarely had guests. At least not of the overnight paying variety, the mainstay of all bed-and-breakfast residences. I could probably count them on two hands. Not, of course, that I was keeping count. Not my business, you understand."

"But she had guests?"

"Oh, yes. Friends, I think. A steady stream of them. Sometimes they'd stay for a week or so, sometimes for longer. Months some of them. Maybe they paid her rent. I don't know."

"Friends from Romania, perhaps. Maybe while they were looking for jobs?" Penny suggested.

"I wouldn't know. I hardly saw any of them in person, but you knew they were there. Lights on in both the front upstairs windows. Well, you wouldn't leave lights on unnecessarily, would you? I'd see the light when I was taking Billy out for his last walk of the day. He's out in the back garden, sunning himself, probably fast asleep. Nice woman but private, as I said, and kept her friends to herself.

"No complaints. Well, not really. Only the neighbour on one

side. Of course, being on a corner plot, she only had one neigh-bour. Used to complain about the noise sometimes. Babies crying or some such."

"Hardly saw any of them?" Penny said. "So, you did see some of them?"

"Well, just one as it happens. Not exactly met, you know. I was walking past the house, a few weeks ago or it might have been a little longer. Tonya was getting into her car and there was this girl standing on the doorstep. Poor child. Couldn't have been more than sixteen or seventeen. As big as a house. About to drop, as they say. I remember hearing Tonya shout something that I couldn't understand at all. Must have been Romanian, and then the name Helena. A bit of a heated exchange. I think they might have had words. And then the door closed, and Tonya drove off. Listen to me prattling on. You don't want to hear me going on about the comings and goings in this street."

"Helena?" Penny repeated, wide-eyed. A coincidence? Sixteen, seventeen – about to have a baby.

"Pretty name for a pretty girl, isn't it? Tall with beautiful, long blonde hair. Probably quite attractive without the – you know – bump," Daphne said.

"Quite sure she was called Helena?" Penny asked.

"My hearing is excellent. Does it matter what she was called?" Daphne frowned.

"No, not one bit, Daphne. Just that we once thought about calling our daughter Helena. Coincidence, hey?" Stan said.

"She was most definitely called Helena," Daphne repeated with strong emphasis on *Helena*.

Glancing sideways at Stan, Penny raised her eyebrows. Now they might be getting somewhere.

"Dreadful thing to happen to a woman so young, and so kind.

Always seems to be the best who are taken from us. I do hope it wasn't a painful death," Penny said.

"I think it was quick from what the detective told me. It was on the Sunday morning when the doorbell rang. A very nice man introduced himself as Detective Superintendent Handley and broke the news. Tonya had passed away. A fall. Caught her head on something. Instantaneous, apparently. On her own in the house. No one to turn to. No one to call an ambulance for her. Tragic. A nice man. I did offer him a cup of tea, but he seemed to be in a bit of a hurry. Doing the rounds, just letting the neighbours know what had happened. They've located an aunt, so he said."

"But I thought you said that she had a girl called Helena staying with her," Penny asked.

"She must have left." Daphne shrugged her shoulders. "Nobody was there according to the nice Detective Superintendent."

"Did he ask if anybody had been staying there?" Penny persisted.

"Naturally. And, of course, I told him exactly the same that I've just told you. And I also mentioned Tonya's manfriend."

"A man friend," Penny said. "It's nice to know that she had a few friends."

"Very handsome. Hair that shone like gold. My heart would flutter every time I saw him drive past in that posh car of his. Must have been very wealthy. A Porsche. I think that's what it was. He used to visit her regular as clockwork, but now I come to think of it, I haven't seen his car there for quite a few weeks. I'm sure the aunt will know him and have broken the news to him. And has probably managed to get word to Helena as well. More tea?"

"Kind of you, Daphne, but we really need to get on our way. Thank you for your hospitality," Stan said, getting up ready to leave.

"But you haven't seen the room, yet," Daphne said.

"If it's as welcoming and clean as this kitchen, then we don't need to take any more of your time. They're going to love it here," Stan said, taking Penny's elbow.

Penny glowered and gritted her teeth. There were plenty more questions she'd liked to have asked, given half the chance.

"And you haven't told me what dates the family want to book in. I get booked up well in advance."

Stan hesitated and picked a date out of the air. "October 28th and 29th. Two nights. And thank you again, Daphne. Best scones ever," Stan said, manhandling Penny towards the front door.

18

ENGLAND

2022

Leaning forward, eyes glued to the screen, Duncan stroked his chin. A master at navigating the internet, there was nothing he liked better than a challenge. And that morning he had challenged himself to learn all he could about crime in Romania. It was as good a place to start as any. Other than that the girl was Romanian, young, a mother, and troubled, they knew little about her or her background. No identifying documents on her; they didn't even have a name. And, as he had just learnt from Stan and Penny, the owner of the B&B had also been Romanian. The only common denominator.

In the space of a couple of hours, he had learnt more about crime in Romania than he had in his lifetime. It was an eye opener. Naïvely, and he was far from naïve, he'd thought that the Mafia operated primarily out of Italy with strong presences in the USA, Japan, and Venezuela. Not so. The Mafia had a very strong presence in Romania as well. Drugs, child abuse, prostitution were everywhere. And much as the Poliția Română apparently did their best to maintain and law and order, they were losing, big time.

Delving deeper and deeper into the internet, going to places that those less skilled might never find, the morning had been profitable. Very profitable.

"Afternoon, Duncan." Gabby walked straight in through the front door and on into the lounge, planting a kiss on Duncan's silvery mop of hair.

"I suppose I ought to knock these days. I wouldn't like to walk in on anything inappropriate. You look well." And he did look well. The happiest and most content she had seen him for months. A combination of married life and yet another mystery to unravel. "You're positively glowing. What are we googling this time?"

"Watching Toy Story 3, if you really want to know!" Duncan swivelled around and held out his hands to her. His favourite woman apart from Jennifer, of course. Hetty and Max's niece was as much part of the Magnolia family as any of them. Six years since she'd first come into their lives, and since their first spectacular success when Trumper finally got what was too long coming to him. Without her, it wouldn't have happened. Down to earth, resourceful, level-headed, and inquisitive, she was also a well-respected investigative journalist.

"That would be the day." Gabby laughed. "No Jennifer? What time will she be back?"

"Hours probably."

"So, I've got you all to myself. What fun."

"Behave yourself, young lady. I'm a respectable married man now, you know. Missed your chance." Duncan grinned.

"Where is she?"

"She's briefing Hetty and Dot for the next production. Some Tom Stoppard play. They're talking costumes."

"They haven't roped you in yet, then? Which play?" Gabby asked.

"*The Real Inspector Hound,*" Duncan replied.

"Right up your street, I'd say. In more ways than one. Isn't there a wheelchair Canadian brother-in-law baddie in it? Magnum or some such name."

"Magnus," Duncan corrected her. "There is. And before you ask, it will not be me, much as Jennifer would like it to be. When she's finished with Dot and Hetty, she's stopping off at Ros and Paul's cottage to ogle the baby. Women! I was invited to join them, but I declined. Politely, of course."

"And Penny?"

"Not long since been back from checking out B&Bs. We'll come back to that later."

"She sounds fascinating, from what Aunt Hetty's told me," Gabby said, pulling a chair up alongside Duncan. "Is it going to work? Her living here, I mean. No one can ever replace Amy."

Duncan frowned, remembering that there was a conversation yet to be had with Penny. He didn't like contradicting stories. While Penny insisted she was here for good, the son on the other side of the world was equally insistent that she was only over for a visit. And on the basis that, according to her son, she had an open return ticket in her pocket, he was inclined to believe the son. The time hadn't been right so far, but the moment would come when he'd have to ask her outright.

"She's a live wire, alright. Typical Australian. Bit abrupt and rough at the edges, but no one can say she isn't doing her fair share of work. She and Stan haven't long since finished revamping the 19th hole. Doesn't mind getting her hands dirty, I'll give her that. Pretty good with screaming babies too. Treats them like little lambs. I ask you," Duncan said steering away from Gabby's previous question. "No. 19, it's called now. You wouldn't recognise it."

"That's where they found the girl and the baby, wasn't it?"

"Monday. Stan and Penny," Duncan said.

"That's being pretty precise," Gabby commented.

"That, my dear, is because with everything that's going on, you forget what day it is…What day is it today?"

Gabby looked at her watch. "Thursday 24th. All day. She was in a pretty bad state, so Aunt Hetty said."

"Yep. It's not long since she's had the baby. A couple of weeks possibly. Episiotomy performed by a butcher, according to Sam. Had to look it up myself. Cut open and sewn back together with a darning needle, Jas said."

"Painful. And she disappeared when?"

"Last night or more likely the early hours today. Penny was asleep. When she woke up, the girl had gone, taking money and Penny's phone, leaving the baby behind."

"Forty-eight hours. Remarkable powers of recovery, wouldn't you say?"

"Sam thought so. Thought she'd be laid up for a lot longer than that," Duncan said. "And Hetty told you about the B&B as well, did she?"

Gabby nodded. "Yes. Said that Stan and Penny were going to drop by there this morning. No luck, I presume. And it's a missing person report by the end of play tomorrow according to Uncle Max. Bit tricky reporting a missing person when you don't even know her name, but there's always a first time."

"Didn't." Duncan grinned. "Past tense, Gabby."

"I wondered why you were looking so chipper. I should have known better," Gabby said. "Fire away."

"A girl by the name of Irina Albescu was reported missing from Ferentari, a pretty rough suburb of Bucharest, in August 2021. When you want to find an answer, the most obvious place is often the best place to look."

"Don't tell me. Missing persons," Gabby said.

"Got it in one. Missing persons in Romania. A shot in the dark, but look at this." Duncan fired up the computer and pointed to a screen. "That's her. Sixteen years of age at the time. Born 12th May 2005. Not been seen since August 2021. 'Anyone with any knowledge of Irina's whereabouts should contact…' That would make her just seventeen now."

"You're sure that's her?"

"Hold that question for a minute or two. Jas took some photographs while Sam was examining her just in case there were any later repercussions," Duncan said, placing the photograph alongside the screen image. "Identical."

Gabby nodded. "Identical. Irina Albescu. That'll help the police find her. Brilliant."

"But hear this," Duncan said, thoroughly enjoying himself. "When Penny and Stan went to the B&B, it was all locked up. No one in. So, they dropped by a neighbour. The neighbour remembers a girl staying at The Towers B&B. Recently. Heavily pregnant. Tall. Long blonde hair. Fits the description. Swears that the girl was called Helena."

"Helena, Irina – easy mistake," Gabby said.

"That's exactly what I said to Penny, but would she have it? No, she wouldn't. Blasted woman. She's just as stubborn as Amy could be when she thought she was right."

"I'd back your horse, Duncan. Irina."

"Well, I strongly advise you to stay well away from a betting office, because you'd lose your money."

"How so?"

"Penny was so insistent. Couldn't move her an inch. I got to thinking. Could we both be right?"

"Not following," Gabby said.

"Sometimes it pays to think outside the box." Duncan strung it out. "Was it possible that there could be two of them? Irina and

Helena. Twins. Sometimes a long shot pays off, Gabby. Every country has a record of births…"

"And?"

"Irina and Elena Albescu born May 12th 2005. Identical twins. Irina was reported missing August 2021. Age sixteen. There's no missing person report for Elena."

"But if you're right, then which one dropped into Magnolia?" Gabby asked.

"I can even tell you that. I've blown up the photograph of our girl and the one from the missing person's report. You need to look closely. And it could well be a bad photograph, but…they're not identical. Spot the difference."

Glasses perched low on her nose, Gabby peered closely at the two photographs. "Irina, the girl reported missing, has a small mole on her right cheek. Your girl doesn't. Gold star, Sherlock. Am I right?"

"Spot on. Ergo, our girl is Elena Albescu. No mole." Duncan grinned.

"And her sister is on file, reported missing in Romania…"

"A leap of faith, but maybe, just maybe, Irina is in the UK as well, and that's where Elena went. To find her sister and not back to the B&B as we thought."

Gabby frowned, unconvinced. "As you say, a leap of faith. There's nothing to say that the missing sister isn't still in Romania."

"Unless you add the note that we found on Elena into the equation."

"Aunt Hetty mentioned something about a note. How's that relevant?"

"Take a look at this," Duncan said, reaching for the note on his desk. "It's a translation. Original written in Romanian. What does it say to you?"

Scanning the note once, and then again, Gabby said, "Written to someone close, I'd say."

"My opinion precisely. Sister to sister. Possible?"

"Possible. So, potentially two missing people."

"And one dead. Tonya, the owner of the B&B."

"Wow. Sounding like trouble."

"There's got to be a connection somewhere. And then there are the names in the note: Alexandru – possibly another family member? Miriana, a friend maybe. Flaviu, golden boy, involved with Elena in some way or another. Maybe the boyfriend. Any one of them might know where Elena is." Duncan pursed his lips.

"That'll keep the police busy. Are you going to tell the police or will Uncle Max?"

"I've asked Stan and Penny to hold fire on telling Max that the girl wasn't at the B&B," Duncan said.

"Why?"

"You need to hear about Stan and Penny's trip up to The Towers. Ready?" Spinning the wheelchair one eighty degrees, Duncan was away.

"And you're going to tell Penny that she was right after all?"

"Building up courage!"

19

ENGLAND
2022

She was quite adorable. So very like her own Amelia as a baby, she brought back fond memories. Little more than forty-eight hours since the girl and the baby had been found, and not much more than twelve, maybe sixteen hours, since the girl had left, Penny was whacked. All too easy to remember the good times and forget the bad times, Penny was never more relieved than when Ros had volunteered to take over for the afternoon. For a few hours, blessed peace reigned.

Looking forward to a couple of hours' sleep, Penny set off up the stairs. Halfway up, the doorbell rang. Her first thought being that the girl might have come back, Penny turned on her heel and headed for the front door.

"Duncan, I was just going to—" Penny started.

"I thought you'd like to meet Gabby," Duncan said. "She's not long since arrived."

"Pleased to meet you," Penny said, wishing that Duncan had chosen any other time to make introductions. "Amy wrote to me often about you. Thought the world of you. I've got the calligraphy set all boxed up and ready for you."

"I'll treasure it, Penny. Promise. I miss her. She was a wonderful woman. You couldn't help but love her. Mischievous, mind you, but a real trooper."

"Hard act to follow, my sister," Penny said. "I wouldn't even start to try. Come on in, both of you. You'll have to forgive the state of the place. I've given up on housework. No time with a babe to look after."

"Can I see her?" Gabby asked.

"She's with Ros at the moment. We've done a deal. Ros takes her in the afternoon, and I do the morning and night shifts. Tea?" Penny asked.

"I'll make it," Gabby said. "You sit down."

"Coffee for me. How you people can drink that stuff, I'll never know."

Duncan cleared his throat. "You were right, Penny."

"That makes a change," Penny replied, the day looking up.

"Her name is Elena."

"Helena," Penny corrected.

"Actually, it is Elena."

"So, you agree that it's not Irina, as you insisted earlier." Penny smiled.

"I do. My apologies for doubting you."

"Apologies accepted." Penny smiled, remembering Amy telling her that Duncan was rarely wrong and almost never admitted it when he was.

"But I was right too. There are two of them. Twins. Elena and her identical twin sister, Irina. Take my word for it. Elena is the mother of the baby. Irina, we believe, might be somewhere in this country as well. That's not certain, but it's possible."

Penny scratched her head. She was tired. It was all too complicated. Better not to ask. At least now she could stop calling her the girl and refer to her by her proper name. "I'll settle for Elena."

"Tea, coffee." Gabby set the tray down on the coffee table.

"I've just been explaining it all to Gabby," Duncan said. "Why I thought she was Irina, and you thought the girl was called Helena."

"Just hope that Elena or whoever she is walks back in this door pretty damned quick. Her time's running out, if it hasn't already," Penny said. "It's only a few days, but I'm beginning to wonder whether Max wasn't right about handing the whole thing over to the powers that be the very first day we found her. If it weren't for that baby...And now we know that the girl – sorry Elena – isn't at the B&B, I guess it's all over, bar the shouting. Are you going to tell the authorities or will Max?"

"I was telling Gabby about your recce over at the B&B this morning but thought it would be better for her to hear it from you. Out of the horse's mouth, so to speak," Duncan said.

"You're the second one to call me a horse in the last week. I'll tell you most horses I know look a darn sight better than I do right now. What do you want, Gabby? The short version or the long version?"

"Keep it short, then we'll leave you to get your beauty sleep," Gabby said, passing a mug of tea to Duncan and coffee to Penny.

"Short version coming up. Business card found in Elena's jeans pocket. B&B called The Towers. Just on the other side of town. No one in. Stopped by another B&B, a neighbour, with Stan posing as my husband, with a cock-and-bull story about looking for B&B accommodation. Typical single landlady. Loved the sound of her own voice. Wound her up and off she went. Lucky for us.

"Towers – owned by a woman called Tonya Cosmo. Romanian. Dead as of five days ago. Accident. A fall. Alone in the house. No suspicious circumstances, according to one Detective Superintendent Handley. Last known visitor one girl about to drop – tall, long blonde hair, called Helena.

"Interesting set up apparently. A B&B that didn't seem to be used as a B&B but a long stay place, according to Daphne. Had guests who stayed for months at a time. A regular visitor as well. A boyfriend. A bit of a heartthrob, by the sound of it. Hair that shone like gold. I think Daphne took quite a shine to him. Drove a Porsche, to boot.

"Neighbours thought the sun shone out of this Tonya's backside. Just one who used to complain. About noise. Babies crying, so she said. And – not that it's probably relevant – the properties in that road are what you English call desirable or, in other words, big bucks.

"And Daphne makes excellent scones. Lousy tea, but all tea's lousy, in my book."

"And Elena had The Towers card in her jean's pocket?" Gabby said.

"Yep." Penny nodded. "So not unreasonable to assume that she had been there. Would have solved the problem, if that's where she'd stayed. Could have dropped the baby back to her. Sweet little thing that she is. Deserves better. Life's never simple, is it?" Penny said. "And dead people don't speak. End of."

"Did Daphne tell the Superintendent about all this?" Gabby asked curiously. "That name rings a bell."

"Yep. Told him about Helena – sorry Elena – being there up until a while ago and about the boyfriend and his regular visits," Penny said. "Reading between the lines, he didn't seem particularly interested."

"And it was an accident? An accident in the home?" Gabby frowned and sipped her tea.

"And didn't you say there was an aunt they had located?" Duncan asked.

"Forgot that. Yep, that's what the Superintendent said."

"Next of kin, maybe. So most probably organising the funeral," Gabby muttered to herself.

Duncan raised his eyebrows.

"That's about it," Penny said.

"I haven't said anything to Max. Guess that's where you'll be going now. When Ros brings the baby back, I'll get her ready for whenever and whoever comes to collect her. I'll miss her. In the meantime, I'm up those stairs for a sleep."

"Thanks, Penny. We'll talk to Max. Tomorrow at the latest," Duncan said.

Duncan turned to Gabby. "What did you make of that?"

"Weird," Gabby said thoughtfully. "One too many babies. Babies, Penny said. Complaints about babies. Elena arrives here a couple of days after this Tonya dies. An accident. Connection? Golden boy, Flaviu, possibly Elena's boyfriend, dropping in regularly. A DS wandering around chatting to the neighbours...Long-term visitors. Whatever's been going on, I'd guess that Tonya is, or was, in it up to her neck..."

20

ENGLAND

2022

Cooking had never been her best suit. Steak and chips okay. Anything more complicated had a habit of landing up in the bin. Jennifer reached into the fridge and pulled three juicy steaks out. And then oven chips from the freezer. Maybe not the best chips in the world, but it saved peeling potatoes and nasty smelling deep-frying pans. And Duncan could never tell the difference. The steak was an extravagance, but it wasn't often that she got to entertain Gabby, and it was the first time that the three of them had sat down to a meal together since Amy had died.

"What time would you two like dinner?" she called from the kitchen. No reply. Jennifer stuck her head through the door. No surprises there. Duncan and Gabby were deep in conversation, oblivious to all else.

"Is there anybody there? What time would you like dinner?" Jennifer repeated.

"Can you give us half an hour?" Duncan said without turning his head. "Just chewing a few things over."

"No trouble," Jennifer said, retreating to the kitchen. It was good to see Duncan engrossed in another project. Never happier than when he was heads-down with Gabby. For a brief moment she spotted Amy standing over their shoulders, or was it her imagination?

"Not quite the angel that Daphne painted her to be, hey?" Duncan stroked his chin thoughtfully. "She's got a record, this one. What do you make of that?"

Gabby leant forward as Duncan brought up one website after another.

"Tonya Cosmo. Suspected prostitution but no arrests. Seems like she had a charmed life, or friends in high places," Gabby said.

"2017 she ups sticks and moves to the UK. Moves into The Towers and sets herself up in business as a landlady. Why? And where does the money come from? Didn't Penny say that those houses were expensive?" Duncan mused. "And it's no ordinary B&B, according to Daphne. So, what went on behind closed doors? And why was Elena there?"

"A brothel?" Gabby frowned. "Unlikely. A highly pregnant girl in a brothel? The neighbours would have sussed that out pretty quickly. More questions than answers. Dead end?"

"Not quite. I've got an idea." Duncan's eyes lit up. "Gabby, go and talk to Jennifer for an hour. will you? Have a glass of wine. Have two. Just buy me an hour. Tell Jennifer to put dinner on hold. Ask her about that Stoppard thing. But watch it. She'll have you and Greg in leading roles before you can say jack knife."

"How's married life, Jennifer?" Gabby asked. "You're looking after him too well. I'm sure he's put on a few pounds."

"He's up to his tricks again, I presume?" Jennifer said.

Gabby winked. "What tricks?"

"To answer your question, as perfect as it could be. We're very happy."

"And you're staying in your cottage?"

"And my husband in his cottage? Yes, I know some people were horrified when we told them we were both going to continue to live in our own cottages but it's the most perfect solution. At our age, and when you've got used to your space, it's very hard to give up. We have the best of both worlds. When I want to stay here, I stay. When I want a bit of peace – he does snore you know – I retreat to my own cottage. We eat either here or at my house. Could there be a better solution?"

"It obviously works for the two of you. The wedding was great. Amazing, in fact. All those guests. Anyone heard from Ahmed?" Gabby asked, putting her arms around Jennifer and giving her a hug.

"Sam keeps in touch. Ahmed's back in India. We've all got an open invitation to visit. You should see the photographs of the house. Out of this world. Pity, but I don't think the bus would get us that far. Austria, yes, but India, no."

"Maybe one day," Gabby said.

"Where's Greg by the way?"

"Off on another of his jaunts. Just six days this time. Swanning around Dubai. I've got a few days off. The last assignment was hard work. 24/7 for almost two weeks. It took me a good couple of days to get over it when I got back. I'm taking a break," Gabby said.

"Some break. Busman's holiday, I call it. But this is a really dreadful situation, isn't it? That poor girl. That poor little mite. What's to become of them? Do you think she'll come back, or we might find the girl soon? Your uncle's none too pleased about keeping the baby here."

"He's made that pretty clear to me. I'm definitely not top of his popularity list right now." He had indeed and in no uncertain terms. What made it worse was that he was probably right. Keeping schtum about the girl for a day or two was one thing, but if it all went pear-shaped, it wasn't going to reflect well on Magnolia and neither would it do anything for her career. With a bit of a reputation for sailing close to the wind, she had to watch her step.

Gabby changed the subject. "And how's the play coming on? Good cast?"

"Funny you should ask, but I do have a couple of parts going begging. I don't suppose…"

"I was right," Duncan yelled. "Gabby, in here."

"Right about what?" Jennifer asked.

"Your guess is as good as mine, but I think I might be needed," Gabby said, heaving a sigh of relief. In the nick of time. A few seconds longer and she'd have found herself in a leading role in Jennifer's play. One of these days she'd learn how to say no.

"What have you got?"

"The connection," Duncan said, his eyes glued to the screen.

"Between?"

"Tonya and the letter. It's all connected, Gabby. I knew it. Guess who the aunt is?"

"The aunt? You mean Tonya's aunt? The one Daphne said was going to organise the funeral?"

"The very same," Duncan said, eyes shining. "The funeral's taking place tomorrow. A burial. No service. South Bristol Cemetery and Crematorium. Organised and paid for by"— Duncan paused—"Miriana Constantin."

"Miriana? As in Miriana in the note?" Gabby said.

"It has to be, doesn't it? How many Mirianas do you know

living in England? So, Tonya and Miriana are aunt and niece, or so we're led to believe. Elena stays with Tonya. Golden boy as mentioned in the note is Tonya's regular visitor. Miriana is mentioned in the note. How many connections do you want?" Duncan sat back, a broad grin on his face.

"But connections to what, Duncan?" Gabby asked. "I'm not sure this gets us any further."

"Take a look at this?" Duncan pulled up another saved screen. "It's a newspaper cutting. August 2013. Does that answer your question?"

Miriana Constantin solicită scuze. Miriana Constantin, bine-cunoscută și respectată proprietară de imobiliare din București, cere scuze după ce poliția a percheziționat una dintre reședințele sale din oraș. Poliția și-a cerut scuze în scris, explicând că informatorul lor s-a înșelat. Nu s-a găsit nimic semnificativ în interiorul reședinței. Șeful poliției a declarat că toate rapoartele de infracțiuni sunt luate în serios, în special cele legate de prostituție sau orice fel de abuz asupra copiilor. Doamna Constantin, văduva regretatului Nicolae Constantin și fiica decedatului Henric Dragnea, se gândește să dea în judecată poliția pentru calomnie.

"Stop winding me up, Duncan," Gabby said. "Translation, please!"

Miriana Constantin demands an apology. Miriana Constantin, well known and respected Bucharest property owner and landlord, demands on apology after police raided one of her city residences. The police issued a written apology explaining that their informant had been mistaken. Nothing of significance was found within the residence. The Chief of Police stated that all reports of crime were taken seriously, especially those related to prostitution or any kind of child abuse. Mrs Constantin, widow to the late Nicolae Constantin and daughter of deceased Henric Dragnea, is considering suing the police for slander.

"And there's a photograph of her. That's not all," Duncan said, tapping away at the keyboard. "Miriana Constantin upped and left Bucharest in 2014. She now owns five properties in the UK. Four in and around Bristol and one in Stroud. The Towers. Tonya's house. Land Registry, before you ask."

"Time to make the call, Duncan," Gabby said.

"Tomorrow? Another day won't make much difference. Haven't been to a good funeral for years. Aren't you just a little curious to see who turns up?"

21

ENGLAND

2021

Flaviu's fifth-floor apartment located near Clifton Village was the most beautiful space Elena had ever seen, and surely the size of a football field. It was what was called minimalist, he had said. The walls were white, the carpet a pale shade of grey, the sofas made of soft black leather; the only colour in the two paintings that hung from the wall. A glass-topped dining table and four chairs occupied a tiny corner at the back of open-plan space. The kitchen area was a sea of stainless steel and shiny glass. Sliding patio doors to the front with a glass balustrade and decking opened up overlooking the street beyond. The master bedroom alone could have slept the whole of her family, comfortably. There was another bedroom as well with equally as extravagant proportions. It was a palace. Another world. And so different to Flaviu's cluttered, albeit cosy, little studio apartment in Bucharest. So far removed from her own home. So far from Bucharest.

Elena had rarely left the confines of Ferentari, other than on that one day when she'd met Miriana and then when Flaviu had taken her to the pizza restaurant on the other side of the city. Both school and the office where she worked were within easy walking distance of home. And then suddenly she had travelled across the whole of Europe, a journey that held few fond memories.

It had been the longest two days of her life. Up through Hungary, Austria, and Germany, finally into France, crossing and recrossing borders, Flaviu had driven from dawn to dusk in the little grey Skoda. Picking up sandwiches as they stopped for fuel, there were no nice little pizza restaurants, no cosy dinners, and no time to stop to explore or admire the wonderful cities they had passed through, all cities that she had learnt about at school, but never visited. They had made two overnight stops at small hotels close by the main roads. The first room had been no larger than the room she had shared with her sister, and the second, little better. They'd slept in twin beds; Flaviu had been asleep before his head hit the pillow.

Eventually they had arrived at a town called Calais in northern France and followed the signs for the Channel Tunnel, the high-light of the journey. Waiting in one of the huge car parks, it had been just thirty minutes before they had been called to go to the next waiting point, the last before the train. And then just fifteen minutes until, remaining in the Skoda sandwiched between two other vehicles, the train had glided away from the station before descending into darkness. Thirty-five minutes later, it was light again, and they were in England. After showing their two pass-ports to the immigration authorities, they were waved on their way.

A memory, now wiped away by the first step she had taken into her new world.

The days had flown by. It hardly seemed possible that it was less than two weeks since she had left her other world behind. She'd simply packed her small backpack, thanked Mama for her packed lunch, kissed the boys and Irina for the last time, and set off for work, with no plan to return home that night or again anytime soon.

It troubled her that she had not entirely kept her word to Miriana or Flaviu. Agonising about the rights and the wrongs of what she was about to do, she had decided to leave a short note for Irina, asking her to read it to Mama and Tata when she did not return that evening. It said no more than that she was going abroad to continue her education, and that she would then be able to get a really good job. When that time came, they would never have to worry about money again and maybe they could then afford to move away from Ferentari and find a nice house in the country and in a safe area where the boys could grow up without fear. In the meantime, they would receive a small amount of money each month, at least equal to that which she regularly contributed from her job in the Bucharest office. She'd ended the note with 'Please forgive me but I am doing it for all of you. Your ever-loving daughter, Elena.' On the reverse side of the note, she had written: 'Irina, in a few days' time I will be in England. I will write to you the moment I get there. Please do not tell Mama and Tata where I have gone.'

Quickly she had slipped into a routine, Flaviu's routine. Rising at six thirty each morning, they ate breakfast together. At seven thirty, he left for work, locked the door from the outside, and pocketed the key. Strange as it had seemed in the beginning, she soon learnt that, as always, he had her best interests at heart. When all the paperwork was complete, he said, they would go out together – to cafés, bars, shops, restaurants – wherever her heart desired. In the back of her mind, she remembered Miriana mentioning that there would be a lot of paperwork, and that it might take time. It was for her own good. There were times when she stood by the patio doors, envying the passers-by. Men and women rushing for buses, mothers with toddlers and prams taking their children to school, groups of teenagers of similar age to herself, giggling and shouting as they shared secrets, while she could do nothing but look on.

The moment he left the apartment, Elena made herself a hot drink. After spooning fresh ground coffee into a cafetière, she added boiling water from the tall tap set into the stainless-steel sink, and then set about writing her diary. It had been Flaviu's idea. It would improve her written English and remind her of all she had learnt from him.

He'd taught her so, so much. About her body, about his body; it was almost too difficult to put into words. He had taken her places that she had never known. Taken her to the stars and back. Laughed as he'd witnessed her first orgasm. Brought her to a high, teased her, made her wait until, finally, he had let her come. Blessed relief. Bliss. Taught her the art of stroking, kissing, and sucking his private parts so that he stood proud once more. At times, he was tender. Whispering in her ear, he told her how beautiful she was, how desirable, how utterly irresistible, and even that he loved her. Those were the moments that she treasured most. There were others she preferred to forget. Where there is pain, there is pleasure, he would whisper to her. She had found muscles she had not known existed. She had not complained. All that mattered was that he loved her, and she loved him.

Where once she had been shy, she was no longer.

She would have liked for her diary to be filled with descriptions of all the adventures she had had, but there were none. She knew no more about him than that which they shared in the bedroom. She would have liked to have known where he went each day, how he spent each day, and with whom. Learn about his exciting world. Not because she doubted him in any way but simply because she wanted to share, make memories. But it had not happened. There were days when it had been difficult to fill a page and then she was tempted to write about her sadness that Irina had never replied to the letters that Flaviu had dutifully posted first class to Bucharest. But it was not what he would want to read. It would sound ungrateful, and that she was not.

He showered her with presents, clothes that took her breath away. Fine lace underwear that looked as though it might blow away in a breeze. Jeans that hugged her neat hips. Stretchy low-cut tops that revealed her breasts. Dresses that clung to her hour-glass figure. High-heeled stilettos that, at first, had pained her ankles and toes. He dressed her and he undressed her, stroking her body, sucking her breasts, running his hand high between her thighs, all the time devouring her with his eyes. He bought her sweet-smelling body creams, face creams, nail and hand creams. She no longer bit her nails. That was forbidden. And he had bought her a suitcase.

She wrote about all the wonderful gifts he had given her in such a short space of time, how much she loved every one of them. She wrote about his never-ending generosity. She wrote that she would never, ever, be able to repay him, nor Miriana who had made it all possible.

It was her last day in the apartment. The following day, Miriana would be coming to pick her up to take her to the house share where the next phase of her life journey would begin. The thought of leaving Flaviu – though he had assured her he would visit her, and she too could come to visit him – tore her apart. The thought of finally restarting school and the future that lay ahead buoyed her spirits and, in part, dulled the pain in her heart.

That evening they made love long into the night. Tender love. Love that spoke words. They talked. For the first time since she had known him, he shared his dreams. And he told her she was brave, had the capacity to do anything that life threw her way. That whatever happened she should stand tall knowing that she was a fine woman.

As his final gift to her, he had told her he had organised for Irina to come for a short visit. That her parents had readily agreed. That they now understood why she had had to leave Romania, wished her well in her future, and looked forward to being reunited one day. Miriana had agreed. Irina would be arriving the following day.

Elena fell asleep dreaming of the reunion with her twin sister. She loved her so much, and apart from Flaviu and Miriana, she was the most important person in her life.

22

BUCHAREST

2021

Irina's hands shook as she accepted the package from the Poşta Română courier and signed for it, her signature almost illegible. It was postmarked 15th August and had been sent from England, addressed to Irina Albescu. Closing the door behind her, she listened for sounds from the kitchen. On the other side of the door, there was a loud argument in progress. Serghei was refusing to eat his lunch. Mama would be spoon-feeding him the bean soup she had prepared for the family. Praying that her mother had not heard the doorbell, Irina stole silently up to her bedroom and propped the envelope against her bedside lamp and then headed back to the kitchen.

If the letter was from England, then it had to be from Elena, but the handwriting on the address label was unfamiliar. Either from her sister or someone who knew of her, to whom she had given her home address. It was weighty, the weight belying the notion that it was a letter only.

Ten days since Elena had left, leaving nothing more than a short note, Mama still railed at the very mention of her name. Elena was not missing, Mama had said. She had left of her own free will. They would not be submitting a missing person report. She was no longer her daughter, and her name was never to be mentioned in the house again. Stoically, Tata had said little, but Irina knew he was hurting badly and that he would find it hard to forgive her.

The first instalment of the promised money that they were to receive each week had not arrived. Had it done so, Irina was almost sure that it would have been returned to sender. Neither Mama nor Tata wanted anything to do with Elena's dirty money, as they called it. They would not be bought off by a few measly leu. On the day she disappeared she had ceased to exist. She had made her bed and now she had to lie in it. There would be no help from the family and no grieving over or search for a lost daughter.

Nothing Irina had been able to say had made them change their minds. It had been at no small expense to herself that she had tried to plead Elena's case, and it was evident that they still did not believe her when she told them she knew nothing of her sister's plans. To this day, she had still said nothing about Flaviu.

Peace resumed. The kitchen was quiet. Mama was sitting in front of the television watching a daytime soap, her legs propped up on a cushioned stool. In a matter of weeks, even days, the next edition to the family would be lying in the cot under the windowsill variously screaming for sustenance or a change of nappy. Lego was spread across the kitchen floor and the boys were building a castle.

"Mama. Is there anything you need me to do this minute?" Irina asked. "I have a mild headache. I thought I would lie down for an hour," she said. "I won't be long."

Mama nodded.

Back in her room, having quietly closed her bedroom door, Irina reached out, picked up the package, and carefully slit it open. Within, there were two envelopes, one she instantly recognized as being written in Elena's hand. The other in the same hand as on the outer envelope.

It was the first communication of any kind she had received from her sister, who had promised faithfully to write the moment she arrived in England. Had she received any correspondence, she would have written back, whether Mama and Tata had liked it or not. With no address, the notepad and envelopes that she had bought for the purpose remained in the top drawer of the dressing table they'd once shared.

Taking the letter out of the envelope and unfolding it, Irina mustered courage.

One of two things. Either Elena had written to say that she was alive and well and missing them all – maybe on her way back – or someone else had written to notify the family that her sister was dead. But if that were the case, why would the package be addressed to Irina Albescu and not Mama or Tata? Irina prayed that against all the odds, the news would be good so that maybe she could sleep without being woken nightly by the same recurring nightmare.

The same dream, time after time. A small inflatable boat rose on its bows before crashing back on its stern, driven on by twenty-foot waves that threatened to engulf them all. Sitting on a rain-sodden wood-slatted bench at the back of the boat, hanging on for grim death with the rain stinging her face and the cold wind chilling her body, Elena vomited. Terrified men, women, and children of all ages – forty or more, packed like sardines in the small boat – none of them wore life jackets. The one lifejacket on board was worn by the skipper, who fought to maintain their course to a never-ending nowhere. A sudden wave caught them on the starboard side and bodies disappeared into the deep and angry ocean. There one minute, gone the next. A second wave caught them. The boat overturned.

A frightening dream, and consistent in its detail with every recurrence. It was happening daily in so many parts of the world. People leaving their home countries in pursuit of their dreams.

Maybe this letter would allay her fears. Give her the unworried sleep that once she had known. Whatever the contents, it would be closure – for better or for worse. She needed to open it uninterrupted.

Draga mea, Irina,

I miss you so much. I miss Mama and Tata and the boys. How are they all? Mama's new baby must be due soon. I hope for your sake that it's a boy so that you can keep our room for yourself.

Everything in England is wonderful. My joyful news is that I start school in mid-September. I have seen the brochure. It lives beside our bed, and I read it from cover to cover each night before we switch off the light.

I will be joining the sixth form and if (no, when!) I get my A levels I will be going on to university. My English is coming on leaps and bounds (that's an English expression. I believe they call it a cliché). I have a beautiful wardrobe of clothes and shoes for the summer months...

Irina let her thoughts drift back to that life-changing moment when Elena had told her that she was in love. Flaviu was his name. *It lives beside 'our' bed.*

I will shortly be moving from this apartment, which I shall miss dreadfully, to share a house nearby the school with five other girls. It was Flaviu who suggested that you might come over for a few days. I am told that there is a spare room that you can have for your stay. Do come. We can catch up and giggle together just like we used to after Mama and Tata had gone to bed. You can see for yourself that I have done the right thing.

Say you will.

Toată dragostea mea,

Elena

Tears ran down her cheeks. Elena was alive and well and full of optimism for the future. Thank God for one small mercy.

Irina opened the second envelope. It contained a ticket for a Lufthansa flight leaving from Henri Coandă Airport on Monday 23rd August, flying via Frankfurt and landing at an airport called Bristol. It was a return ticket with the return dated three days later. Pinned to the ticket were details of travel arrangements to Otopeni and from Bristol to the house share. A taxi would pick her up and take her to the airport. In England she would be met at arrivals. She should look out for someone holding a board bearing her name. If immigration were to ask, she should simply say that she was visiting family and would be staying at The Beeches, Avon Road, Bristol.

Irina pulled out a small burgundy red book with the words 'European Union', 'Romania', and 'passport' inscribed above and below the coat of arms in Romanian. Opening the passport to the centre page, Irina stared at the photograph of herself. But it was not she. Only she and Elena knew of the one tiny mark that differentiated one from the other. She had a tiny mole on her right cheek. Elena did not. The photograph was of Elena. The name in the passport was Irina Albescu.

Dropping her head in her hands, Irina dug her nails into her forehead. Whatever else she had been expecting, it had not been this. How could Elena possibly expect her to drop everything and go for a visit? Of all people, she, her twin sister, would know that Mama and Tata would never agree to such a trip. And the very thought of going through an airport, let alone boarding a plane, was the most terrifying of all.

Angry and confused, Irina shoved both the letters in the dressing-table drawer, her head throbbing. There would be little or no point in asking Mama or Tata for advice. She knew what their answer would be. The clock was ticking. She had five days to make a decision.

There were just the two of them sitting side by side at the kitchen table. Distracted, Tata had one eye on the sports page of the Gazeta Sporturilor and the other on Irina. "Irina, can we have a word?" Tata said.

Irina looked up from her mending and smiled. Tata, the kindest man in the world, rarely ever raised his voice in anger. His family meant everything to him. She knew that. "Yes, Tata, what is it?"

"You are still my little girl, you know. Maybe not so little anymore, but to me you will always be. I care for you deeply and now that…"

"Elena has gone." Irina finished his sentence, knowing how hard it was for him to even mention her name.

Tata nodded. "I am worried about you. You've become distant in the last few days. This is not like you. Mama has noticed it too. She too is worried. Is there something on your mind, *draga mea*? You can tell me," he said softly.

Irina bit her lip. More than anything, she needed someone to talk to. Someone who would help her make the right decision. But Tata was the last person in the world she could confide in, especially since she had already made her decision – one that he would most certainly not condone. She would go to England. Speak to her sister. Listen to her sister. Even try to persuade her to come home. After three days, she would return home with or without Elena. She would then know that she had tried or at least that her sister was safe. It would be soon enough for explanations to Mama and Tata when she returned.

"It is nothing, Tata. Just the time of the month." Irina leant over and kissed Tata's cheek.

23

BUCHAREST

2021

"Loser."

"Wanker."

"Big girl's blouse. Go home and cry to Mama."

"Saddo."

Dropping down onto his knees, Alexandru covered his head with his hands and fought to wipe the memory of the past ninety minutes from his head. By half time he'd saved three attempts on goal and let in one. By full time he'd saved another two goal kicks and had let in a further three. It was always the goalkeeper's fault when the final whistle blew and the score was four–nil. The other side, the visiting team from Otopeni, had wiped the floor with them. No one ever blamed the forward, midfielders, or defenders for a loss. Alexandru was in disgrace, and he knew they would never let him forget it. Bad enough if it had been one of the earlier rounds, but for the final of the inter-schools' annual football tournament, it was unforgivable. And it was a home match at that.

Twelve years old, he was too old to cry, but he did. Tears flooded his eyes and streamed down his cheeks. Wiping the tears away with his sleeve, he sniffed and looked up. His so-called teammates had disappeared into the changing room. Half of the school, who'd stood behind the sidelines for ninety minutes praying that the team would bring home the coveted trophy, filed off the field to the jeers of the supporters of the opposite side. The pitch was empty of all but one man, who stood on the sideline with arms crossed, legs akimbo, staring at him.

With knees and elbows bruised from the saves he had made, Alexandru slowly hoisted himself up on his two feet. Going back to the changing room was not an option. He'd be pilloried by the team and hung, drawn, and quartered by the sports teacher. The only option was to walk home as he was – muddied and dirty – and if he was lucky, get into the house without an interrogation by his mother or brothers. They would all no doubt hear about his humiliation before the day was over.

"Hey, you," Alexandru heard the man call out. "You going to let them walk all over you or are you going to grow up?"

Alexandru ignored the man.

"I'm talking to you, Alexandru," the man shouted.

Alexandru turned. He had never set eyes on the man before, but the man knew his name. Face lined, hair black and slicked back, curling up over his collar, he was tall, well-set, and striding towards him. He'd had enough trouble for one day. The last thing he needed was a lecture from some stranger or more like a dressing down from one of the other player's fathers.

"What do you want?" Alexandru called.

"You don't recognise me?" the man said. "Bogdan Lung?"

Alexandru shook his head. "Should I?"

"Probably not. Doubt that you were a twinkle in your Mama's eye when I played for Romania. Goalie. Just like you. Coach now. Always on the lookout for talent, and maybe you've got it, kid. You just need the balls, if you'll excuse the pun. You want to be a goalie? You want to show those prats what you're made of? You want to rub their noses right in it?"

Alexandru nodded. The answers were yes, yes, and yes.

"Call me Bogdan. And tomorrow you tell all those boys that you just had lessons in goal keeping from the one and only Bogdan Lung.

"Eyes, Alexandru. Take your eyes off that ball for a split second and it's over. Looking at the totty out on the sidelines, were you? Sure, you made some saves today, but that was a whole lot more luck than skill."

Alexandru smarted at his comment. Right at that moment the only memories that were preventing him from crumbling completely were those of the five saves he had just made, for which he had the scars.

"When someone's firing a ball at you, you close down. You don't hear the shouts from the crowd. There's no one on the field except you and that bastard whose about to kick that ball between your goal posts. I watched you. In those crucial split seconds, your eyes were everywhere. It doesn't matter if your hair is all over the place or you've wet your pants, you don't think about it, you hear me?"

The man was right. He had let himself be distracted, two times at least. First by the referee hammering down the field with the defence, and second by one of his own defences telling him to go right when he knew he should have gone left. The others he refused to own up to.

"When you catch that ball, you hang on to it. Wrap your arms around it. You any idea how many goals have been scored by goalkeepers simply dropping the ball after saving it? It doesn't matter if you're winded or the ball's broken your bloody ribs, you hang on to it. Want to give it a go?"

Hopping from one foot to another, Alexandru narrowed his

eyes and watched the man as he walked back almost to the side-line. He'd show him what he was made of. Taking a deep breath, filling his lungs, he prepared to receive the shot. The man stepped back from the ball, ran forward, and kicked. Alexandru watched as the ball travelled at speed and low level across the pitch and timed his dive accordingly. His eyes never left the ball and yet the man scored his first goal.

"Again," the man shouted.

Alexandru kicked the ball back to him.

"You'll never make a goalie if you don't look like one. Man up. Make yourself big. I want to see a mean look on your face."

Having had more than a bellyful of humiliation for one day, Alexandru wasn't going to let this man get under his skin. Flexing his neck, back, arms, and leg muscles, he planted his feet firmly on the ground, leant forward, and rested his hands on his thighs and engaged the ball.

"Reach," the man yelled as the ball flew faster than the speed of sound across the pitch and high up in the corner of the goal, inches from Alexandru's outstretched arms.

"Again. Jump."

"Again. Reach."

"Again. Dive."

And again and again, until, exhausted, Alexandru sank down on his knees.

"Get up," the man said, towering over him. "Penalty kick. It's going to come fast. Be ready." Dribbling the ball back near the goal line, the man placed the ball carefully on the ground and stepped back. "Ready?"

Alexandru struggled to his feet and nodded. The ball flew straight and fast, four feet above the ground. He was ready for it, but nothing could have prepared him for the impact. Thump. The pain was excruciating. Lights flickered in front of his eyes, then darkness, then more lights. Reaching up, he felt the swelling on his forehead and blood trickling down from his nose, his head pounding, thump, thump, thump. His left eye had closed completely. The right eye struggled to focus. He was sinking, sinking to the ground, sinking away. The last he remembered was the man leaning over him, phone in hand, camera flashing, once, twice, three times.

The man turned and walked slowly away. Alexandru's humiliation for the day was complete.

Some months later, Alexandru learnt that Bogdan Lung had died in a car crash some five years earlier.

24

BUCHAREST
1999–2014

BUCHAREST

I n 2013, Henric passed away quietly in his sleep. It was more than he deserved. If Miriana had had her way, it would have been a slow and painful death. One that was long overdue. She was under no illusions. After the sudden accidental death of his only son, Anton, at no more than two years old, and with no prospect of further sons following the death of his wife while bearing Miriana, Henric had made no secret of the fact that the business would pass into the hands of his brother's eldest son, a once callow youth, who over the years, he'd taught everything he knew.

Miriana's first-class honours degree in business studies had done nothing to change the status quo. Old school, Henric stood firm on his principles. Men ran businesses. Women made babies. Preferably male. Boys and then men who would, generation after generation, maintain and grow the family's business interests.

There was no place for a woman in business. Well qualified, Miriana applied for jobs in finance and banking, her chosen careers, only to have her applications turned down without explanation. Some years later she learnt that Henric was solely responsible for her lack of success.

Getting tired of his daughter's wilful, wild, and increasingly debased lifestyle that was endangering the good name of the company, Henric decided he would find her a husband within the company. Like it or not, she would do what women were brought into the world to do. Offered two candidates, Miriana declined both and instead set her sight on one of her father's business associates, a man of considerably older years – a man she had known since her teens and whose wandering hands were more than familiar to her.

Flattered beyond measure at her proposal, the following day Nicolae Constantin had asked Henric for his daughter's hand in marriage. Henric had been enraged. It was not what he wanted for his daughter. On the contrary, with Nicolae's age and the family line in imminent danger of extinction, it was the last thing he had expected and the very last thing he would have wished for. Had it not been for the fact that Nicolae had more dirt on him than the other way about, then he would have refused point-blank. Instead, he gave his blessing, forked out for a society wedding, and washed his hands of her.

In Miriana's mind, Nicolae had ticked all the right boxes. He was wealthy, old, well connected in Bucharest society, and judging from his incessant coughing, in ill health. With a fair wind, not long for this world. That it seemed highly unlikely she would bear fruit from his loins was a bonus. Nevertheless, Miriana took precautions to ensure that it did not happen. Two years of baby Anton had been more than enough. That she had underestimated Nicolae in the bedroom stakes came, as it turned out, as a pleasant surprise. Determined to get his pound of flesh, he was amazingly virile for a man of his age. More than enough to satisfy her needs.

To Nicolae, all his Christmases had come in one. When he was in his forties and had first been introduced to her, she was a teenager. He had watched with growing interest and lust as she had developed into a very beautiful and accomplished woman. That she might even show interest in him was quite beyond his wildest dreams, but he was not naïve. He knew there would be a price. A price he was more than willing to pay.

Miriana made heads turn. A fine-looking woman, Nicolae was delighted to parade his new wife in society. Showering her with gifts, not least a three-carat diamond ring on the first anniversary, he also gave her a monthly allowance that would have fed half the poor in Romania for a year.

The price was predictably high, and it hadn't taken her long to raise the subject. She wanted in. Into his businesses. But one particularly. At first, he had declined to either discuss it or answer her questions, but it had been to no avail. Little did he know at the time that Miriana's plans were already well advanced.

Map in hand, Miriana walked the streets of Bucharest. At the top of her list were ten residential properties each owned and rented out by her husband. Unlike the rest of the properties in his portfolio, the rentals were way below market value. It was strange. She had her suspicions born of eavesdropping on her husband's conversations, rifling through his paperwork, breaking into his computer, and of the infrequent visits to the marital home by a series of unsavoury characters.

Miriana's father had his legitimate, wholly respectable businesses, but far more could be classed as seedy and, at worst, criminal. Nicolae's business spread was based on a remarkably similar model.

Watching the comings and goings at each of the ten residential properties, her suspicions were confirmed. Each of them brothels. Unlike the usual brothels, of which there were many across the length and breadth of Bucharest, these were operated out of houses of good proportions, set apart from adjacent properties and in their own grounds, which in turn were well maintained. Gardens were set to lawn with mature shrubs and trees. Located in desirable locations, they nestled inconspicuously with the great and good and the aristocracy that had risen from the ashes since the fall of the Communist regime. Those who entered generally left within the hour. Smartly dressed, for the most part they drove expensive motor cars. Aimed at the more discerning clients, these were brothels at the very top end of the market. A highly lucrative business.

Running a brothel was a criminal offence in Romania. It spoke volumes that none of the residences had been closed down. Without friends and acquaintances in very high places paid to turn a blind eye, it could not have been the case.

Her research complete, Miriana was ready to confront Nicolae. If he had any common sense, he would acquiesce to her demands. The alternative was to find himself behind bars for the rest of his life. Hopefully she would not have to resort to such threats. Hardly appropriate for a newly married woman.

When confronted with her findings and suggestions, he had been impressed that she had been both resourceful and diligent. Despite the fact she had accessed his private files without permission, which had initially angered him, he heard her out. There was little that she said that he could disagree with. A tweak here, a tweak there, and they could double their profits. What was there to lose?

Miriana took charge of the operation.

Day by day, she became more and more hands-on while taking care to remain unseen in and around the residences. Only the best and most beautiful. Only the young. All to be well educated and well spoken. Each one to have received appropriate training in the art of pleasuring the opposite sex. Those that did not live up to her exacting standards were shown the door, given a modest handshake, and informed in no uncertain terms of their fate if they should decide to speak to the authorities. A few disappeared and were never seen again.

Word was soon out that she was a woman not to be crossed. Those house managers who deviated from her exacting model and standards paid the price. Those who met and exceeded her expectations were well rewarded.

It came as a shock, although it perhaps should not have, that Nicolae died of a heart attack in his sleep after what had perhaps been the most amorous and physical night of his life. She had made sure of that. Perhaps she had pushed him too far, but he had died happy, and who could argue with that? A short marriage of ten years, it had nonetheless been amicable and hugely rewarding.

Unbeknown to Miriana, while her side of the business flourished, the same could not be said for her husband's other business interests. Forgetful and careless, he was well behind with his taxes, and it was not long before the vultures smelt blood and swooped. Had she not been so totally engrossed in her side of the business, she might have been able to ward them off. At the top of her list of suspects for informing the tax authorities and contributing to her husband's downfall was her very own father, Henric. Miriana silently vowed that one day, his day would come.

Miriana inherited what was left of the business. After taxes had been paid, it amounted to the value of just twenty of his properties. Keeping ten of the properties in Bucharest, she sold the rest and banked the proceeds.

It was 2009. She was thirty-six at the time.

Dedicating the years that followed to both rebuilding what had been their joint business and simultaneously working on the destruction of her father's business, Miriana kept her nose to the grindstone, building an enviable network of loyal contacts from all walks of life.

In August 2013, Miriana sat beside her father's bed as he took his last breath. The last words he heard were those of his daughter. "Who's the winner now, Tata?"

He had always had the last laugh. With his dying breath, he told her that word had got out that she was the madam behind a string of Bucharest high-class brothels. Fortunately, it was a risk she had planned for and had been able to mitigate almost on the spot. The following day, one of her residences had been raided by the police. It had been a narrow escape. They had found nothing. With potential damage to her reputation, Miriana insisted on a public apology and put her lawyers to work. Two subsequent raids had followed. Whoever knew about her business had no intentions of letting matters rest.

A dutiful daughter, she wept at her father's funeral and, after all the guests had departed, spat on his grave.

It could not have happened at a better time. Word was out that the UK government would shortly announce that, at the beginning of the following year, on the first of January 2014, to be precise, Romanian citizens would be free to live and work in the UK. A change that might significantly simplify international business between the two countries, an opportunity not to be missed. It was time to move out and move on.

Miriana sold the residences in Bucharest, ensured that none of her employees would talk, and moved to England. With the proceeds from sales, she started house hunting. The first residence, she decided, would double as her home, office, and business premises. It would also have a basement – a mere precautionary measure. The second and third would be purely for business. The fourth, a more modest establishment, for a new business start-up based on a model that she had recently tried and tested. The fifth, a staging post for recruits where they would learn their skills. The choice of location for the operation had been trickier. London was the wealthier and potentially better capture area. It was also expensive and it was likely that others might already have entered the market. Finally, she settled on the city of Bristol. With excellent fast links south, north, and east to London, it was a fast-growing city. The pickings were ripe.

Keeping staff to a minimum, a house manager would be appointed for each of the residences. Already she had names in the frame. Ladinas Popescu would be one. Other services brought in. Marku and Codrin, long-term employees of Nicolae, had already volunteered to manage all aspects of security.

Finally, she needed an ambitious and personable young man to work and travel between Romania and the UK, and to run the staging post.

A young man recently finished school, taking time out before university, came strongly recommended. Miriana flew to Bucharest to interview him. His name was Flaviu.

Legs outstretched, he'd sat opposite her, with a fixed smile on his face. Totally at ease with himself, he had answered all her questions with such confidence that it bordered on insolence. Had he not been so attractive, she might have taken offence. It had been a long time since she had felt such an attraction for a man who was scarcely more than a boy. Tall and muscular, his hair a mass of pale golden curls, he was sex-on-legs.

As the hour struck, he had got up to leave. "An hour, you said." Flaviu checked his watch and reached for the tan leather jacket he'd thrown carelessly over the back of a chair. "I have another appointment. Thank you for your time." At which he left.

"There'll have to be a follow up interview, next time I am in Bucharest. There is more we need to talk about before I can offer you the job," she called after him. The door closed. Miriana sat back and let out a deep sigh. She had to have him. For herself, for her business. With a little knocking into shape, he would make the most perfect staging manager, and more.

The trip to Bucharest included an overnight stay. Sufficient time to check up on her other business interests in the city. By late afternoon, mission accomplished and finding time on her hands, Miriana hailed a taxi. "Stander Street. 1311." It was the address on his job application form.

Stepping out of the taxi, she looked up at the three-storey block before checking each of the names listed at the main entrance. The house was divided into ten apartments. Against the bell for the top-floor flat was the name, Flaviu Dumitru. Miriana rang the bell and stood back from the door and waited with growing desire.

"Hello again," he said, arms crossed, leaning casually against the door frame. "I hadn't expected you quite so soon. If I'd known you were coming, I'd have got changed."

Her eyes swept over him. He was perfect as he was. A short-sleeved open-neck shirt, unbuttoned to the waist and tucked into his jeans, revealed a carpet of rich golden hair. Longing to claw her nails through it, Miriana stepped past him and started up the stairs.

It was a small studio flat, shabby but clean, with a kitchenette to one side and a door that she presumed led to the bathroom and toilet. The bedclothes lay thrown back as though he had not long since got up.

Three hours later Miriana noticed the time. An hour to Henri Coandă Airport and a two-hour check-in for her flight back to England. It was past time she made tracks.

Cupping his face in hers, she kissed his lips. "You are beautiful, you know that?"

"I do." He grinned. "So, have I got the job?"

Miriana nodded. "You're the best candidate so far. Yes, but the job description has changed. You will add me to it."

"I'm liking it more all the time. I get a well-paid job, accommodation, a car, and I get to fuck a beautiful woman. What's not to like?" Flaviu said flippantly, making a mental note to let Tonya down lightly. He was in her debt. Without her tutelage, Miriana would not have that smile on her face. He would not have a job.

"Passport?" Miriana asked.

Flaviu reached over, opened a small bedside drawer, and pulled out the maroon passport of Romania.

"Check."

In June 2014, Flaviu closed the door to his studio flat and pocketed the key.

25

ENGLAND

2014

Sometimes Miriana wondered whether the world would be better off without them. Men, that was. From a personal point of view. Certainly not a business point of view. He was late. No, forget that – he was way past late. She'd met him recently on a return flight from Bucharest to London Gatwick. Both had been travelling in business class, occupying adjacent seats. Comfortably but smartly dressed, a seasoned traveller, he was in his mid-forties and reading *The Times*. She'd sat in the aisle seat, he in the window seat, and thirty minutes into the flight he had apologised profusely. An unavoidable call of nature. Don't get up, he had said, carefully manoeuvring past her but not carefully enough to avoid brushing her legs. Miriana watched as he strolled down towards the toilets. Tall, broad-shouldered and muscular, he had exceptionally neat buttocks tucked away under his close-fitting trousers. Her hands itched to squeeze them.

The conversation started, as did all polite conversations, with her asking whether his trip to Bucharest had been successful. He had been delightfully forthcoming. If spending three days at a convention about drug trafficking could be called successful, then, yes, it had been, he had said, adding that he was in the police force working out of Bristol. Suddenly, she was all ears. He was a detective superintendent, with responsibility for major crimes. In comparison, she had said, her job would sound very dull. She had a recruitment consultancy firm, recently established and coincidentally also based in Bristol – Exclusivity – and had just returned from Bucharest having interviewed several excellent candidates for a client – an investment bank in the city.

Neither offered any information about their personal circumstances. She could tell the attraction had been entirely mutual. Before disembarking, they had exchanged business cards and agreed to meet up.

It should have come as no surprise that he had not turned up. Seven p.m. and going on for eight, no phone calls or texts; it was annoying to say the least. Miriana reached into her handbag, opened her Gucci wallet, pulled out a credit card, and waved it at the barman.

"Allow me," a voice said, setting down another credit card over the top of hers. "I didn't think you'd still be here, but I hoped. The least I can do is pay for your drinks before you leave."

Feeling a warm breath on her neck and the strong hand that squeezed her shoulder, Miriana swivelled around and faced him. Sandy-coloured, well-cut hair, high forehead, steely blue eyes, clean shaven, and immaculately dressed, he was even more handsome than she remembered. He kissed her first on the neck and then on her cheek and then on her lips.

"A murder case. A fight down by the docks. One dead and two seriously injured. My luck to be SIO this week. No choice. But I'm off-duty until tomorrow and at a loose end. Maybe you could help?"

Straight to the point. Miriana liked a man who knew what he wanted and rarely failed to get it. Presumptuous. Confident. More than a little arrogant. A man who she suspected had yet to meet his match in a woman. A man due a lesson.

"I've taken the liberty of booking a suite at the Avon Gorge. Room with a view. The champagne is on ice. I'd prefer not to drink it alone."

Born Sean Handley – mother and father, Mary and Patrick Handley, staunch Catholics – he was the only son and one of five offspring. He was sixteen when he first started to take any real notice of his sisters. Susan was thirteen, filling out into a shapely and attractive teenager, wearing her first bra with great pride. Not unattractive, either. Sufficiently attractive to cause his loins to stir. At school the boys of his age spoke endlessly of their latest conquests. Sean had had several fumbles, most of which had resulted in slapped hands and no more. Not that he ever admitted that to his friends. The fact of the matter was that, try as he did, he remained a virgin, his only comfort self-administered under the sheets at night.

And then Susan came home from school one day and proceeded to educate the family in human biology, specifically – and very specifically – about how babies were made. His mother and father had been appalled. To their mind, there was plenty of time to learn all about that when a girl met a nice man and got married. There was no need for schools to interfere and certainly no need at the age of thirteen for a young girl to know what a penis was, let alone that it might be the instrument of pleasure. Sean begged to differ but kept quiet. Curious to learn more, Susan was ripe for picking. What better way for his sister to learn than first-hand from her brother?

An eager pupil, Susan saw no harm in Sean's proposal. She was no telltale, and neither were her younger sisters when their time came. In his opinion it was a harmless part of their education. Instructing each of them in the importance of always using contraceptives, strictly forbidden in the Handley family, along with underage sex and sex before marriage. None of them, fortunately, bore seed.

As the years passed and his confidence grew, Sean branched out, testing the water with older girls and with older women. It was then that he made his first mistake. A drunken one-night fling with Felicity bore fruit. Twenty-five years old, five years his senior, Felicity was looking for a husband. With a promising career ahead of him in the police force, dependent upon his good reputation in the locality, at the age of twenty, Sean had no choice in the matter. One month later they were married. Three months later Felicity walked across a road without looking and was killed instantly. Sean grieved neither the loss of his wife, who had given him no sexual pleasure whatsoever, nor the loss of his unborn child.

He had never married again, content to find his pleasures in other directions. The younger and sweeter the better.

A woman excelling in the art of sex, uninhibited and fearless, Miriana was the one and only exception. Of mutual benefit one to the other, they had remained firm friends and business colleagues. She provided him with an unending supply of his preferred delights. He provided her with the protection that she needed for her business.

26

ENGLAND

2021

Elena shook the duvet and carefully positioned it over the bed, taking care that the overlap was equidistant on each side, the way Flaviu liked it to be left. A tear sliding down her cheek, she plumped up the silk-covered pillows and placed them at the head of the bed. It was the last time – at least for a while – that she would feel the smooth silkiness of the sheets on her naked body and feel the warmth of Flaviu's body beside her own.

The next phase in her life was about to begin. With mixed feelings, she checked that she had left nothing in the wardrobe or drawers, in her bedside table, in the dressing table drawers, or in the bathroom. Her heart was heavy. Had he asked her not to leave, then she might have stayed. With some regret. But he had not asked.

She had everything to look forward to. New friends that she would meet in the house share. A new school. University. A career. The prodigal daughter one day welcomed home. And then Flaviu by her side for the rest of her life. And maybe a family of their own. He loved her more than anything in the world. She never tired of hearing those words. There was nothing that she wouldn't do for him. He had only to ask.

Elena closed the bedroom door behind her, wandered through to the lounge, stood by the sliding patio doors, gazed out over the treetops to the Clifton Suspension Bridge beyond, and waited to hear the key in the front door.

Miriana pulled up in the basement car park, parking alongside Flaviu's little grey Skoda, checked her make-up in the mirror, and headed for the lift. Flaviu had called not an hour since to say that the girl was ready and would be waiting, her suitcase packed.

Having selected one of the many keys on her key rings, Miriana inserted it into the lock.

Her head in the clouds, Elena had not heard the door. Turning, she saw Miriana standing silently behind her, looking even more glamorous than she had when they'd first met at that coffee shop in Bucharest. A waft of Chanel Chance filled the air. Her face was smooth and unlined, framed by jet-black hair, cut shorter than Elena remembered. Miriana wore a fine white cotton shirt with dark-blue skintight jeans, red painted toenails peeking out through the open toes of three-inch-high white sandals. She was the epitome of elegance.

"Darling." Miriana held out her arms. "Is that my little Elena? I would hardly have recognized you. Look at you! You're glowing, and that dress. It's perfect. Welcome to England. Has Flaviu been looking after you?"

Elena smoothed the skirt of the blue floral-print dress that Flaviu had chosen for her to wear that day and looked up shyly.

"That's not a tear, is it?" Miriana held her close.

"No," Elena said, wiping the tear away with the back of her

hand. "It's just…" Elena stumbled over her words. "He's been so wonderful. So kind. The loveliest man in the world."

Narrowing her eyes, Miriana reflected briefly on Elena's words. Flaviu was not employed to be wonderful but to do his job. "He wanted to drive you to the house share himself, but I needed him elsewhere. Blame me," Miriana said. "Don't worry, you'll be seeing plenty of him. Are you ready?"

Elena nodded, followed Miriana to the door, and picked up her suitcase. "It's not heavy. They're all summer and evening clothes that Flaviu bought me. I might need a few others for the winter."

"Really? A summer wardrobe. How nice," Miriana replied. Neither was Flaviu paid to splash money about unnecessarily.

Locking the door to the apartment as they left, Miriana smiled as she noticed Elena turn left out of the door. "This way to the lift," she said, turning right. "And then the car is in the basement." At least Flaviu had done that part of his job as instructed. "Welcome to the world."

Elena nodded. "Does this mean that all the paperwork has been completed?"

"It all came through yesterday. You're legit, now." Miriana pressed the lift button for the basement. "Free as a bird."

Taking a key fob out of her pocket, Miriana pointed it in the direction of the red Audi parked in the underground car park.

Elena stood back as the boot glided open to reveal the plush red interior of the car. Cream-coloured carpets, white leather seats front and back, walnut dashboard, it was the height of luxury. One day she would be as successful as Miriana, and she would have a car just like this. If Irina could see her now. She had counted off the days, hours, and minutes to Irina's arrival. In twenty-four hours, they would be reunited. It hardly seemed possible that she could have found love, be given the opportunity to continue with her schooling, and be back with her sister and dearest friend, all in the space of a couple of weeks. If she had one more wish, it would be that Irina would stay in England for ever, but she knew that would never happen. Irina was a home bird. Sinking down into the passenger seat, Elena stroked the white leather. So soft, so cool, so unbelievably beautiful.

"It's not far. It shouldn't take us more than fifteen minutes, traffic allowing," Miriana said, as the car roared into life.

Elena sat back and watched the world go by.

"Your new life is about to begin," Miriana said, leaving Clifton Downs behind, and picking up the A4018. "We're on our way."

Elena gazed left and right, her head on a swivel. "I've never seen so many schools," she said, pointing out one after another. "English Language, Westbury, Redmaids, Bristol Free…Which one is mine?"

"Your school is just a couple of miles north of the house. A private school, if you remember rightly. Nothing but the best for my girls." Miriana grinned. "Excited?"

"Excited and nervous, at the same time," Elena said, her eyes sparkling, memories of the hardship of the journey from Romania in the dim and distant past.

"No need to be. You'll be fine. We'll get you settled in first, and then I'll introduce you to the girls a bit later today. Party time last night. They were all fast asleep when I left earlier. They're all longing to meet you – and your sister. I bet you're pleased as punch that she's coming to visit." Miriana reached out and took Elena's hand.

"I can't tell you how grateful I am. It's the first time we've ever been apart for longer than a few hours, and that's because I went to high school and Irina took up vocational education," Elena said. "We've so much to catch up on."

"There'll be plenty of time for that, don't you worry," Miriana said, changing down before flooring the accelerator to overtake the car in front.

"I will repay you. I promise," Elena said.

"I know you will, my dear." Miriana flicked switches on the steering wheel and the car filled with the gentle sound of mood music. She grinned.

Her heart filled with gladness, Elena settled back in her seat and let the music wash over her.

"Nearly there. This is Passage Road and we're not far from the motorway. It's a very pleasant district. Coming up on the left. It's called The Ivy."

"But it's fabulous," Elena exclaimed excitedly. "Am I really going to be living here?"

"You are. It's what the English call a period property. There are seven bedrooms, three reception rooms, a self-contained apartment, which is where I live, and my office," Miriana said, signalling left and pulling in past two brick gateposts onto a spacious driveway enshrouded by trees.

"And is there a garden where we can all sit out?"

"Out at the back. A huge lawn bordered by shrubberies. South facing, it catches the sun most of the day. Let's get you settled in. And don't forget that the girls are having a sleep, so we'll not wake them up."

Elena followed Miriana as she led the way up the front steps to the door and took out a bunch of keys. She inserted the first of the keys into a Chubb lock at eye level, the second into yet another Chubb lock set two feet above the ground, and the third into a Yale lock. Miriana opened the door.

"Where's my room?" Standing in the hallway, Elena glanced up at the staircase.

"Follow me. Up the stairs and along the corridor."

"Should I take my shoes off?"

"They're not dirty, are they?"

Elena shook her head.

At the top of the stairs, the corridor branched off left and right. Miriana turned left. "Your room is right down at the end. It's one of the best rooms with views to the side of the house and over the car park at the front. Now, remember what I said," Miriana said, putting her finger to her lips.

Elena soaked it all up. The carpet was plush, a dusky pink bordered by grey. The walls were hung with landscapes and paintings of horses like the five-star hotels she had seen featured in magazines. On the first door to the left, the name 'Anya'. On the second door to the right, the name 'Petra', and then, dead ahead, her door – with her name on it, 'Elena'.

Miriana unlocked the door and ushered Elena in front of her. "You see, I told you that it would be nice. A lovely carpet, a big comfy bed, a nice dressing table, and there's plenty of space for your things in the wardrobe and in the drawers. It just needs a few personal touches," Miriana said, holding open another door. "And you've got your own ensuite toilet, basin, and shower, and a big pile of soft fluffy towels."

"It's beautiful. Irina will love it," Elena said, a tear sliding down her cheek. "Can we share for the few days that she's here?"

"I've already made arrangements for Irina. A pretty bedroom just down the road at another of our house shares. It's called The Beeches. It's walking distance."

"I just love it. Everything about it." Elena sighed, twirling in front of the floor-to-ceiling mirror on the wardrobe door.

"Elena, that is music to my ears. Now, how about I leave you

for half an hour to unpack and settle yourself in, and then I'll
come back, and we'll talk some more?"

Elena stared at the closed door. Miriana had locked it from the
outside.

Click, click. The sound of a key being inserted into a lock and then
being turned.

Miriana sat down on the bed and patted the space beside her.
"Come and sit with me, Elena. We need to have a little talk. As
two adults. What do you think of it? Do you like it?" Miriana
asked.

With an increasing sense of foreboding, Elena shivered. Something was wrong. Very wrong. Why was there a lock on her door?
Why had Miriana locked it when she had left, and then unlocked
it? Why were the windows locked? Why were there no keys for
the windows to let the fresh air in? Why were there three locks on
the front door? Why did each door bear a name? Why was the
building so silent?

"I see you haven't unpacked your things," Miriana said,
glancing at the unopened suitcase on the carpet.

"I'd like to see Flaviu, Miriana. Can you call him for me?"

"Flaviu is away, dear. That's why I collected you earlier. He
probably won't be back for a week or more. He's a busy man.
Much as he might like to, I'm afraid that he won't have much time
for you in the future. He's done his job, Elena. You're here and
ready to start your new life. Time to move on."

"He will have time for me," Elena said slowly and deliberately. "He loves me, and I love him. I will go back to his apartment and wait for him to come home. I don't like it here."

"Let me correct you, there, Elena. The apartment that you have
been staying in belongs to me. I decide who stays there and who

does not. And you, my dear, have been staying there entirely at my expense. Flaviu is one of my employees and does what I tell him to do. Do you understand?"

"No, I don't understand. Why do you lock my door?" Suddenly frightened, Elena jumped up and ran to the front window. The car park was deserted. Not a soul around. Even if she had been able to open a window to call for help, there was none to be had. "I want to leave. Now."

"Let's both stay calm and talk this through as two adults," Miriana said, patting the bed beside her again. "Listen to me, Elena. I have only ever had your best interests as heart. You deserve the same chance in life that I had. I too had to work for my success. Nothing came easy. It was a long hard road but worth it in the end. I may have put it slightly differently when we met. You can go to school, university, whatever you like, further down the road, but first you have to earn your passage, as I did. Do you understand what I am saying?"

Elena shook her head. "Earn my passage? But you said…"

"I'm sorry if I didn't make myself clear," Miriana said.

"You lied."

"I said I'd help you realise your dream. That was no lie. You were a virgin when you left Bucharest. You told me that yourself. You are no longer a virgin. In the space of two weeks, you have learnt the art of sex. Flaviu tells me that you have passed with flying colours. That you are ready. You have all the skills you need to earn your passage. I have a job for you. You will soon be earning good money. My clients pay well. You will receive a small percentage of everything you earn. It may take a year. It may take two. That will be up to you."

"You lied. It was all lies. There never was any school…" Elena said, shaking her head in disbelief. In the space of thirty seconds, everything she had believed in had turned to ashes. Empty promises. Dreams shattered. The man she thought she loved. The man who loved her. "Never!"

"It's time to grow up, Elena. The world isn't always a nice place. Welcome to your new home. This room will be your home for the foreseeable future," Miriana said, tiring of the conversation.

"I trusted you. I hate you. You can't do this…How could you…? Nothing, nothing on God's earth would persuade me. Nothing. Do you hear me?"

"Your first client will be with you this evening. I shall bring him to you personally. Don't let me down, Elena," Miriana said, reaching for her handbag and extracting her mobile. "Do you recognise this young man in the photo?"

It was a photo of a boy. His face was covered in blood. Tears were streaming down his face, a look of terror in his eyes. Alexandru, her brother. Twelve-year-old Alexandru. Shocked and stunned, Elena searched for the words.

"We can do this the nice way, or we can do it the hard way, Elena. The choice is yours, and don't forget that your sister arrives tomorrow. You wouldn't like anything to happen to her, would you?"

27

ENGLAND

2021

The door shut with a resounding thud. A key turned in the lock, once around and then again, ever a reminder that henceforth she would live within the same four walls. A waft of perfume hung on the air – Chanel Chance. Miriana's signature that once filled her heart with gladness and with hope. That now sickened her. Misplaced hope. Girlish dreams. A fresh start in life. An exciting future. A career. The opportunities to make her parents proud of her, repay them for the hurt she had caused. Dashed by naïvety. Dashed by vanity. Dashed by liars and cheats. The truth was staring her in the face, although too painful to accept. Maybe Flaviu would…

Elena glanced at her wrist, the pretty silver bracelet that Flaviu had given her no longer there. Miriana had taken it off her wrist for safekeeping. No clock. The room was timeless.

She had unpacked her case. Hung her dresses in the wardrobe; folded her clothes and put them neatly away in the drawers. It was time to think of her family. Alexandru's little face swam before her eyes. The laughter of them all rang in her ears: Alexandru, Luca, Danut, and Serghei. In her mind's eye she pictured her mother cradling the baby. Had it been a boy, or had it been a girl? Maybe it was yet to be born. Perhaps she would never know, and Irina...A sob escaped her lips, followed by another, and another, until her whole body heaved. Tears streamed down her face, wetting her neck and breast and the dress she wore. What would happen to Irina when she arrived? There was nothing. Nothing in this world that she would not do to prevent any of them from being hurt.

A sharp rap on the door. Miriana calling "Five minutes." Fear permeated every fibre of Elena's being, such fear as she had never experienced. *Boom, boom.* She could hear her heart thudding as she counted the seconds and minutes, steeling herself for the ordeal ahead.

A gentle rap on the door. A key slotted into the lock. Turning. The door opening slowly. A face around the door. He did not look like a monster. Older. Much older than Flaviu. Tata's age possibly. Sandy-haired. Tall, slim, and well dressed, he stood holding a small black leather holdall. The type that a man might carry with him on an overnight business trip.

"How old are you?" he asked.

"Sixteen," Elena replied, her legs turning to jelly, her head held high.

"Sweet sixteen. And are you sweet?"

Elena did not know how to reply and said nothing.

"Take your clothes off. Slowly. I want to see you. All of you. Step out of the dress. Leave your panties and your shoes on. Hair over shoulders."

"Please don't hurt me." The words came out before she could stop them, her fear turning to terror as he advanced slowly and deliberately towards her. Holding her fast with one arm, he ran his fingers down her body and inside her panties. Sharp nails dug into her soft sensitive skin as he thrust two fingers and then three into her body. Fighting to break free, Elena screamed. The more she fought, the tighter he held her. Probing. Probing until she felt herself being lifted off the ground. Terrified, hurting, and desperate to break free, Elena summoned her last reserves of energy. Bringing her knee sharply up between his legs, the blow hit home. Withdrawing his fingers from her body, his hands flew to his genitals. Elena screamed and ran for the door. But the door was locked.

Eyes smouldering, he fisted his hand and lashed out. His first blow struck one side of her face. Her head snapped right. The second, the other side of her face. Her head snapped left. Agonising crunching blows. He hauled her up onto the bed before admiring his handiwork. Powerless to prevent what might come next, Elena stared into his eyes and wanted to die.

"I wanted to be nice to you, Elena. I'm a nice person. I wanted to give you pleasure. Show you how good it can be – for both of us, but you've spoilt that," he said, reaching for the leather holdall. "And now I shall have to teach you a few lessons."

Her head throbbing, eyes barely focusing, Elena stared in disbelief at what he held in his hand. It was twelve inches long, fat and round. Whipping her legs out from beneath her, he pinned her down to the bed, face-down. Searing pain. Burning. Ripping her apart. Time and time again.

"Are you sorry, Elena…?I'm waiting for an apology…Or perhaps you are enjoying it," he whispered.

"I'm sorry." Agonising pain searing through her body, Elena whimpered, "Please. Please."

"Turn over," he said.

Shaking, frightened, and hurting with every slight move, gasping for breath, Elena rolled over and lay looking up at him.

And down at him. Climbing up on to the bed, forcing her knees apart, he held his penis in his hands and brought it to her face.

"Later," he said, unwrapping the condom that he had placed on the bedside table. "I'll keep that pleasure for later."

Beyond caring, Elena closed her eyes as he entered her and pushed his shaft further and further inside her, paused, withdrew, thrust, withdrew, thrust, withdrew, thrust. On and on like a man possessed. Momentarily her thoughts returned to Flaviu. He had never hurt her. At least not really hurt her. Not like this man. And then in the final frenzy, he crashed down on top of her, his whole weight on her chest.

It was over, but it was not over as she felt his hand take hers and steer it towards his penis. "Make me hard," he said. Again, and again.

Elena lay like a limp rag. She had done it for Alexandru. For Luca, for Danut, for Serghei. For the baby brother or sister that she had never seen. For Mama and Tata. And most of all for Irina.

A key turned in the lock. Elena crawled towards the bathroom before slipping into blessed unconsciousness.

28

ENGLAND
2021

At the end of the day all he wanted to do was stick his feet up in front of the box with a plate of fish and chips. He didn't have to go far to fetch them. The flat was right above Dolphins, the fish and chip shop. Accessed by a door to the left of the fish shop, stairs, bare of carpet and permanently in need of a good sweep, led up the flat. On the door, he'd fixed a doorbell and a small handwritten sign that read, 'Laddie Popescu'. Not that it served any purpose. In all the years that he had lived there, there had never once been a visitor. Except the man who used to come to read the meter, but that was before smart meters had been invented. The flat stank, but he was used to it. It was familiar and strangely comforting. Elena had laughed when he described it to her – a little shabby but always tidy and immaculately clean.

It didn't matter what he watched on TV so long as it helped him switch off. Soaps used to do the job best – lots of family stuff, but nice family stuff. Now they didn't. Packed end-to-end with violence, all they did was remind him of his day job.

. . .

Back in the day, Nicolae had been the boss and had called the shots. A hard taskmaster, but beneath that hard exterior, a decent bloke who knew when to draw the line. Unlike Miriana.

He'd been there at the wedding of the great Nicolae Constantin and Miriana, the daughter of the powerful and feared Henric Dragnea, albeit only driving the wedding car. A big society event, the great and the good had filled the pews in the church of Stavropoleos, later showering the happy couple with unwanted and unneeded gifts. Laddie was thirty-five at the time; he'd been Nicolae's right-hand man since he was no more than a lad.

Twenty-three years since he'd first met Miriana, and thirteen years since he'd started working for her following the sudden death of Nicolae, there was little he didn't know about her. She was bad news. The worst. People were no more than pawns in her game. If anyone ever thought themselves special in her eyes, they were fools. If anyone crossed Miriana, then either they or their nearest and dearest met an untimely end. But she was clever. Nothing that happened in Miriana's sordid little world could ever be traced back to her. Except by word of mouth from one of her more trusted employees, each of whom she held on a tight leash. Nicolae would be turning in his grave if he knew the half of it.

Laddie's leash was the promise that in five years' time when he reached the age of sixty-two, there would be a golden hand-shake and the slate would be wiped clean. He would never hear from her again. He had a fancy for a smallholding. Back home in Romania but way out in the country. Away from the hustle-bustle of Bucharest, the city that he'd grown up in. And he'd keep a couple of dozen chickens, a few goats, and pigs, and grow what crops he needed to feed himself and his family. At fifty-seven years of age, Laddie hadn't given up on a family. There was nothing lacking in that quarter. Okay, so he was no picture book. There were the pockmarks from the acne way back in his teenage years and a red-veined nose, witness to the not-so-occasional overindulgence in alcohol. And the paunch. Those things aside, any good woman would snatch him up, when the time came.

If he kept his nose clean, then maybe it would come to pass. And Laddie had his mother to consider as well. Living on her own, she was vulnerable.

He wasn't paid to like his job. And he wasn't paid to like any of the residents, as he preferred to call them. Mostly he didn't. Treated him like dog dirt. His title was house manager, his job to clean up the mess. Always the mess. The girls and the rooms. Clean, clean, clean. Make them whole and presentable ready for the next bastard who walked through the door, while Miriana secured and managed the bookings and reaped the rewards.

The odd one of them got under his skin – in a good way. Elena was one of them.

She'd earned her stripes had that one. No way that he'd thought she'd stay the course. Not after that first night. Bloody man. He was the worst bastard of the lot. Walking out with that smarmy grin on his face, leaving him to put the pieces back together week in, week out. Miriana knew exactly what made that man tick. Likely taught him the tricks of the trade, or at least, broadened his knowledge. And she gave him the pick of the bunch. It was Elena's bad luck that the bastard had taken a sadistic liking to her. But there was always a day of reckoning. His day would come. Laddie had eyes and ears and, on the quiet, made it his business to find out about the so-called clients.

If he'd had his way, that particular bastard would have been six feet under by now. But burying clients wasn't his job, either.

Elena grew on him right from that very first day. Probably the worst beating he had ever seen a girl take and survive. An hour of

his life and an image that he'd take with him to the grave. He'd
done his best that day…

~

"This room's in a pretty rubbish state, Elena." Laddie glanced
around at the mess. Bedclothes strewn all over the place, clothes
on the floor, drops of blood trailing from the bed to the bathroom.
"Put up a fight, did you? Silly girl. And Miriana told me you had
brains. Well, you didn't use them, did you?

"Nothing to say for yourself. Let's get you up on the bed."
Laddie took a step forward and reached out his hand.

"Don't touch me. Get away from me." Elena bent over and
wrapped her arms around her legs, a desperate attempt to hide her
swollen breasts and nudity. Her hair slid down over her shoulders,
reaching her waist.

"Look," Laddie said softly, moderating his voice. "I'm not one
of them. I work here. It's my job to look after you girls. I'm just
going to pick you up and lay you on the bed. And then I'm going
to put you back together again. No funny business. No jumping on
top of you. I'm just here to help."

Turning her head away from him, Elena whimpered, her
mouth forming words without sound.

"What's that you're saying? You're scared. Yes, I know that,
but you don't need to be scared of me. I'm not going to hurt you.
You're going to have to trust me," Laddie said, easing her out of
the bathroom before slipping one arm under her legs and the other
under her shoulders.

Laddie lifted her from the floor, light as a feather.

"Stay away from me!" she yelled. "Let me go!"

Once he'd lay her on the bed, he picked up the quilt cover and
gently draped it over her. "See? I'm not here to give it to you. I've

got a daughter much your age," he lied. "She's got herself in some scrapes in her time, let me tell you. Bloody noses. Bloody knees. And it's always me not her mum she runs to when she needs somebody to patch her up. Past master I am. So, are you going to let me help you?" Laddie paused. No reply. "Then I'll take that to mean yes."

Elena watched out of the corner of her eye, the other too swollen to focus. He was dipping a towel in a bowl of water, folding it up, and resting it on one cheek and then on the other. He had big hands and chubby fingers but they were gentle.

"This'll take the swelling down. We'll leave this on while we deal with the rest of you."

Elena grabbed the quilt and held it tight across her body.

"If we don't put something on those bruises, you're going to be one sorry little girl. This stuff"—Laddie held a tube up to her eyes—"will start work on them in no time. Couple of days and the soreness will be gone. So do I put this cream on or not?"

Elena nodded. Through a mist of tears, she watched as the man squeezed cream out of a tube and gently rubbed it into first her arms and then her legs. Almost instantaneously, the pain dulled.

"Now, the difficult bit. Let's get you turned over and see what we can do with the back of you."

"No!" she screamed, as Laddie rolled her over. "Don't touch me."

It was as he had thought it might be. A trickle of dried blood ran from her private parts down onto her thighs. If he ever got his hands on that bastard, he'd stick that bloody dildo right up his ass as far as it would go…And then kill him, slowly.

"Painful?" he asked. It was a rhetorical question. Filling the palm of his hand with the cream, Laddie reached far into her crutch, leaving a thick layer of cream behind.

"Now swallow these," Laddie said, wiping his hands before

passing her a glass of water and two small white pills. "They'll help you sleep."

"Thank you," Elena said, as the pain started to ebb away, and her eyes closed, the tears staining her cheeks.

Glancing back as he unlocked the door, he wondered how and when it had ever come to this. But he was in too deep and there was too much at stake. However much he might want to save the world, and these girls in particular, it was not in his power to do so. There'd been others who'd crossed Miriana and lived to regret it. One day...

It was early morning when he next looked in on her. After placing a mug of tea and a plate on the bedside table, he switched off the bedside light before crossing to draw the curtains back. One eye flickered. The other remained closed, but the swelling was a lot less than it had been the previous evening.

"Brought you a cup of tea and a sandwich," Laddie said.

Elena turned her head away.

"Come on, girlie. You've got to eat."

Elena shook her head.

"It's ham and cheese. I cut the crusts off for you. Make it easier with that sore mouth. Come on, just for me." Sitting quietly by her side, Laddie watched as she ate, and drank. "That good?" Laddie asked. "It'll make you strong. The world will look a whole better place with something in your belly...That's better."

Elena ate before handing the empty plate back to him. "Where's Irina?" she whispered. "Irina will know what to do. Irina always knows what to do."

"She's not far away," Laddie replied.

"Is she here? Is she safe?"

Laddie nodded and smiled reassuringly. "She's safe and sound down the road. She asked me to pass on a message. Finish that tea and I'll tell you all about it." What could he say? That Irina had arrived in England full of hope, only to find her life changed. Best guess was that she was in The Beeches. It was not long since one of the former residents had disappeared overnight.

"What did she say?"

"She's living in a lovely house and she's got a beautiful bedroom with her own bathroom…" Laddie started, anything that might bring the tiniest bit of comfort to this poor, wretched girl.

"I'm glad she likes it. Not like our bedroom at home," Elena said from a faraway place.

It was all too familiar. Denial. The need to block out the truth. The desperate need for reassurance that all was well. He'd seen it time and time again. It was in those moments that he did his best to bring comfort to the girls. The reality of the situation would kick in soon enough.

"It was so small we could reach out from our beds and hold hands," Elena continued, locked in her own little world. "The bathroom was down a long cold corridor. Eight of us shared it. I think there are nine now."

Indeed, Laddie knew there were nine in the family – at least for now. Miriana had made it her business to find out. "And Irina asked me to pass on a few other messages."

"Tell me." Elena reached out for his hand.

"She said to tell you that she understands. Understands that none of this is your fault. That you must be brave. That she thinks of you from the moment she opens her eyes in the morning until the moment she closes them after dark, and then she says a little prayer for you."

"I'll say a prayer for her tonight too. Was there anything else? Did she say anything else?"

Laddie hesitated. "She did say that she wouldn't be able to

catch up with you for a while because she's really busy, but she will as soon as she can. She said that in the meantime you're to be a good girl and do everything that is asked of you."

"She sounds just like Mama," Elena said. "Be a good girl…"

"And I hope you won't mind but I did mention that you'd been just a bit poorly," Laddie added. "I told her that I'd look after you."

"Thank you, and what about Flaviu, is he well?"

Laddie ground his teeth. Bloody Flaviu. Miriana's golden boy. Miriana's toy boy and right-hand man. Both possessive and obsessive about him; Flaviu could do no wrong in Miriana's eyes. "Out of the country so I hear," Laddie said.

"He'll be back soon, won't he? He's going to take me out, you know, and then I'll be going back to the flat. Have you seen the view from his balcony? You can see for miles, right across the Avon."

"I haven't had that pleasure, Elena. Maybe one day, I'll pay him a visit." Laddie bit his tongue. If ever that day came, it wouldn't be a social business but to throw him headfirst off that balcony.

Elena rested her head on the pillows. "We're not expecting any visitors for a couple of days, are we?"

Laddie shook his head. It hadn't been easy, but finally he'd persuaded Miriana that Elena needed three days' rest before her next assignation. "No, you rest," he said. "I'll bring you your meals and we can chat as much as you like."

"Are you going to lock the door?"

"Just following orders. Irina said I was to keep you safe."

Thankfully, Elena had since got the bastard's measure. He liked a good fight and, since that first encounter, Elena had never given him that satisfaction. Word had it that he was looking to move on to a newcomer in one of the other residences.

Two months on and she had most of the clients eating out of her hand. Sex wasn't everything for many of them.

Elena...Laddie liked her.

Elena was special. He really liked her and, he thought, she liked him. Genuinely. She liked to talk about her family. Missed them. Cared for them. Always asking about her sister, Irina. He'd lied to her right from the beginning. Irina was in The Beeches on the other side of Bristol. He hadn't set eyes on her since she'd arrived, but he kept his ears to the ground. She was doing great, he always said. A real trooper. Always asking after her twin sister. Dreamt up little messages from her – that she'd got some lovely friends, that she'd had a lovely day. Stupid stuff. Stuff that only someone desperate to hear good news would ever believe. Elena did, or at least appeared to. She soaked it up and in return asked him to deliver little notes that she had written back to her sister, telling her about the beautiful trees she could see from the windows, the morning sun as it streamed in, and the flame red of the dying sun. And always that she couldn't wait for the day they would be together again.

Sometimes she'd ask him about Flaviu. Was he well? Was he in the country or off on his travels? Might he come to see her soon? Laddie didn't like it when Elena asked about Flaviu.

And Elena was a loner. So long as she had some paper and pencils, she was happy. A relative term. It was beyond him. Algebra, she called it. And then there was geometry, and then something called trigonometry. It kept her dreams alive.

She'd even taught him to play chess. Laddie Popescu playing chess! Who would ever have believed it? He'd found an old set in a charity shop. Maybe once, twice a week, they played whenever she had a good break, and he wasn't busy clearing up somebody else's mess. Kings and queens, bishops and knights, castles, and pawns, they sped across the black-and-white board unknowing of their fate. In return, he'd taught her how to play poker. Poker for matchsticks. Matchsticks that were always returned to their box at the end of a game. She could read him like a book. Beat him hands down almost every time.

They were good days. Not all days were like that. There were days when she was rock-bottom, sobbing her heart out, hating herself, wishing she were dead. That's when he'd find her in the bathroom scrubbing her body from top to toe with a nailbrush. On those days he did what he could to console her, but there wasn't much he could do. To tell her it would all soon be over would be the biggest lie of all. There would be no golden handshakes for Elena. The end would come. It did for all of them. Threatened and then transported back across the channel before being dumped to find their own way home, for ever looking over their shoulders. Mostly that was as far as they got. Sleeping rough. Scavenging. Drugs to erase the memories. More abuse.

He liked Elena. She was special. One in a million. Maybe, just maybe, one day he'd take her back to Romania. She'd make a good wife.

29

ENGLAND

2021

Laddie tapped lightly on the door. Then louder. He inserted a key into the lock. *Click. Click.* From within, the sound of a girl singing. Happy. Laughter.

"Sorry, late today. Truth is I didn't want to get out of bed. Freezing cold it was in that flat," Laddie said, tray in hand. "Breakfast."

"You shouldn't be cold. It's not good for you. Why don't you move?" Elena sat upright and leant against the pillows.

"It's home and there's everything I need. Right above The Dolphin, like I told you – fish and chips on the doorstep. One Stop right next door for milk and stuff. A petrol station across the road. Next door to The Bull. Nothing fancy, but a good pint. And it doesn't cost much. What's not to like?"

"And Flaviu?"

"Haven't seen him about much," Laddie said. All part of the daily conversation with the same questions and answers each day.

"Now, how's my favourite girl today?" Laddie asked, steering away from his least favourite subject. "Breakfast. Muesli, yoghurt, toast, and honey, just as you like it. I hear you had a late night?"

"Quite late. Three visitors, but they were no trouble." Elena shrugged her shoulders. "Did you say yoghurt?"

Laddie smiled, recalling Elena's first assignment, one that he truly thought she would never get over. It was as though she had wiped it from her memory. Now, she rarely received less than a five-star rating from her clients. Polite, intelligent, beautiful, sexy, helpful…The accolades kept coming in. Miriana was delighted.

"It's strawberry."

Elena pulled a face. "I can't eat yoghurt, Laddie. It's not good for me."

"It's healthy food. The best."

"If it's no trouble, I'd prefer to have fruit instead. Prunes. Yes, prunes would be perfect."

Laddie frowned. If that was what she wanted, then that was what she could have. Tomorrow. He'd pick up a tin or two from the One Stop.

"How's Irina?"

"She's fine. Busy as usual. Sends her love," Laddie replied. Residing at The Beeches, as far as he knew. He still hadn't seen hide nor hair of her. Neither had Miriana made mention of her, which was, on the whole, always a good thing. "Now come on. Bought this yoghurt specially for you."

"You're too good to me, Laddie. Do all the girls get this treatment?"

"You're the only one that gets five-star service. The rest have to make do with what I give them." Laddie laughed.

"I'm going to miss you when I'm gone."

"Gone?" Laddie frowned.

"Yes, gone. I can't stay here for very much longer."

Sitting down on the edge of the bed, Laddie reached out and stroked her hair. "You've only been here for a couple of months. It'll take a year, maybe two before you've earned enough money to move on," he said. Wasn't that what Miriana told all the girls? "You just let me take care of you and the time will fly. You'll see."

"I'll keep in touch. Promise."

She was flushed and had a glow about her that he hadn't seen before. Excited.

"Well, that's nice," Laddie said.

"Can you get a message to Irina for me?"

"Probably."

"Tell her that she's going to be an auntie. I'm having a baby, Laddie. Isn't it marvellous?"

Staggered by her words, Laddie was momentarily speechless. It wasn't possible. It simply wasn't possible. Clients were strictly forbidden to have sex with the girls without using condoms. They all knew the price of breaking the rules. A non-negotiable fine. A huge one. What they didn't know was that there were hidden cameras in every room.

"That's not possible, Elena. You're on the pill. One day you'll have a baby. After school and uni and that career you're always talking about. Then you'll have babies and a family. Maybe..." Laddie stopped short of saying what was on his mind. "Now eat this yoghurt like a good girl and let's be hearing no more of this nonsense."

"It's not good for pregnant girls, Laddie," Elena replied, smoothing down her belly.

"It's all in your imagination. Happens sometimes," Laddie said, looking in her eyes. They sparkled like he had never seen them sparkle before.

"But I am, Laddie. I didn't tell you about the morning sickness. I didn't want you to worry, but I'm better now. It'll all be fine..."

"No, Elena, you think you are, but you're not," Laddie persisted.

"I have four younger brothers, maybe five now, at home. I knew when my mother was pregnant almost before she did. She was always very open about it. Talked about how she was feeling all the time. And now I've got a craving for prunes. Prunes of all things." Elena laughed as if she didn't have a care in the world.

"You're sure?" Laddie said, his brain spinning.

Elena nodded. "You need to get a message to Flaviu as well. Tell him about the baby."

Feeling his temper rising, Laddie felt his face drain of all colour. "Flaviu?"

"We weren't as careful as we should have been before we left Bucharest. That's what happens when you're in love. I'm sure you can understand that."

Laddie ground his teeth. "And there was no one in your life before Flaviu, back home in Bucharest. Nobody else who could be the father of this baby you think you are having?"

"I'm not like that, Laddie. I've never been like that. Flaviu was my first. I need you to give him the news. He'll be so happy. We talked about it, you know. That one day we'd have a family. Three, we agreed. Two boys and a girl. We even chose names for them. But only after I'd finished school and uni. He wanted me to get my qualifications first. He thinks I'm at school now, you know. That's why he hasn't visited yet. Studies first, fun afterwards, he always said. But now we're just going to do things the other way around. I wish I could see his face when you tell him."

Her words echoed in his head. We talked about it, two boys and a girl... Fuck Flaviu. If there was one man he hated above all other, it was Flaviu Dumitru, Miriana's golden boy, and now he hated him more than ever before, if it were true.

"You will tell Irina and get a message to Flaviu, won't you, Laddie?" Elena said.

"I'll get the message out, Elena. Trust me."

"And we'll always be friends, won't we?"

"Friends. Yes," Laddie said.

Laddie wrestled with his conscience. Nothing was certain, but Elena was convincing. If, as she had said, she conceived back in Bucharest then she was already over three months gone, maybe three and a half months. Miriana would be beside herself. Not only had one of her precious commodities got herself in the family way, but she was also claiming that Flaviu was the father. There'd be no mercy for Flaviu. Few people crossed Miriana, but when they did, they lived to regret it. Flaviu would rue the day that he'd got Elena pregnant.

"Miriana." Laddie knocked quietly on the office door before entering. "Can you spare a few minutes? I need to speak to you."

"If you must," Miriana replied, indicating that he should sit and wait.

Laddie took the hard wooden chair opposite her desk and fiddled with his hands. With Flaviu out of the way...

"Elena's pregnant." The words burst out. "She says Flaviu is the father."

Miriana looked up from her papers, her eyes boring into his. "What did you say?"

"I can't be a hundred percent sure, but she says she's pregnant and I believe her. She says Flaviu's the father. Says that it happened in Bucharest before Flaviu brought her over to England. She asked me to get a message to him. I've said nothing."

Steely-eyed, Miriana took a deep breath and slowly exhaled. "Thank you, Laddie. I'll deal with it. In the meantime, you will continue to say nothing to anybody. This conversation has not happened. Understand?"

"What will you do?" He knew it was a foolish question. If she deigned to answer the question at all, almost certainly, he would not like the answer.

"You'll find out in the fullness of time. In the meantime, I shall be doubling her visits and selecting them myself. You'll need to be on your toes. I have my investment to consider. Close the door behind you. And thank you, Laddie. Nicolae always trusted you. He was right to do so."

Miriana looked out of the window. It was a cold November day. Clouds scudded across the sky, the trees bent low by the wind. The first drops of rain pitter-pattered loudly on the glass. Loyalty was everything.

30

ENGLAND
2017—2022

ENGLAND

Miriana lay on Flaviu's shoulder. "I'm thinking about branching out, Flaviu. Into babies."

Flaviu flinched.

"Not me having babies, you know my views about that. A business based on a model I perfected back in Bucharest. A service to young girls who don't want their babies but have left it too late to do anything about it. Maybe their parents threw them out. Maybe they've got nowhere to go, no one to turn to in those last months. Maybe they are prostitutes in desperate need of help. Call it charity, if you like. I just need a suitable house and someone I can rely upon to run it. The sort of person I need will be tough, streetwise, have empathy and patience, and…be hungry for good money, a regular income, and a roof over her head."

Flaviu nodded. Tonya's name sprang to mind. It was almost

three years since he had seen her before leaving Bucharest for England. He had promised to get in touch when he next visited, but time had never been on his side.

"Miriana," Flaviu said, "I've got a name that you might like to check out for the new business. Her name is Tonya Cosmo. We met way back in Bucharest. She's in her late twenties. Streetwise. Tough, and she speaks English fluently. I can get a number for you…"

"How did you meet her?" Miriana asked.

"Through a friend at a party. An exclusive party. She's on the game but very selective about her clients, which let me say, did not include me." Flaviu grinned. "I'll leave it with you. If it works, it works…"

Tonya leant forward into the mirror, turned her face this way and that, and nodded in satisfaction at her reflection. Thirty-four today. In full war-paint, she could be, and often was, mistaken for late twenties. On a really good day, early twenties. Today was a good day.

Only too aware that Flaviu could still have his pick, Tonya wanted to look her best. So far, she'd come up to scratch on all counts, friend, lover, and confidante.

They had first met in 2013. He was in his late teens. Happy-go-lucky. Carefree. Popular among his peers. Blessed with good looks. But naïve, still to make his first conquest with a woman, as she soon learnt. An escort, as she preferred to describe herself; she was twenty-five at the time. It had been in a club. He'd brushed past her on his way to the toilet. He was not her regular type of customer. Far too young. For a second, they'd locked eyes. A mutual attraction. She had waited until he passed by on his return, slipped her arm in his, and led him away from the smoke and noise of the club. On occasions she had been happy to waive her fee. That had been one of them.

Flaviu was eager to learn and eager to please; their relationship had flourished.

On the anniversary of their first meeting, Flaviu had failed to show. It had saddened rather than angered her that he had disappeared without so much as a word. But that was life. She had a living to earn. There had been no commitment between them. He had her number if he wanted to call. Move on.

Three years later, she had received a call, the caller's name displayed on her mobile. *Flaviu.* Piqued that he had not so much as rung her in all that time, she had been sorely tempted to cut the call, but curiosity prevailed.

First apologising, he had gone on to tell her that he had given her mobile number to a business associate who might well contact her in the next few days. Her name was Miriana. Asked why, he had said that there was a job opportunity. In England. Likely to be well paid. A regular income. House and car. All found. Finally, he had said that he missed her, but that when and if this person rang, she was not – not – to mention that they were old friends.

Coincidentally, it had not been far from her mind that her professional days might soon be drawing to an end. Her entries in her diary were becoming fewer and fewer. Indeed, there were weeks when there were no entries at all.

The call came. Two days later. Miriana Constantin. She was a woman of few words. Without further words of introduction, she had said she was looking for a mature woman to run a bed and breakfast located in Stroud, Gloucestershire, England, and that from time to time she would be required to accommodate longer-staying guests. Tonya had come recommended, Miriana had said. Far from anything Tonya had expected to hear, and streets apart from any thoughts she had had about a future career, it had left her speechless. But she had listened as Miriana had explained more about the job, but by no means the full extent, as she was later to find out. At first, she had said that she would need to think about it. Leaving no uncertainty, Miriana had said that she could either take it or leave it. The offer would not be repeated. Tonya accepted the offer. If it didn't work out, then she would simply return and probably take up where she'd left off. At least while she was in England, she'd have Flaviu to turn to. He'd always had a place in her heart.

Saying goodbye to the streets, Tonya packed her bags and departed Bucharest for England.

A woman of the world, it had still come as a shock when Tonya had found out about Miriana's line of business and Flaviu's own role in it. It had been a hard pill to swallow but one that she had no choice but to accept.

Five years on, Tonya had her own feet firmly under the table, albeit in one of Miriana's fringe but highly lucrative businesses. Despite all the obstacles, her relationship with Flaviu, long since revived, continued to flourish, and she believed it had reached an all-time high. At the express wish of Flaviu, Miriana remained blissfully ignorant of their relationship. According to him, she was vehemently opposed to mixing business with pleasure. Several times Tonya had come near to letting the cat out of the bag but had stopped herself in the nick of time. The more she came to know

Miriana, the more she appreciated that she was not a woman to be crossed.

Thirty-four years of age, Tonya found herself wanting more. To be married and have a family of her own before it was too late. With Flaviu.

31

ENGLAND

2022

The summons to The Ivy had not been expected.

"She claims that you're the father of the baby. That you're in love with her. Is that so?"

Miriana's accusation rang in his ears.

Taking a moment or two to gather his thoughts, Flaviu said, "No chance. You know me better than that."

"Do I?" she persisted, her eyes blazing with anger.

"How many girls have I brought into this country for you and trained? Did one of them ever get pregnant? No, is the answer."

"So, she wasn't special to you as she claims?"

"Just one more job. The same as the rest," Flaviu insisted.

"Then you'll have no trouble in following my instructions now. I want you to get rid of the girl and that bastard she's carrying. She's past her sell-by date with the clients. Eight months pregnant. And she's trouble. And I don't want any temporary solution. She disappears. Permanently. I want them both dead."

Flaviu took a deep breath, choosing his words carefully before he spoke. "The baby is worth money. I can get rid of the girl when the time comes…"

"Not this one. I've made my decision, and it's final. Today."

"If that is what you wish, then that's the way it will be," Flaviu said.

Miriana smiled. "And there must be no mistakes. They must disappear without a trace. We go back a long way, Flaviu. We are good together. Don't spoil it now. Make your family proud of you."

Flaviu nodded. He understood. There would be consequences, severe consequences, not only for himself but his family too, if he messed up. "You can trust me."

"She's waiting for you in the hall with her bag. I've told her you are coming to collect her. She's so happy. A pity that it will be short-lived, wouldn't you say?"

"I'll take your bag," Flaviu said, walking towards the car. They got in and pulled away from the house. Glancing in his rear-view mirror, he watched as Miriana waved them farewell.

Pulling on a body-hugging, low-cut dress, Tonya twirled in front of the mirror before slipping her feet into a pair of high-heeled Jimmy Choos, shoes that not so many years ago she would never have dreamt of owning. They were her pride and joy, along with the other three pairs in her wardrobe. It was her birthday. In the background, Adele sang 'Love In The Dark' from her latest album. After drawing the curtains across the window, Tonya turned and reached for her mobile. It was Flaviu's ringtone.

"Hi, honey." Tonya kicked off her shoes and lay sprawled on the bed, her hand slipping between her thighs in anticipation.

"Getting fuel. Fifteen minutes at most," Flaviu said.

"You've got your key. I'll be waiting. Come right up."

"I've got a surprise for you," he said. Her heart leapt. In her mind's eye she pictured a small leather box. Inside lay a diamond ring.

Tonya took a deep breath and slowly exhaled. The last time she had seen him, she'd dared ask if there might be a future for them both together. He hadn't said yes, but neither had he said no. Simply rolling her over and straddling her, he had whispered, "You're my soulmate. You know that." It was as close to a yes as she could have hoped. Soulmates were for life.

"I've got a job for you," he said.

"And I've got a job for you, too, and it's going to be a very long job," she said playfully. "We've got all day. No residents. No visitors. Just you and me."

"No, I mean a proper job, Tonya."

Tonya's face dropped. They were words that she simply didn't want to hear. It was no more than a matter of days since she'd concluded the previous job. She needed a break. She deserved a break. And right at that moment, she needed Flaviu. Deep inside her. Not another job. To hell with the business for a day. "But you know it's…"

"Your birthday. I haven't forgotten. If it could have been any other day…This can't wait. I need a favour. A big one," Flaviu said.

"I'm listening."

"A girl. She's eight months gone. One of Miriana's girls. Coming up to seventeen. I need you to take her in," Flaviu said. "I know I can rely on you."

Tonya sat bolt upright and held the phone at arm's length. Jobs came through Miriana, no one else, and certainly not direct from Flaviu. "Miriana hasn't mentioned any jobs to me."

"No, and she mustn't know about this one. There's a lot hanging on it," Flaviu said.

"What's so special about this one that it can't go through the normal channels?" Tonya frowned, knowing full well what the consequences might be if Miriana were to hear of it.

"Miriana told me to kill her and the baby. Killing the girl is one thing but killing a baby is another. It's not good business sense. We both know that."

After a moment, Tonya asked, "Whose baby is it?"

"I don't know. Could be anyone's. She's in the car. Her name's Elena…I brought her over in August last year. She's insisting that the baby is mine. Believe me, Ton, it's not. I'm not that stupid. She must have got herself pregnant before I met her…Are you still there?"

"Yes. Just thinking," Tonya replied. She'd known Flaviu for nearly ten years and, to the best of her knowledge, he had never lied to her. So why was she doubting him now? "And the girl. What about her, after the baby is born?"

"Let's cross that bridge when we get to it," Flaviu said. "I'm on my way right now. And Tonya, I want to know the moment the baby is born."

"And why would that be?" Tonya asked.

"I want my cut of the proceeds, and I've got a buyer lined up."

32
ENGLAND
2022

Eight months pregnant and as big as a house. Seventeen years her junior, the girl was undeniably beautiful. Life was a bitch.

"Flaviu." Tonya nodded in his direction.

"Thanks. Let's get her inside," Flaviu said, looking over his shoulder.

"Expecting someone?" Tonya leant into him and whispered in his ear. "Miriana, by any chance?"

"I wouldn't put anything past her," Flaviu whispered. "You know her as well as I do."

"You're welcome, Elena. Any friend of Flaviu's is a friend of mine," Tonya said, turning to Elena before planting a light kiss on her cheek. "My home is your home until we've got you through this, and you are ready for whatever the world holds for you... Flaviu seems to have forgotten his manners. I'm Tonya."

"You're very kind, and if I may say so, very beautiful. That dress...it suits you. Were you going out somewhere?" Elena asked.

"No, nothing special planned for today." Tonya laughed, seething inside.

"Flaviu told me that he must go away on business for the next four or five weeks. He'll be coming to collect me and the baby when he gets back," Elena said.

"Really?" Tonya glanced sideways at Flaviu. Not only was she expected to look after this girl, but she was also expected to do it single-handed.

"You'll be fine here, Elena. Take care of yourself and the baby," Flaviu said, turning back to Tonya and whispering, "I can't afford for Miriana to see me anywhere near this place, and neither can you. I have to go now."

"You're not stopping, Flaviu?" Tonya raised her eyebrows. "Isn't there something that you've forgotten?"

Flaviu pulled an envelope out of his pocket. "I bought you a birthday card. And there's a gift voucher to go with it."

"A gift voucher. How thoughtful of you," Tonya said with as much sarcasm as she could muster. So much for a diamond ring.

"I'll ring. Keep in touch on the phone." Flaviu turned and, without so much as looking back, climbed into his Porsche and drove away.

"Drive safe." Tonya waved as she watched the car disappear out of sight. He was a liar. It was written all over his face. He had eyes only for the girl. With or without the baby.

A four-bedroomed house with two double bedrooms to the front, one double and one single to the rear; the rear double was reserved for long-term guests. The first of the two front doubles was reserved for B&B guests, of which there were few, and never at the same time as long-term guests were in residence. Tonya occupied the second double. The single bedroom, little larger than a box room, was used as a storeroom. It was kept locked at all times.

Inaptly named The Towers, it had been established as a B&B long before Miriana had bought it and Tonya had taken up residence.

"Let me carry your case upstairs, I'll show you where your room is and where the bathroom is, and then you can have a rest before unpacking. I expect you're tired," Tonya said, leading the way.

Walking across to the window, Elena reached out for the window catch. "Do you mind if I open it? It's not locked, is it?"

"Of course not. Fresh air is good for you. Be my guest." Tonya shrugged her shoulders. "I'm no gardener as you might notice."

"It's full of wildflowers. So different to Ferentari. I can see butterflies and hear the birds. And I'll be able to see the stars at night. I'll be very happy here. And this room is so pretty…"

"I'm pleased you like it. And there's an armchair by the window, so if you want to snooze during the day, you'll be nice and comfortable," Tonya said, hoping that her guest might do precisely that. Anything preferable to having to put up with the girl 24/7 and under her feet. "Why don't you unpack and take a rest now. Come down and join me later."

Stopping by her own bedroom, Tonya pulled the red dress over her head, slipped the Jimmy Choos off her feet, and threw both of them in her wardrobe. Slipping on her dressing gown, she padded downstairs. What she needed was a very, very large vodka and tonic and time to think.

"Do you mind if I join you?" a quiet voice said. "I couldn't settle. The baby's kicking."

Tonya gritted her teeth. "Do you want one?" she said, pointing to her glass.

"I'd love a glass of water," Elena replied, politely. "I can fetch it myself. Is that the kitchen?"

"Yes," Tonya replied. "Glasses are in the cupboard above and to the right of the sink. Help yourself. Make yourself at home." The one thing she would not do was wait on this girl hand and foot.

"It's a lovely little kitchen. Not as big as Flaviu's but more cosy," Elena said, returning glass-in-hand before sitting down on the sofa within inches of Tonya.

Tonya shifted away, draining her glass.

"I did some cooking for Flaviu while I was staying with him. Not often, but sometimes. I'd make him a nice hot meal for when he came home."

"And had his slippers ready by the fire?"

"He doesn't wear slippers. You don't need them on his carpets. Maybe I can cook a few meals for you? I'll wash up as well."

"Good idea," Tonya said leaping up. "Just going to get myself another glass of water." Closing the kitchen door behind her, Tonya reached for the vodka bottle and half filled her glass before throwing the empty bottle in the bin.

For the next four weeks it was Flaviu *this*, Flaviu *that*, Flaviu *the other*, until she was ready to scream and close to wringing the girl's neck. Instead, she practised counting to a hundred and then counting backwards.

She was never so pleased as when she heard the sweet sound of Elena yelling that the baby was coming.

It was a false alarm, but Tonya had had enough. More than enough.

33
ENGLAND
2022

Elena was two days past her due by date. May 4th, she said. Nine months to the day since she had slept with Flaviu for the first time. In Bucharest. In his flat, the girl insisted.

Paid a modest salary, Tonya took a modest ten percent of the profit on sales while Miriana scooped the lion's share. A small cut for the huge responsibility of running a business from a residential property without arousing suspicion. Miriana dealt with the related paperwork. The B&B was a cover for what had proved to be an extremely lucrative business.

Pouring herself a large glass of vodka – her now daily go-to – Tonya sat down at the kitchen table, going over it all in her mind, checking that she hadn't misread the situation and that her plan was sound.

Flaviu. Was he telling the truth that he was not the father of the baby, and that his only interest was to share the profits from the sale of the baby with her? Doubtful. Flaviu was well paid for his services to Miriana.

Miriana. Why had she instructed Flaviu to dispose of Elena

and the baby rather than simply send them direct to The Towers for processing through the normal channel?

There could only be one rational explanation...And if she was right, then Flaviu was lying to her and deserved to be punished.

She'd stood by him through thick and thin. Slept with him whenever he wasn't *on the job*. Rarely complained. And if everything went according to plan, Flaviu would be no wiser of her role in the outcome and maybe they might still have a future together.

A three-stage plan; it was neat. Stage 1, get the baby born and the sooner the better. Stage 2, in two weeks' time, complete the sale and deal with Elena. Stage 3, deal with Flaviu. It was all a matter of keeping her nerves.

If she had learnt one thing over the past five years, it was that babies came when babies were ready and due dates meant little, particularly for a first born. From knowing nothing whatsoever about pregnancy, childbirth, or looking after newborns when she had taken the job in 2017, she now considered herself to be a world authority with a fairly impeccable record, having only lost one baby along the way, and that the child of a long-term drug user. Letting nature take its own course on this occasion was not convenient.

Finally, she was ready to make the first call.

"Dr Sharma?"

"Speaking."

"Tonya Cosmo. I have business for you."

"Good evening, Tonya," he replied.

She could tell he was smiling to himself. She was probably one of the few people – probably the only person – who ever addressed him by his proper title these days. Struck off the medical record four years previous, he had not practised in the NHS since. But a man had to make a living.

"I want a girl induced," Tonya said. "Today."

"Short notice, Tonya. I'll have to check my diary."

Drumming her fingers on the table, Tonya waited with growing impatience. He was winding her up.

"Sorry to keep you. Yes, it appears that I am free later."

"After dark. The side gate will be unlocked. I'll have her ready for you."

"And payment?"

"On completion. Cash. I'll double your normal fee, and in return, you will forget that this conversation or the birth ever happened. Do you understand?"

"I've already forgotten, my dear. Nice to do business with you."

"And then I will ring you the moment she starts," Tonya said, cutting the call before rerunning the story that she was about to tell Elena.

The following day on 7th May at 10 a.m., Elena started. First calling Dr Sharma, Tonya then went into the storeroom and took out everything that might be needed for the birth.

By 5.00 p.m., a healthy girl weighing 7 lbs 10 oz had been born. An episiotomy was needed to assist the birth, and Elena had fared less well.

Thanking him for his time, Tonya took the small bottle of morphine from Dr Sharma and started the clean-up process.

Elena felt blessed. She had a beautiful baby girl and a wonderful friend who fed and changed her little girl while she was unable to do so herself.

Elena slept and dreamt of the future. Flaviu would look after both her and her baby. Her mother and father would welcome her and the baby with open arms and be so pleased that at last there was another girl in the family. And one day, she would introduce the baby to her Aunt Irina, who was never far from her mind.

34

ENGLAND
2022

There was always a waiting list. Desperate people taking desperate measures. And then living the rest of their lives wondering if their decisions might come back to haunt them. Like a piranha, Miriana fed on them.

Occasionally plans went awry as had happened not six months since. Miriana had asked Tonya to call the expectant parents of a promised baby and 'let them down gently'. Miriana had sold the baby to a higher bidder. The name of the unhappy couple remained in Tonya's notebook and their phone number in her contact list. She was about to make their day. It was 21st May and time to invoke Stage 2 of the plan.

"Tonya Cosmo here. Maybe you remember me? I'm so sorry that we let you down earlier in the year…" Tonya said. "But I have news for you. Exciting news. In the late afternoon on Monday 7th May we had a new arrival. Caucasian. White. Of good stock. Seven pounds ten ounces at birth and putting on weight nicely, she is in need of a new home. She is yours if you want her."

Tonya listened to the conversation between man and wife and the tears shed by both.

The only question they asked was "When?"

"Tomorrow. I'll have her ready for you by ten o'clock tomorrow night…We can sort out the money transfer once you arrive…Perfect, and may I just remind you that you must keep this to yourself. I've stepped a little out of line in jumping you up the queue. It would be more than my life was worth if the firm were to find out…Thank you…Making people like you happy is worth more than anything to me."

Tonya finished the call, punched the air, and poured herself a glass of vodka – straight.

Had Tonya been aware that Elena had been standing outside of the door and had heard everything, she might not have been celebrating quite so soon.

Elena had needed a fresh nappy for the baby. There was no need to disturb Tonya. Having watched Tonya going in and out of a room that she called the storeroom, Elena knew where to find them. But the door was locked.

After padding quietly down the stairs in her slippers, Elena leant against the doorframe. Tonya didn't like to be interrupted when she was making phone calls. And a few minutes more wouldn't make much difference to the baby. Tonya was loud. Excited.

"May 7th…Caucasian. White. Of good stock. Seven pounds ten ounces at birth and putting on weight nicely…in need of a new home…Tomorrow…"

Elena felt the blood draining from her face as she sank quietly to her knees and listened to the rest of the conversation. It couldn't be true. Tonya was her friend. Flaviu's friend. Selling *their* baby? Maybe she had misheard? Perhaps her head was still muzzy from the latest dosage of morphine...Seven pounds ten ounces, born 7th May....

Elena stood rooted to the spot, her heart pounding as she listened to the final words of the conversation. Her mind in turmoil, her legs turned to jelly as she heard laughter. And then a glass being filled. And then more laughter. And then a glass being refilled. And then...then...loud snoring. Stepping silently into the room, she found Tonya, the woman who she had thought to be her first friend, lying prostrate on the sofa. Her fingers were clutched around a glass, an empty vodka bottle within arm's reach on the coffee table. Not for the first time, drunk and out for the count. A bunch of keys lay alongside the bottle on the table. Elena picked up the keys, crept silently back upstairs, and unlocked the storeroom.

Fresh linen bedding, towels, and nappies piled high on shelves. Elena reached up and tucked three nappies under her arm. Having opened the mirror-fronted medicine cabinet that hung from the wall, her eyes alighted on a row of small amber bottles labelled 'Morphine', together with a box labelled 'Syringes'. It takes the pain away. It helps you sleep...Tonya's words.

Hands shaking, Elena unscrewed the top of one of the bottles before removing a syringe from its wrapper. Pushing the plunger down as far as it would go, she inserted it into the bottle and slowly drew it out again until the amber liquid filled the glass.

Tonya felt nothing.

Elena switched off the light.

Beside the front door on a small reception table lay a visitors' book and a small number of business cards. After pocketing one of the business cards, Elena turned the key in the front door and stepped out into darkness. With a small backpack over her shoulder and the baby nestled close to her chest and hidden beneath a loose cardigan, Elena started walking. No one was going to take her baby away from her.

35

ENGLAND
2022

Almost six weeks on and he still hadn't heard from Tonya that the baby had been born. And now, she wasn't picking up his calls, and neither was she responding to the voicemail messages that he left at regular intervals. It was out of character. Tonya always kept in touch. Flaviu was getting irritated and not a little worried. If Miriana had found out about where Elena was, then there might have been trouble – trouble for all of them. Anything could have happened.

Pacing backwards and forwards in the apartment, Flaviu rang again. Once more it went straight to voicemail. "For God's sake, Tonya, how many messages do I have to leave?"

It was late – past midnight – but he knew of old that Tonya rarely retired before one in the morning, and she'd often welcomed him into her house in the early hours. He had his own key. If, although unlikely, she was asleep, he would have no need to wake her. It would be sufficient to know that they were all safe.

Jumping in the Porsche, Flaviu set off in the direction of the M5. Thirty-five miles and less than an hour on the road was a small price to pay for peace of mind. Picking up the motorway at junction 18, and leaving at junction 13, he'd reach the house well before one.

The street was in darkness, the streetlights long since switched off, the pavements deserted. Approaching The Towers, he could see that it too was in darkness. Suddenly he felt foolish. Creeping around in someone else's house in the early hours was sheer madness. What would he say to her if she awoke thinking that there might be an intruder in the house? Better to drive on by. Better to trust Tonya as he should have done in the first place. Better to go home and call her again in the morning. Instead, Flaviu parked the car kerbside right outside The Towers.

Opening and closing the gate behind him, Flaviu reached into his pocket for his mobile, switched on the torchlight, and started to ease the key into the lock.

The key didn't turn. The door was unlocked. Tonya never left the door unlocked. There was always too much at stake to be careless, and that was one thing Tonya was not.

Flaviu stepped in through the front door. Silence. You could hear a pin drop. And certainly, no sound of a baby crying.

Opening the kitchen door, he flashed the torch around. Beside the sink waiting to be washed and cleared away were two dinner plates, knives and forks, and two saucepans. So, they'd been in and not long since. Had lunch or supper and gone to bed?

Closing the door again – just as he had found it – Flaviu returned to the hall before carefully opening the door to the lounge.

Her body lay on the rug in front of the fireplace, blood trickling from her scalp down behind her ear and onto her cheek and the rug. Her eyes were open. On the coffee table, an empty bottle of vodka and a glass, and blood splatters on the marble fireplace and down the wall. Disbelieving and believing at the same time, Flaviu dropped to his knees and felt for her pulse. Nothing. She was cold to the touch but the blood on her head had not yet coagulated. She had not been dead for long.

Stroking her hair, he whispered in her ear that she had always been precious to him and that he would never forget her. He kissed her lips and smelt her breath, heavy with alcohol.

The scene before his eyes told the story. Intoxicated, she would have tripped and hit her head on the mantelpiece. An accident.

Wiping the spent tears away with his arm, Flaviu stopped and listened. It was the silence that wasn't right. Surely Tonya would have cried out when she had fallen. Elena could not have failed to hear. Where was Elena?

Flaviu took the stairs two at a time, flinging open doors as he went. First Tonya's room. Empty, the bed unmade. Second, the 'business' room, empty. The third double, empty. The storeroom door open. There was no sound from the bathroom.

Where was Elena? What the hell was he going to do? If he called the police, it would be game over for all of them. If he called Miriana, it might well be game over for him. How would he explain to her that he had turned up at Tonya's at one in the morning? And what if she were to discover that Elena had been at The Towers? Only six weeks ago, he had looked her in the eye and told her that Elena was dead as per her instructions. For the past five years, Tonya and he had kept their relationship away from Miriana – successfully, as far as he knew. Or he could walk out the same way he had come in, drive away, and let somebody else discover that Tonya was dead. Three options. None of them good. On the positive side, Miriana had contacts in the right places. He might just get away with it.

Flaviu rang Miriana. Mercifully, the call rang out eight times before she answered. Little time to get his story straight but better than none.

Miriana rolled over, checked the time. And picked up the phone. Flaviu. It was 1.00 a.m. "This had better be good," she snapped.

"I'm at The Towers. Tonya is dead. Looks like an accident. A fall." Flaviu paused. "She rang me earlier. Asked me to come over. Some emergency, but she wouldn't say what. I couldn't get here sooner."

"How did you get in?"

"The door wasn't locked. What do you want me to do?"

"And you've checked the house? There's no one else there?"

"Nobody."

"I'm on my way," Miriana said. "The house needs to be cleared out – of everything."

"I'm here, right now. I can do it. The car's outside. There's nobody about. I can store everything at my apartment until you decide what to do with it."

Miriana hesitated. This was too important to be left to chance. It was also time-critical. "If you let me down, Flaviu, it will be the last time that you do. Papers, computers, mobiles, files…Every bit of paperwork you can find. And there's a storeroom upstairs. Leave the linens and get rid of everything else. Check her hand-bag. Get it done and get out and ring me the minute you leave. Understand?"

"Trust me," Flaviu said with a sigh.

Computer, phone, files, letters, papers, the visitors' book, Flaviu bagged everything up in black dustbin bags before going upstairs.

After first checking Tonya's bedroom, Flaviu moved quickly

on to the business room – the room that Elena would have occupied during her stay. Elena gone, he had not expected to find the wardrobe and drawers full of the clothes that he had bought for her all those months ago. Flaviu filled more dustbin bags. And then the storeroom. Finally, the bathroom.

There on the bathroom floor, beside the toilet, lay a dirty nappy.

Wishing that on this one occasion he had driven the spacious little Skoda, Flaviu re-parked the Porsche around the corner, near the side gate, away from prying eyes. He loaded up the dustbin bags, forcing them in one by one, before returning to lock the front door, the whole job completed within the hour.

"It's done. Everything cleared. I'm leaving now," Flaviu said, as he pulled away and headed back the way he had come.

But where was Elena…and the baby?

At 3.00 a.m. a police car drew up outside The Towers, responding to an anonymous call.

36

BUCHAREST

2012

A brothel. Six girls. Clients arriving, clients leaving. It was an accident waiting to happen. Ten brothels and sixty girls, sometimes more. Ten times as many clients.

Back in her university days, Miriana had learnt the power of anticipating risks and putting in place plans to mitigate them as and when they might arise. And as often as not, one or more would. No matter how unlikely, each one deserved reasonable consideration before dismissal. Those that remained were the real risks.

Miriana took over Nicolae's residential operations and went through each of the businesses with a fine toothcomb. While there were innumerable risks in running a legitimate business, their numbers paled almost into insignificance in the case of an illegitimate one. Surprise visits and raids by the Poliția Română, a disgruntled client or employee, a word out of place, a nosy neighbour, an over-inquisitive bank, not to speak of the common day-to-day hazards of fire and flood, sickness, and failing technology, all had to be considered. Satisfied that she had addressed every conceivable risk, Miriana congratulated herself on a job well done, one that had so far proved worth its weight in gold. But the clue was in the word. Conceivable.

The possibility that one of the girls might conceive had not been ignored – far from it. There were rules in the residences. Clients must always use condoms. Each of the house managers was responsible for ensuring that each room was well equipped and the stock level maintained, and that none of the products were ever past their sell-by date. For the safety of the girls. For the safety of the clients. An outbreak of gonorrhoea, chlamydia, or syphilis would be disastrous for the business. When a client signed up for membership, he signed a declaration taking full responsibility in the event that such a situation was to arise. A declaration that included a heavy financial penalty. As an additional safety precaution, there were minute cameras invisible to the eye installed in each of the rooms, providing an additional level of insurance in the event of a pregnancy-related dispute. And that particular investment had paid dividends in more ways than one, especially when Miriana needed an influencer on her side. However, and notwithstanding her extensive precautions, it had happened. A sixteen-year-old was in the family way.

Miriana reviewed the risks and doubled, trebled the precautions. All girls were immediately put on the pill. House managers were instructed to stand over each girl as they swallowed them. In the event that a condom split, as the client claimed had happened in the case of the sixteen-year-old, the girls would have double the protection.

Faced with a pregnancy, Miriana thought long and hard about the options. Raised in a staunch catholic family, however much she disagreed with many of her parents' doctrines, abortion she, too, believed to be wrong in the eyes of God. A second option was to pay the girl off and return her from whence she came, running the risk of bringing the strong arm of the law down on her head. The remaining option was to keep the girl in the house, work her for as long as it was possible, and then deal with the consequences when the time came. The baby would have to go. Adoption was a strong possibility.

Sitting up late into the night, Miriana learnt all there was to know about the government-led Romanian adoption process and dismissed it out of hand. It would involve the authorities, social workers, and all kinds of time-wasters. What went on behind closed doors stayed there.

Unable to find an answer to the problem, she googled 'unwanted babies'. Dozens of websites popped up. The first, claiming postnatal depression as a significant factor preventing the bonding of a mother and child, offered one-hour counselling sessions, weekly counselling sessions, and even mother-and-baby retreats. Nothing that she didn't already know and nothing that was of any interest whatsoever. The second, sponsored by the Catholic Church, reminded the reader that abortion at any point during a pregnancy was a sin in the eyes of God and there were prayer meetings that women could attend. That she couldn't disagree with, but it was unhelpful for what she had in mind. The third website was entirely different. It called itself an adoption agency, purporting to work wholly within the law, claiming that they could acquire a child for those who had failed to conceive or had been unsuccessful with fertility treatments. There was a contact number guaranteeing the anonymity of the caller. Her interest piqued, Miriana called the number.

Exhausted by the process, fifty minutes later, she cut the call and reread the notes she had made. Patiently, she'd answered endless questions. Patiently provided endless information – all of which was credible, although untrue, and none of which could be traced back to her. And then patiently listened to the verdict – the likelihood that they could help her find the baby that she was unable to conceive for herself. It was not out of the question, they had said. The service they offered was all-inclusive and totally thorough, but it would be costly. For a white Caucasian baby complete with all necessary paperwork, she would be looking at slightly in excess of two hundred and fifty thousand leu. She had written the sum down on her notepad and underlined it three times. Alongside the sum, she had written 'opportunity'. Selling a baby was a criminal offence but probably no less criminal than running brothels.

The girl worked right up to her thirty-sixth week. Men whose wives did not let them near them during their pregnancy wanted to know what it was like, how it felt. According to the books, gentle sex would harm neither the mother nor the baby – not that that was within her powers of control. Miriana had no reason to turn them away. Instead, she charged a premium for visits.

Born in the residence under the care of a retired midwife, little Rasvan found a new and loving family. Miriana cleared two hundred thousand leu after expenses and nobody was the wiser. Three weeks later, the girl returned to work.

All Miriana now needed was a regular source of supply.

Mătăsari. Bucharest. Bustling streets. Late evening. Clubs and bars as far as the eye could see. Queues to gain entry. Men and women alike falling out of clubs, intoxicated or high on drugs, laughing as they picked themselves up from the pavement before staggering on. The skunky, burnt rope smell of marijuana in the air. Chemical smells – cocaine and crack cocaine. Dogs rummaging in overflowing bins. Stray dogs that hunted in packs – the risk of rabies. Gypsies hustling on street corners. Standing kerbside, girls and women of all ages. On the lookout. Vehicles crawling slowly by, windows open. Money exchanging hands.

Prostitution was illegal in Romania – both soliciting and picking up – but the Poliția Română were ill-resourced to do much about it. Strada Mătăsari was the centre of the red-light district of Bucharest and not for the faint-hearted.

Having removed her rings, necklaces, Rolex, and earrings, Miriana unlocked the safe, deposited them carefully inside, and relocked it. She checked her appearance in the mirror; she was ready. In a long grey padded jacket over a dark-blue rollneck and jeans, and with flat, black boots on her feet that were warm and comfortable, she would not stand out in a crowd. Just another curious tourist checking out the infamous Strada Mătăsari.

The car would be left in a secure, monitored car park close to Scoala Lancului. From there, she would take the No. 55 tram to Mătăsari, one stop further down the line. And then she would walk, keeping her eyes and ears open. In her pocket she carried a small but lethal knife in case she might have need of it.

A long shot, but if she struck lucky, it would not be a wasted trip.

It was ten o'clock when she left home. Ten forty-five when she stepped out of the tram.

Hands firmly in pockets, Miriana strolled down Strada Mătăsari, weaving her way through the dregs of humanity.

A BMW slowed down alongside of her. Pooped the horn.

Pooped the horn again as he crept slowly along, keeping pace with her.

"How much?" he called, winding down the window.

Ignoring the caller, Miriana walked on.

"Clear off," a voice yelled from behind. "Who d'you think you are?"

Something sharp poked her in the back; a firm hand gripped her arm. Miriana turned sharply.

"Not what you think," Miriana replied.

The woman wore a thin, low-necked, body-hugging jumper and a black leather mini skirt. On top of laddered stockings, pink slingback stilettos slopped off the heels of her feet. Her hands were blue with cold, her nails ingrained with dirt. Heavy black make-up rimmed her sunken eyes. Lines criss-crossed her face, her neck scraggy. She was old. Far too old to still be on the streets.

"I saw you. Turning him down. Too posh for him, are you? That pickup was mine," she yelled.

"I'm not for sale. That's not why I'm here," Miriana said, removing the woman's hand from her arm.

"Then, what are you doing here?" she demanded.

"I'm looking for my daughter. A prostitute. She's pregnant."

Showing teeth badly stained by nicotine, the woman laughed in her face. Miriana stepped back from the foul-smelling breath.

"Her and plenty others. Comes with the territory. A hazard of the job. Or didn't you know?"

Miriana nodded, wiping a tear from the corner of her eye.

"How far gone?" the woman asked, softening her voice.

"Seven months."

"And still on the game. Tough. Blokes don't care so long as they can get it up them or down them, whatever turns them on. What does she look like?"

"She's sixteen. Tall. Long dark hair. Straight. The last time I saw her she had red streaks in her hair. Stands out in a crowd."

The woman shook her head. "Rings no bells. Ask that girl," she said, pointing to a girl wearing a loose brown coat. "She'll be dropping soon, that one. Hiding it, but it's there right enough under that coat of hers. They stick together – the pregnant ones, help each other out. Have to or they wouldn't survive."

"Thank you," Miriana said, first looking around and then reaching in her inside pocket. "You've been very helpful. I'm sorry I lost you your pickup. Take this. Small compensation, but I hope it helps."

Her eyes lighting up, the old woman snatched the one hundred-leu note out of Miriana's hand and disappeared into the crowd.

Miriana watched the girl in the loose brown coat from the shadows.

Three times she stepped out into the road, knocked on windows, ran alongside vehicles, grabbed door handles, shouted to the drivers, but without success. She turned and tottered away. Left down a side street, stopping to catch her breath every few minutes, stilettos clip-clopping on the pavement.

Keeping her distance, Miriana followed her. Finally exhausted, the girl sank down to the ground in a doorway littered with bottles, rubbish, and spent syringes. She buried her head in her hands.

Squatting down beside her, Miriana wrinkled her nose at the stench of urine and dogs. She reached out and stroked the girl's hair. "You need help?" she asked quietly. "Do you want this baby?"

The girl shook her head. "How can I bring up a baby? Look at me," she said, her black mascara streaking down her cheeks.

"I can give you shelter and look after you until the baby is born, and then you won't have to worry anymore."

Tears ran down the girl's face. "Why would you do that for me?"

"Because that's what I do. Help girls like you…"

The following day, Miriana searched for and found her eleventh residence in Bucharest.

37

ENGLAND

2022

Thirty-six hours since he had taken his seat on the Quantas flight to Perth before changing for the nonstop to London Heathrow, Gary felt completely bushed. He'd flown economy to save precious money and now lived to regret it. Six foot four, he had barely been able to sit in his seat, let alone stretch his legs out. And then he'd had to find his way from Heathrow to Stroud. He'd opted for public transport and had regretted his choice. Few trains ran in the early hours and those that did were worse than a slow boat to China. Heathrow to Reading and then Reading to Stroud, it had been little short of a nightmare. In the early hours of the morning, finding a taxi at Stroud station that would take him to Magnolia Court had been no easier.

Thirty-six hours and there was no one in. Gary checked the number of the cottage that Penny had given him. Yes, he had the right cottage. It was eight o'clock in the morning and there wasn't a soul about. The place was deserted.

Remembering the boyfriend's name, he knocked at the next-door cottage. An elderly gentleman dressed in lemon-and-blue striped pyjamas, clearly quite bewildered at seeing six foot four blocking the doorway at that time of the morning, looked up at him as though he had descended from Mars.

"I'm looking for Stan," Gary said. "Point me in the right direction, mate?"

"No trouble. You'll find Stan over there," the man replied, pointing to one of the other cottages.

Stan was up and dressed and on his second mug of tea and, as always, debating whether to do a bit of housework or get out and enjoy the morning air, when he heard a loud rap at the door, followed by a second, and a third.

"G'day," the man said. "You must be the boyfriend."

He was a big lad, although lad was probably not the right way to describe him. There was only one person with an Australian accent who would describe him as the boyfriend – and that was Penny's son.

"Gary, I presume," Stan said. "Just dropping in for a cup of tea?"

"Come a long way, Stan, to see what's going on for myself. Just been over to that cottage. She's not answering the door."

Stan hesitated. Normally he wouldn't keep any visitor standing on the doorstep, but from what Penny had indicated, this one was trouble.

"Penny expecting you?"

"She won't be surprised, if that's what you mean."

"Don't count on it," Stan said, starting to close the door on him. Penny certainly hadn't made any mention of the imminent arrival of number one son. Maybe she did not know and had kept it from him. There were times when he didn't know if he was coming or going with the woman.

"Look, Stan. Mind if I call you that, cobber? Maybe we got off on the wrong foot." Gary stuck his size fifteens in the door. "If Mum wants to have a boyfriend, it's no business of mine…It was just…"

"A surprise, hey? Right. Apology accepted. No need for that," Stan said, pointing to the foot. "It's too early for Penny. She probably had another sleepless night."

"At home she was always the first up. Up with the sunrise and never to bed before sunset. Every day. Not like her to change her habits," Gary said. "Still, she's getting older."

"Well, sometimes we can't choose what time we get up," Stan said, grumpily. "And she's not that old. You can come in for a brew if you want." He held the door open. "And take your shoes off."

"Got a stubby by any chance?" Gary said, following him inside.

Stan chuckled. A chip off the old block. There was no doubting that this man kicking off his shoes was who he said he was.

"I was worried about her. Really worried."

"Really?" Stan said, unconvinced. "And why would that be?"

"She sounded odd. Okay, so she does have a boyfriend, and you don't seem like a bad bloke, but a baby?" Gary said. "If your old mum came over all broody at seventy-four, wouldn't you be concerned?"

"Tea?" Stan asked.

"Prefer a beer, if you've got one. Need something to keep me awake."

He had a point. Penny had milked it a bit. "Broody, she isn't.

Kind and generous, she is," Stan said, getting Gary his drink. "And just to put the record straight, she does have a baby."

"What! For real?" Gary said, taking the beer off Stan.

Stan nodded. "She's a good woman. So, you've flown all this way to check up and see if she's losing her marbles, have you?"

"Yep, put it like that," Gary replied. "Well, not entirely."

"Now we're getting somewhere. Why have you come?"

"I'll be honest with you, Stan. I came over to persuade her to come home. She's been gone for four weeks now. She's needed at home," Gary said. "That's where she belongs. We all need her...I need her. I want to take her home."

"Needed, hey? Needed like how?" Stan probed.

"To knock some sense into my head. That's how. And to knock some sense into the rest of the family as well."

"Trouble back on the ranch, hey?" Stan asked.

Gary took a gulp of his beer. "Why would you say that? What's Mum told you?"

"Not a lot. Not my business. I keep my nose out of other people's business. Just reading between the lines. And Penny's just come into some money. Got herself a nice little cottage and a tidy little sum."

Gary stroked his forehead. "I can see that's how it might look. Probably what Mum will think too. Yes, the ranch is in a bit of trouble, but what Mum doesn't know is that I've got plans and that's what I wanted to tell her about, as well as take her home. She's pretty pissed off with me and the rest of the family, and she's right to be. Even agreed the plans with Ronnie, Mum's mate. Ask her about Ronnie...Pretty close the two of them..."

Stan's face dropped. It was the first time he had heard of a mate called Ronnie. Maybe the rumours about her going back home were true after all. Ronnie. Stan stared at the ground.

"They go back years. Dad's best mate. Mum's best mate. He's had his eye on Mum for years…Everything alright, mate?"

"Couldn't be better," Stan barked. "You're here now, but don't be surprised if you're on the next plane back to Australia."

"About this baby…" Gary started, draining his beer.

"You can ask her about that yourself," Stan said, checking his watch. "I'll take you over there at ten. Make yourself comfortable. I've got some work to do."

Stan looked back over his shoulder as he headed up the stairs. Gary certainly didn't mind making himself comfortable. He leant his head against the back of the armchair, put his feet up on Henry's chair, and dozed off.

38

ENGLAND

2022

S tepping back from the front door, Stan looked up at the windows and frowned. The curtains were closed, and Penny wasn't answering the door. His heart missed a beat. Little more than a month ago, he had stood in exactly the same place wondering why Amy hadn't opened her curtains. And then he'd found her lying in bed, passed away in her sleep. It was the last time he'd wept, and he'd never forget that moment. She'd meant everything to him. But he was being maudlin. This was where Penny lived; larger-than-life Penny. To hell with Ronnie or whatever his name was.

"Looks like she may have had a rough night," Stan said. "Curtains drawn. Doesn't look like she's up yet." Reaching out and turning the front door handle, Stan felt a shiver run down his spine. "It's not locked."

"Don't always lock our doors back home," Gary said.

"Your mother is meticulous about locking and unlocking the front door, the Chubb and the Yale, especially since she took the girl and the baby in," Stan said, glancing anxiously at the upstairs windows.

"Well, maybe she just hasn't drawn the curtains back. Not a hanging offence, at least not where I come from. Calm down, mate. You look as though you lost a dollar and found a cent." Gary raised his eyebrows. "Deffo not a crisis."

"Penny's routine. Gets dressed, makes the bed, draws the curtains back, and then – only then – does she ever unlock the door," Stan said anxiously. "And I know that for a fact, so don't you go telling me…"

"…That's another reason I want her home. She's been getting more and more forgetful."

At other times he would have told this jumped-up Aussie where to get off and in no uncertain terms, but right now he had more pressing things on his mind. "Penny," he shouted, barging in through the door. "Penny. I'm coming up just to make sure that you're okay. It's me, Stan."

Gary stood back as Stan took the stairs two at a time.

"She's not here," Stan said, shouting down from the top of the stairs. "The bed's not made. Clothes on the chair. The cot's gone. No baby…"

"Must have taken her for a walk then. That's what people do…" Gary said.

"In her bloody dressing gown?" Stan yelled.

"Crikey, Stan, calm down, mate. There's most likely a simple explanation," Gary said.

"And how do you explain that then?" Stan pointed to the floor. "For fuck's sake, Gary, this is serious."

"Ketchup," Gary said as Stan left the room.

Puffing and panting, Stan raced first up to Ros and Paul's cottage. No, they hadn't seen Penny. And then on to each of the other cottages. No one had seen Penny. Getting more desperate by the minute, he hammered hard on the door of the Old Forge. "Gabby. We've got trouble. Penny's gone and the baby. There's no one in the cottage and no one's seen hide nor hair of her since last night. And…and…there's blood on the hall carpet. And Gary's turned up from Australia. Penny's son. He's there now."

"Oh my God," Gabby screeched. "Right, listen to me, Stan."

Stan stood, staring and unseeing. It wasn't possible. Not Amy and then Penny.

"Listen to me, Stan. Look at me. You've got to hold it together. We'll find her. Right now, I need you to go back to the cottage, get Gary out of there before he touches anything. Then go down to Duncan and get the key to the Mansion House. I'll be there as soon as I can sling some clothes on, but I need to make a phone call first. And tell Duncan I need him there as well."

Dazed and near tears, Stan turned and walked away.

She should have seen something like this coming. It had all the signs of trouble right from the beginning. She was the bloody investigative journalist, and she'd made a wrong call. Uncle Max had been right. They should have called it in much sooner, sooner than last night.

"I need to speak to the Chief Constable, Barry Hardcastle," Gabby said. "No, I don't have an appointment to speak to him. Can you please just let him know that Gabby Olsen is on the phone and needs to speak to him as a matter of urgency…Yes, I'll wait," Gabby said, pulling on a jumper.

"Gabby. What's so urgent? I can give you ten minutes, no more."

His voice was music to her ears, even though she knew full well that he would not be at all pleased with what she had to say.

"It's complicated, Barry, and I wouldn't be ringing you direct if it weren't sensitive and even a matter of life or death," Gabby said, organising her thoughts.

She got him up to speed, telling him about the appearance of the girl and baby, her subsequent disappearance without the baby, and now Penny and the baby's disappearance, the blood on the carpet, and the Romanian connections. "I'm not going to make any excuses. We should have reported the whole thing to you days ago. Now I think we might have a critical situation on our hands."

"Romanians. Prostitution. Trafficking. Gabby, what were you thinking of?" Barry said.

"I wasn't, or at least I wasn't thinking clearly enough," Gabby admitted.

"This is a job for Major Crimes. Do you want to call it in, or shall I get someone to ring you back?"

"That's just it, Barry. I rang in to report Elena's disappearance yesterday evening, and I also mentioned that the baby was being looked after at Magnolia Court. The caller took down all the details and said that she would pass them on to Major Crimes straight away. And that I should expect a call back from Detective Superintendent Handley. I didn't get one."

"He's a good man, Gabby, but busy. You'll be in good hands," Barry said.

Gabby took a deep breath. "I'm not so sure. I think he's involved in some way."

"That's a serious allegation. I hope you've got something to back it up."

"It's tenuous, I know, but DS Handley recently attended an accidental death in St Mark's Road, Stroud. That death was Tonya Cosmo. A Romanian who apparently ran a B&B. That was Elena's last known location before she arrived at Magnolia. He also attended Tonya's funeral yesterday. I know because I was there. Together with Miriana Constantin, suspected of running brothels when she lived in Bucharest, and a man called Flaviu Dumitru. We had all their number plates checked out. DS Handley and Miriana looked very pally to me. So, I ask you, Barry, is it usual for one of your DS's to attend an accidental death and wander around the neighbourhood talking to the neighbours, and then to attend the funeral of the deceased, unless they knew of each other?"

Gabby paused to give Barry time to absorb what she had said.

"That's more than tenuous, Gabby."

"Last night I made some calls to contacts. I can't divulge my contacts. You know that. But one of them reminded me that ten years ago DS Handley had been under investigation for inappropriate behaviour with minors. His name was cleared."

"I'm aware of that. And since that time his career has been exemplary."

"Other than Elena, myself, and the residents of Magnolia Court, whom I would vouch for with my life, there was only one man who knew that Elena had been at Magnolia Court and that Penny Reilly was looking after her baby. DS Handley. From the report that I rang in yesterday evening. If Elena had returned to take the baby, she would not have taken Penny Reilly. Particularly wearing her dressing gown. I can't give you chapter and verse, but I think that someone wanted to find Elena very badly. They arrive at Magnolia. She's not there, but the baby is. The baby is taken. Penny Reilly, who is also taken, is collateral damage. Elena's last known port of call was that B&B owned by Tonya Cosmo. DS Handley is the only person who knew where to find Elena."

"Slow down, Gabby. DS Handley may well be on his way to Magnolia Court as we speak."

"I refuse to share any more information with him," Gabby said.

"What you're asking, Gabby, is highly irregular. If it weren't for the fact that I know you have a nose for trouble, I'd put this phone down right now."

"Please, Barry, anybody but Handley. I'm not going to say 'Trust me', because I should have spoken to you sooner."

"As it happens, I do. Trust you, that is. We've got another murder on the patch. Last night. A knife fight, outside one of the bars. The assailant got away. I'll put Handley on that case. Expect DS Neil Rogers. And, Gabby, no heroics. You do nothing without consulting my people. And keep me informed. My mobile will be on."

39

ENGLAND

2022

"**D**S Neil Rogers is on his way," Gabby said breathlessly, bursting in through the Mansion House doors. "If a DS Handley arrives, no one is to speak to him. Don't ask but it's important."

"Understood," Duncan said.

"Well, I'm glad you understand, because I for sure as hell don't. Would somebody like to tell me what's going on here? Isn't this all a bit extreme, or is this the way you do things over here? Surely, we can find an old lady and a baby. It can't be that difficult. Maybe she's gone wandering. Sleep walking..." Gary interjected. "And who the hell are you?"

"Gabby Olsen," Gabby said, noticing the expression on Stan's face. At any moment he was about to explode. "And you're Gary, I presume. Nice to meet you. To answer your question, we are not dealing with a normal situation here."

"Well, you can say that again. There's nothing normal about my mother having a baby. Nor a boyfriend, for that matter..."

"Let's all calm down," Gabby said quietly, looking at her watch. "Shouting and arguing isn't going to help anyone, let alone

Penny. The police will be here in a minute. I've just called them. Someone needs to let the residents know that we're about to have visitors…Duncan, can you call Jennifer? Ask her to just knock on doors and let them know that something's happened but they're not to worry. And that I'm asking that they stay all clear of Penny's cottage and the Mansion House until further notice."

"That'll be popular, particularly with Max," Duncan said, pulling his mobile out of his pocket. "But if that's what you want."

"That's precisely what I want. Thank you, Duncan."

Stan paced the carpet while Duncan gathered his thoughts and Gabby stood waiting anxiously by the open door, deep in thought about how she would handle it if DS Handley was the first to arrive. Stretched out on the sofa, Gary was catching up on his sleep.

It was just ten minutes before the first car turned in from the road. It was a black BMW followed by a marked police car and then a white van. Gabby strode out to meet them.

"Detective Superintendent Neil Rogers and this is Detective Sergeant Atkins."

"Gabby Olsen." She heaved a sigh of relief. "That one," she said, pointing to the row of cottages. "Penny Reilly's is the one with the blue door. It's unlocked. Other than Stan Morrison, one of the residents, and Gary Reilly, Penny's son, nobody else has been in there this morning."

"Tape it off, PC Mariot. You boys," the DC called to the occupants of the white van, "see what you can find. I'll be down in a minute."

"Stan and Gary are in the Mansion House waiting for you. I've asked a resident by the name of Duncan Gillespie to join us," Gabby said, leading the way without further explanation.

"Duncan Gillespie and Stan Morrison, and Gary Reilly, who flew in from Australia not more than a few hours ago," Gabby said, making the introductions. "This is Detective Superintendent Neil Rogers and Detective Sergeant Atkins."

"Right. I understand that you, Mr Morrison, and you, Mr Reilly, discovered that Mrs Reilly was missing. And at what time would that have been?" Rogers asked.

"Ten this morning," Stan replied.

"And you're quite sure that Mrs Reilly has not just gone off for a walk with the baby?"

"Hundred percent," Stan said. "Her dressing gown's missing. Her clothes for the morning are always laid out on the chair in her room. They're right where they should be. I think she's injured. There's blood on the carpet. It wasn't there yesterday," Stan said, seeming barely able to contain his patience.

"So, what was the last time any of you saw Mrs Reilly?"

"Had tea with her in the afternoon. It would have been about six when I left. She was going to get an early night. There was a routine, you see. She'd be up again at two and then up again at five to feed and change the baby," Stan said.

"And did any of you see or hear any vehicles entering the site during the night?"

Gabby, Duncan, and Stan shook their heads. Gary shrugged his shoulders. "Count me out, mate, didn't get here until eight."

"Atkins, make a note and check to see if any of the other residents saw or heard from her after six," Rogers said. "And ask about vehicles heard entering the site between 6.00 p.m. and 8.00 a.m. this morning.

"And there's no reason that any of you can think of why somebody might want to kidnap Mrs Reilly."

They all shook their heads. "None," they replied in chorus.

"It's got to be the baby they were after," Gabby said impatiently, just wanting to get on with it. If he'd only let her explain the big picture...

"Let's just take this step by step if you please, Mrs Olsen. Do you have a photograph of Mrs Reilly?"

"There's one on the bookshelf in the cottage. Penny with her family. That'll be her in the middle," Stan said.

"And the girl who went missing, the mother of the baby, I am told?"

Duncan picked up his phone and clicked on the image of Elena that Jas had taken. "I can send it to you. Taken when we first found her here when Sam – he's a doctor – was cleaning her up."

"The girl's full name?"

"Elena Albescu. Former resident of Bucharest, Romania. Turned seventeen two weeks ago. She has a twin sister called Irina who we also believe might be in the UK. She's on the missing persons list in Romania," Duncan said.

"How long was Elena here at Magnolia?"

"Me and Penny found her down at No. 19 – that's a Portakabin we just refurbished – last Monday, 23rd May. Penny looked after her and the baby here in her cottage. Then Elena disappeared sometime in the early hours on the 26th, leaving the baby," Stan said.

"And you didn't think to report her missing at the time?" Neil asked.

"We all thought and hoped that she'd come back of her own accord," Gabby interjected. "At the time we didn't even know her name."

"And she's definitely the mother of the baby?"

"Elena is the mother. As far as we know the child has no name as yet. We believe the baby to be about three weeks old," Duncan continued.

"Photograph?"

"Yep, took this one just a couple of days ago." Stan pulled out his phone. "Pretty little soul, isn't she?"

"So, isn't it just possible that the mother returned overnight and took the baby?" Rogers said. "If so, we might have one missing person – Mrs Penny Reilly? Not three after all."

"Yes, that's one conclusion you could draw, but when Elena disappeared, we decided rather than just wait for her to walk back in, we might try and find her ourselves," Gabby said. That it had been Penny, Duncan, and Stan's initiative was neither here nor there. They were all in it together now. "We found a couple of things in the clothes that Elena was wearing when she first arrived here. She disappeared wearing some of Penny's clothes.

"We found a business card for a B&B in her pocket, and we also found a handwritten note, which we think could have been written by her sister. We thought that, for whatever reason, Elena might have gone back to the B&B so Penny and Stan went over there. It's called The Towers. There was nobody at home, so they spoke to a neighbour—"

"Daphne," Stan interrupted. "Owns a B&B in the same road. Told us about the woman up at The Towers…"

"A woman called Tonya Cosmo, who died – accidental death – two days before Elena turned up here." Gabby picked up the story. "Romanian. Tonya, I'm referring to. Moved to England in 2017. Known prostitute." Gabby paused, correctly anticipating Rogers' next question.

"Are you suggesting that this B&B owner's death and the arrival of the girl here at Magnolia are somehow related?" Rogers raised his eyebrows.

"We think there's a connection," Gabby replied. "And then there's the note that we found in Elena's pocket. It was written in Romanian. Duncan translated it."

Duncan passed the note across to Rogers.

"And the significance?"

"Written, and we can only speculate, by Elena's twin sister, Irina. A leap of faith but it's just possible that Elena might have gone off looking for her sister."

Frowning, Rogers reread the note. "Miriana, Alexandru, Flaviu..."

"That's where it gets interesting again. The person who organized Tonya Cosmo's funeral is one Miriana Constantin. Left Bucharest in 2014 shortly after the police raided one of her properties. Nothing specific, but the implication was that it had something to do with minors. Now owns five properties, four in and around Bristol, one in Stroud – the house in which Tonya Cosmo was found dead."

"Alexandru?"

Gabby shook her head.

"Flaviu?"

"The note indicates that Elena and he might have been in some sort of relationship," Gabby said. "From the description and according to Daphne, he was a frequent visitor to Tonya Cosmo's house."

"Anything else?"

"Flaviu Dumitru. Born 20th September, 1997, Bucharest. Now resides at an apartment block called The Downs in Clifton, a property owned by Miriana Constantin. Drives a white Porsche. Registration number F1 DIM. Registered in the name of Miriana Constantin. Blond curly hair onto his shoulders. Height approximately five ten," Duncan said.

Raising his eyebrows, Rogers glanced first at Duncan and then at Gabby.

"I have my contacts," Gabby cut in. It was best that Duncan's best-kept secrets remained precisely that.

"Duncan and I went to Tonya Cosmo's funeral yesterday. Well, not to the actual funeral, you understand, but we happened to be at the crematorium laying flowers on another memorial when she was laid to rest," Gabby said before continuing the story. "There were – how shall I describe them – three mourners? First, Miriana Constantin. We recognized her from a cutting in one of Bucharest's newspapers. Second, Flaviu Dumitru. It had to be. And the third…well I believe the Chief Constable might have briefed you on that. And there were two other men, who stood apart from the mourners. Dumitru arrived in the white Porsche, Miriana and two of the men arrived and left in a black Audi A8—"

"Registration number BS73 GVH," Duncan interrupted. "Also registered in Miriana Constantin's name."

"And then the other man…he left in his own vehicle."

"BS72 HYT. BMW 5 Series. Black," Duncan added.

Narrowing his eyes, Neil glanced back down through the notes he had made. "Could this Flaviu be the father of the baby? If so, he'd have a motive for taking her."

"Possible," Gabby said.

"Then we'd better try and find him. Excuse me while I make a call.

"All roads between Stroud and Bristol Clifton area between 6.00 p.m. yesterday evening and now. White Porsche, F1 DUM. And black Audi, A8, BS73 GVH. And put out a call to all vehicles to be on the lookout for the same. If anyone picks either vehicle up, then to follow at a distance and to keep me informed…I want to know the minute you hear anything. Report back in. No action until I say so. Thank you.

"Now if you'll all excuse me, I need to get down to the scene. We'll need statements from all of you later," Rogers said, turning to leave. "Atkins, house to house enquiries please. Now."

Gary dropped his head in his hands. "Jesus! What a bloody mess. But I'll tell you one thing. My mother may be small but she's gutsy, and wherever she is, she isn't going to go down without a good fight."

"She's not been gone long, sir. We'll throw everything we've got at finding them," Rogers said.

"I can't just sit here." Stan jumped up.

"Me neither," Gary said. "It's my mother we're talking about."

"That is precisely what you are all going to do. I suggest that you all return to your homes and I would be grateful if you did not leave Magnolia Court until I say so. This is now a police matter."

"Would it be acceptable if we were to stay in the Mansion House?" Gabby asked. "The residents like to be together at times like this."

"Fine," Rogers said. "Mrs Olsen, I'll contact you as soon as we have any news."

Pulling up in the car park, Gwen did a double take. It was almost as though she was on set and about to shout *'Cut'*. In the near distance, marked and unmarked vehicles, a white transit, scene of crime tape, white suited figures wearing goggles, gloves, and shoe protectors wandering back and forth between a cottage and a van. No cameras. No lighting. No actors. It was no film or TV set. Whatever had happened here was for real.

Having locked the car door, Gwen started across the short distance from the car park to the cottages, stopping briefly to admire the Mansion House as Penny had described it. They'd had a good chat in the end after a ropey start. Penny's story had been quite a revelation and Gwen was looking forward to meeting her.

"Perhaps you can help me," Gwen said, walking up to a police constable. "I'm here to meet a friend. I don't suppose you could point me in the right direction."

"I suggest you head over to that big house," he said, pointing her back in the direction she had just come. "There's a few of the residents in there. You'll probably just catch them. They'll know."

Door open, she could hear voices inside. Whispered conversations. No one noticed as she stepped in through the door. She cleared her throat. "Hello, I came to see Penny Reilly. I'm Penny's niece. She invited me over here this morning. For coffee…"

"Penny, as you call her, hasn't got a niece, and I should know. I'm her son."

"Gary, that would be you," Gwen said, holding out her hand. "She obviously hasn't had time to explain. If I'd known that and known that you were visiting, then I'd have been a little more tactful with my entrance. I do apologise. Where's Penny?"

40

ENGLAND

2022

"More tea," Hetty asked, wandering aimlessly around, teapot in hand.

"We'll all be swimming before long," Max said, catching her arm as she passed by the umpteenth time. "Time you sat down and had one yourself."

"A nice piece of lemon drizzle?" Totally unaware that Sam had already declined, Dot cut a thick slice of cake and placed it on his plate. "And you, Jas?"

Jas smiled and nodded her head, knowing full well that a no thank you would have made little difference. In times of crisis, they ate cake. It was what was expected. Ate cake and drank tea. Except Penny, of course, who hated both tea and cake...Poor Penny.

"Dot," Dennis whispered, "I don't think anyone's got room for any more cake. Come and sit down. And stop working yourself up about it."

"It's just that I feel so guilty, Dennis. Saying all those things behind her back. Doubting her when she said that she wanted to stay with us. What kind of friend am I?" Dot flopped down onto the sofa next to her husband.

"A good one. You had reason to doubt. A return ticket. And now the son turns up on the doorstep expecting to take his mother home. Just heard him talking to that Gwen, and she's a turn up for the books as well. Two of them seem to be getting on well."

"And now we might never know," Dot said, blowing her nose. "What if?"

"We'll have none of that, Dot Gardener. Blow your nose. Any more of that lemon drizzle left?"

Dot smiled. She was lucky to have him.

"Don't know about you, Thomas, but I'm ready for a G&T. Early I know. For medicinal purposes. Sound good?" Gerald said, eyeing the bar.

"Hmm, yes, I think I'll join you," Thomas said.

"You can't blame yourself, Duncan," Jennifer said.

"I can. It was me, not Gabby, who suggested that we wait another day and go to that funeral. If we'd reported the girl missing the same day she disappeared, none of this would have happened. You see, I was caught up in the thrill of the chase. Enjoying myself, Jennifer." Duncan hung his head in shame. "And it was me who let the cat out of the bag about the return ticket. Should have kept my mouth shut instead of sowing seeds of doubt here, there, and everywhere. I suspect that after all this, she'll want to be on the first plane home."

Jennifer smiled. "That's more like it. When and not if…"

"It's the waiting that I can't stand," Gabby said. "How long is it, now?"

"Five minutes later than when you asked me the last time, Gabby. Two o'clock," Max said.

"You were right, Uncle Max. We should have listened to you."

"And Hetty, Duncan, Penny, and Stan were right too. That girl didn't deserve to lose her baby. And as Stan quite rightly reminded us, Amy would have been right up there banging the drum for her too…Is that your phone ringing?"

The room fell silent as Gabby pressed the green button and held her phone to her ear.

"That was Detective Superintendent Rogers," Gabby said, her eyes glazing over. "They've…they've…found Penny and the baby. The baby is fine. Penny"— Gabby hesitated—"is in an ambulance on her way to intensive care at Bristol Royal Infirmary. Penny…Penny…sustained a gunshot injury. That's all he can tell us at this point in time."

"I've got to go to her," Gary said, grabbing his jacket.

"I'll come too," Gwen said. "Family."

Gary nodded.

"I'll drive," Stan said.

"Ring. As soon as you know anything," Gabby said, hiding her tears as she buried her face in Max's chest. Max stroked her hair, just as he had done when she was a little girl.

41

ENGLAND

2022

Sitting on a park bench, Elena watched the buses unload their passengers at the bus stop before waiting for the next group to get on board. That morning had been the first time that she had been on a bus in England. It wasn't so much different to Bucharest except the buses here were nice and shiny, the seats clean, and there was no litter on the floor. That was probably because of the sign at the front of the bus that said 'No eating and drinking.' No jostling for seats. Everybody formed an orderly queue at the bus stop and awaited their turn.

It was thanks to Penny that she had enough money and more to pay for her bus fare from Stroud to Bristol. And she hadn't forgotten that one day she must repay Penny in full. After a long walk from Magnolia Court into the centre of Stroud, with her feet blistered from the shoes she wore, she had been thankful for the rest. And then three more buses to get her out to Clifton. Everybody had been so helpful. For the final ride, unable to remember more than the park, she had described it to the bus driver as she remembered it. A grassy park alongside a main road, shiny black metal fencing around it, a small gate letting into it and a bandstand. "Victoria Square, that's what you're looking for love," he'd said. "I'll tell you when we get there."

Disembarking from the bus, she'd thanked the driver, waved goodbye, and walked into the park for the first time ever. How could she forget it? The long days when she had stood at the picture window on the fifth floor of the apartment block on the opposite side of the road watching people jog along the path, walk their babies in prams, play ball with their children, or just sit enjoying the morning sun on the very same bench that she now occupied. How much she had longed to join them.

Everything had seemed possible the previous night. Flaviu would open the door and hold her tight in his arms. She'd tell him about their little girl. They'd talk about a name for her. He'd tell her why he hadn't been to visit her at Tonya's. A perfectly reasonable explanation. She'd tell him that it was not his fault. That school and university and careers weren't important anymore and that the only thing that mattered was that the three of them would be together as a family. And that when they found Irina, which she knew with his help they would, they'd all go back to Bucharest, to safety, and to start a new life. In her heart, she knew that Flaviu was no saint. He had done bad things. Miriana had made him do bad things. Things that she was sure he regretted but had no power to change. She'd help him change. Find a new way of life. A new job. Stand by him.

He had told her he loved her, and nothing that had happened since, not even Miriana's cruel words – 'He's done his job...' – made her doubt him.

A young couple sat on the bench next to her; a baby in a pram brought tears to her eyes. The girl had long hair just like her own, but she wore it in a ponytail. Dressed in a pretty, floral blouse and white jeans, she wore Croc sandals on her bare feet. He wore a white T-shirt and jeans with sandals and no socks. The baby was crying. The girl reached down into the pram and carefully passed the baby to him. A tiny little girl dressed in a pink body suit with little pink booties. The doting father, he laid the baby over his shoulder, rubbing her back and whispering soothing noises until the crying stopped. And then gently rocked her to sleep.

Wiping the tears away with the back of her hand, Elena allowed herself an indulgent moment imagining that it was she and Flaviu sitting there with their baby. Laughing and joking together, sharing secrets, and planning their future. A sharp reminder that she had left her baby in the hands of strangers. Not strangers, perhaps. Penny was the kindest woman she had ever met. She deserved far better than for her to leave in the early hours of the morning without so much as a by-your-leave. It was bad enough to help herself to Penny's clothes, but to steal money and her phone as well was unforgiveable. She knew that the baby was in safe hands and that she'd be well looked-after while she was away, which would not be for long. One day she'd repay Penny for all her kindnesses.

It all depended upon Flaviu. The one person in the world that she trusted and the only person who could help her find Irina.

Deep down in her pocket, Penny's phone pinged. Elena took it out and read the message. It was not from Penny as she might have expected but from a woman called Gabby. "Call me back, please," the message read.

Building up courage, Elena headed for the pedestrian crossing and pressed the green button. The lights turning to red, she crossed to the other side and walked in through the revolving doors, her eyes firmly fixed on the lift.

"Excuse me, young lady, where do you think you're going?" the man behind the reception desk called.

Without looking back, Elena stepped into the lift, the doors closing behind her, and pressed five. Leaving the lift, she turned left and followed the plush carpeted corridor down to the first door on the right. On the door was a bell and a small brass plaque that read, 'F Dumitru'.

Ringing the doorbell, Elena stepped back and waited but no one came to the door. She rang the bell again, this time harder and longer. Nothing. In desperation she rang it again. That he might be away on business or have left for work had crossed her mind a hundred, a thousand times since she had left that morning, but she'd dismissed it, telling herself that if he wasn't in, then she would wait, however long that might be. Exhausted and overcome by emotion, Elena hammered on the door with her fists, tears streaming down her face.

And then a sound. There was someone in. Flaviu. He was in. Perhaps he'd been in the shower or asleep. Relief flooded over her. Thank God. Dear Flaviu.

"It's me, Elena," she shouted through the door.

"Pleacă." A girl's voice. *"Pleacă."*

"I need to speak to Flaviu. Will you get him for me? Tell him it's Elena," she shouted.

"He's not here. *Pleacă.*"

"No I won't go away. Open the door, please," Elena begged.

"I can't. It's locked," the voice said. *"Pleacă."*

Locked. The door was locked. Just as it had been when she had lived in the apartment with Flaviu. It was for her own safety, he had said. Until her papers came through. Always locked until he came home.

Elena felt the colour drain out of her face. Just another job. She on one side of the door and just another job on the other. "What's your name?"

"Roxana."

"What are you doing in Flaviu's apartment?"

"Waiting."

"Waiting for what?"

"My papers to come through and then I will go to a good school."

"Does he tell you that he loves you?" Elena asked.

"Yes," Roxana said. "Flaviu love me. He tell me every day. He look after me. And Miriana. They are good people."

"Listen to me, Roxana. They are not good people," Elena said, scarcely aware of her words. "You need to get out of there while there's still time."

"Pleacă."

"I will, I'll go…" Elena said, as her world fell apart again. There was nothing to keep her there a moment longer.

Ignoring the receptionist, Elena crossed the foyer, pushed the revolving door, and walked back across to the park. The young couple had gone.

Sitting back down on the park bench, she looked up. A girl stood staring down at her.

As day turned to night, Elena slept, waking the following morning to find that someone had placed a blanket around her.

42

ENGLAND

2022

L addie opened the door, his face turning the colour of alabaster. With his eyes wide, he opened and closed his mouth but no words came out. He held fast to the doorframe as he felt himself sway.

"Laddie," Elena said.

She looked smaller than he remembered, thinner, a shadow of her former self. Her once perfect complexion now blotchy, her hair lank and greasy hanging down in tendrils over her shoulders, her eyes sunken into her face. She wore a check shirt and cord trousers that finished six inches short of her ankles and that were in desperate need of a wash, almost unrecognizable as the eight-month pregnant girl he had last seen leaving The Ivy less than two months ago.

"Elena," he muttered, moving closer towards her, disbelieving his own eyes.

Tears streaming down her cheeks, she felt his hand in hers. Wearing the same familiar sleeveless knitted sweater with the same holes in the neckline, he hadn't changed. His eyes were kind, his voice gentle as she remembered, his hands warm, and his fingers pudgy to the touch.

"Where…where've you been?" he stuttered, gently steering her inside and towards the worn brown sofa in the middle of the sitting room.

"Since yesterday, sitting in a park, thinking," Elena said. "I'm so tired. I need your help. You're the only one who can help me now."

"But where've you been?" he repeated. "Come in." It was a miracle. Nothing short of a miracle. His very own little Elena sitting on his sofa in his flat and asking him for help. There was nothing he wouldn't do for her. "How d'you find me?"

"The Dolphin fish and chip shop. Don't you remember telling me about the flat above, the pub across the road, and the One Stop shop. Maybe I knew that one day I might need it to find you," Elena said.

"But where've you been?" he asked again.

"When I left The Ivy? Flaviu took me to a house owned by a friend of his, Tonya…"

"But Miriana said…"

"What, Laddie?"

Frowning, the lines across his forehead deepened. Had he got it wrong? Had Miriana actually said that? Had he been so troubled about Elena's future and so wrapped up in his own loss that he had misheard? "That…that…that you were dead. The day after you left, she told me you had died in an accident. I knew it was true because I overheard her telling Flaviu…"

"Telling Flaviu what?" Elena asked.

"Telling Flaviu that he was to get rid of you and the baby. That Tonya was not an option. I saw that look on her face. I knew exactly what she meant. Just moments before Flaviu drove you away. I couldn't do anything. She thinks you are dead. Both of you."

"Why did she want me dead?"

"Flaviu. She thought that Flaviu was the father of your baby. She'd thought it for a while. I'd tried to tell her it wasn't true, but she wouldn't listen," Laddie lied. His intention to see Flaviu punished had misfired. If for one minute, he'd thought...

"I don't understand," Elena said. "Only you and Flaviu knew that to be true, and Irina from the notes I sent to her."

"Then Flaviu must have admitted it. It didn't come from me."

"But why would he tell her?"

"His loyalty is to Miriana. Flaviu and Miriana have always been an item. He didn't care about you or the baby. He probably thought that Miriana would dismiss it as a stupid accident."

A day earlier, his words would have cut her to the quick, broken her heart. But almost overnight, that had changed. Flaviu had been no less of a dream than that she might have gone to school, to university, had a career, and eventually been reconciled with her family. All fantasy. A stupid childish fantasy.

"Flaviu did take me to Tonya," Elena said.

"So, he defied Miriana...That was brave of him. He would have had his reasons," Laddie muttered. "Tonya's dead."

"Good. I don't think I killed her, but if I did, I have no regrets." Elena listened to her own words, words that she never thought to hear from her own mouth. Everything had changed. Now she would happily kill anyone to protect her own baby. "She was going to sell my baby."

"Flaviu would have known," Laddie said, turning the knife. "That's how she made her living. Miriana sent her girls. Tonya looked after the girls and then sold the babies. Flaviu knew everything about Tonya. They were close."

Elena nodded. It was all beginning to fall into place. Every sordid detail. Flaviu didn't have the guts to kill her or the baby himself, so he'd asked Tonya to do his dirty work for the two of them to reap the rewards. And what had they intended for her? Thank God she hadn't stayed long enough to find out. The final promise he had made – *'I'll be back for you and the baby'* – was as empty as all the other promises.

"The baby. A girl or a boy?" Laddie asked.

"A girl. She's safe. With friends. Nobody knows where she is. Nobody can get to her," Elena replied.

"Nobody is safe with Miriana. She has contacts. Contacts everywhere. If she finds out, she'll have you both killed. Your family. Irina…They'll all suffer."

"That's where I need your help, Laddie. You once said that if ever I needed you, you would be there for me. I'm asking you now. I need you to help me find Irina and save her."

Laddie felt his heart pounding. He could feel it. So close. What he said and did now would make the difference between a future with Elena or a long and lonely existence.

"You know I'll help you. I promised, didn't I? Have you eaten?" he asked.

Elena shook her head. "Not since I left Mag…" Elena stopped herself just in time. There was still a long road to travel before she would trust anybody with that information, even Laddie. "Not for a couple of days."

"Fish and chips and a cup of tea? Then we can talk some more."

"They used to do it in newspaper. Tasted much better then," Laddie said, stuffing the last of the chips into his mouth. "I've been thinking. We need to get you and the baby somewhere safe. Out of the country…"

"I won't go anywhere without Irina. She's what I came to see you about. I have to get her out of there. She's there because of me. I can't leave her. You know where she is. You've taken my notes to her. You can get her out. We need to go home. Please, Laddie. I beg you."

Laddie nodded. How could he tell her that it had all been lies? Not once had he seen Irina in all the time that she had been in England. He had thought that she might have been taken to The Beeches, but it might well have been The Cedars. And as for the notes…Besides, Irina had no place in his plans, but Elena must never know that.

"I'll do whatever I can, but it won't be easy. Give me tomorrow to work something up," Laddie said, his mind churning. "In the meantime, you'll have to stay here where I know you're safe. Tomorrow, I'll get the baby and bring her here. Then we'll work out a plan to bring Irina here as well. Where will I find the baby?"

Elena closed her eyes and said a silent prayer. Please God, let me be putting my trust in the right person. "You'll find her at Magnolia Court…" It was done.

"You can sleep in my bed. I'll take the sofa. I'll be gone by six in the morning, but I'll be back tomorrow – with the baby," Laddie said. "And then we'll get Irina. Get some sleep."

As Elena slept, Laddie sat beside the bed, lost in his own world, dreaming about their future together. He had a fancy for a small-holding. Back home in Romania but way out in the country. Away from the hustle-bustle of Bucharest, the city that he'd grown up in. And he'd keep a couple of dozen chickens, a few goats, and pigs, and would grow what crops he needed to feed himself and his family, Elena and the baby. And maybe more babies.

And suddenly it was all within reach.

43

ENGLAND

2022

The morning light filtered in through the threadbare curtains. The room was small, no more than eight by ten, the only furniture the bed she lay in and a small wooden table beside it, its once polished surface now a kaleidoscope of white water marks. Her clothes were folded on an old ladder-back rush seat at the foot of the bed. Disorientated, Elena sat up and swung her legs out of the covers. She was wearing a pair of pyjamas that she did not recognize. Hanging low on her shoulders, they swam around her frame, the trousers drawn tight around her waist with a white cord. She didn't remember taking her clothes off or replacing them with any nightclothes. She did remember disjointed parts of the previous night's conversation, and then eating supper with him and drinking a mug of tea. He was going to sort everything out. He would be going out early the following day. He would collect the baby. And then they'd find Irina. His words: she had to trust him and stay safe indoors until he returned.

Padding silently out of the bedroom, Elena opened the first door. The small sitting room with the brown sofa. A small flat-screen TV on the wall. A low, rectangular glass-topped table between the sofa and the TV on which sat the detritus from the previous evening's supper. Flies circled around on the ceiling, hovered, and then returned to the feast. Dust balls drifted silently across the wooden floor, taking temporary refuge in front, alongside, and behind a stack of old newspapers. The curtains still drawn, a single low-wattage lightbulb, shadeless, was suspended from the ceiling and had been left switched on.

The room was dirty, filthy, uncared for. In the dim light of the previous evening, desperate for a friendly face – someone who could help her find Irina, and help the three of them find safety – she had noticed none of these things. Exhausted and tired, she had seen and heard only what she had wanted to hear – Laddie's warm, kind voice reassuring her that he would make everything right.

Remembering how Laddie had once described his flat to her, Elena shivered. 'A little shabby but always clean and tidy,' he had said. A small home but one that he was proud of. Forever tidying, sweeping, and cleaning her room at The Ivy, she had often thought that he was OCD, had a fetish for housework. Never had she thought that he might live in such squalor. He had not told her the truth.

The kitchenette, although smaller, resembled Mama and Tata's old kitchen before it had been lovingly refitted by Tata's own hand. An old Belfast sink set within a wall-to-wall length of cracked Formica work surface was piled high with dirty dishes lined with food in varying states of decay. Half filled with water from the leaking pipes, a bucket had been placed under the sink. There were no under-surface cupboards. No wall cupboards. Half empty and long since soured bottles of milk and empty beer cans filled a large black rubber wastebin. Shiny metallic bluebottles buzzed and crawled over the contents of a second bin while small white maggots waited impatiently to hatch and join in the foray.

The stench was overpowering; Elena covered her nose and her mouth with her hands as she backed away.

Thirsty, Elena searched for a glass. Reaching out, she opened the only cupboard in the kitchen. A ceiling-to-floor cupboard, it reminded her of the old larder back home. Inside were two deep shelves. On the top shelf, high above her head, an ill-assorted selection of crockery and glasses, cutlery, tins, packets, and sauces piled precariously one on top of another, fighting for space. Elena reached up and carefully extracted a glass tumbler. And then froze as her eyes fixed on the contents of the second shelf.

Totally unlike the top shelf, it was organized meticulously and with loving care. The shelf was lined with pale pink paper. Centre-stage stood three dolls. Barbie dolls. Though they were long before her time, Elena knew their names. Hand in hand, Barbie and Ken gazed lovingly into each other's eyes. Both mounted on a wooden plinth, Barbie had long blonde hair down to her waist and wore a floral dress, closely resembling the dress Elena had worn the day she'd arrived at The Ivy. Head shaved of all hair, Ken wore a black dinner suit and bow-tie with a tiny plastic rose in the lapel. Two names had been engraved on the wooden plinth – 'Laddie' and 'Elena'. Stripped naked, the third doll had been beheaded. The name engraved on the plinth: 'Flaviu'.

Photographs in little silver frames. Taken of her when she had been asleep in her room at The Ivy. Naked. Lying on top of the bed, her hair spread out on the pillow.

The chess set that they had played with. The pack of cards that he had used to teach her how to play poker, and a box of matches. Two small notebooks that she had misplaced and never found.

A lock of her hair held together and tied with a small pink bow.

A small pile of notes written in her own hand. Notes that she had written to Irina. Notes that Irina had never read.

A small pile of envelopes addressed to Elena written in a hand that, at first, she could not place until finally it came to her. Flaviu's hand. The same hand that had left notes in the apartment before he left each day.

A small gold band in a velvet-lined box. A wedding ring.

It was a shrine to the past and a window on the future. His intentions were clear. And hadn't he once said to her that he had a wife and a daughter about the same age?

Her thirst forgotten, Elena opened the first envelope and then the second and then the third. There were eight of them. One for each of the months she had been incarcerated in her room at The Ivy. Flaviu had not forgotten her.

Terrified, Elena pulled on her own clothes and sprinted for the door. Laddie had gone to collect her baby. She had to get there first.

The door was locked.

44

ENGLAND

2022

Chewing his nails to the quick, Flaviu sat by the picture window, watching, and waiting. Miriana had summoned him. Not just a summons but a car as well. It did not bode well for him. In twenty minutes, the black Audi would be outside and waiting to take him to The Ivy. He had suggested that he could drive himself, but Miriana was insistent – the boys were already on their way. Fleetingly, he had contemplated packing his bags and fleeing, but few had managed to do so and lived to tell the tale. Whatever it was she wanted to see him about, he would just have to brazen it out and hope that the trust he had earned over the years would see him through.

In the background, Roxana sat repeating words from the TV. Irritating him to death from the moment he had picked her up in Bucharest, he was sorely tempted to pack her bag and boot her out into the street. Unlike Elena, who had rarely, if ever, irritated him. She was still alive and the baby too. If he knew that, then the likelihood was that Miriana might also know – the most obvious reason for the summons. Somehow, she had uncovered the fact that Elena had been with Tonya and that he had taken her there.

It was all such a mess.

Her heart pounding and thumping, Penny's eyes flickered open and closed. In the darkness of her mind, she started trying to work out what had happened and where she might be. A tangle of thoughts. A collection of images dancing before her eyes like an old black and white movie. Words that, the second they entered her brain, deserted her. A whiff of perfume. The smell of a baby. And then slowly the pieces came together, and she remembered. The rattle of the front door handle. The first thought that had entered her mind. Elena had come back. Too early in the morning for it to be anybody else. Her heart filled with joy and hope. Dressing gown on, she had raced down the stairs, unlocked the door, and opened it a fraction. A fraction too much. A man, dressed in a black hoodie and trousers, pushing in through the door. A strong hand covering her mouth. Gasping for breath. Her arm up high behind her back. The pain. The gaffer tape. Seizing the moment before her lips were sealed, tasting blood as she sank her teeth into a hand. A fist striking her face. Her legs collapsing beneath her. Falling. The world going black.

Still as a rabbit caught in headlights and with eyes no more than slits, Penny took in her surroundings. A small below-ground window, barred, to her right, the light of day filtering through. A basement. The air oppressive. A chill in the air. To her left, filing cabinets and boxes piled one on top of another. A basement and a storeroom. Opposite, in direct line of sight, stone steps leading up. Barely visible at the top of the steps, a closed door. Close by, almost within reach, a scrubbed wooden table. A woman sitting in a hardbacked chair to the side of the table. Jet-black hair cut in a short bob, she wore a black blouse and black trousers, a diamond ring on her finger, her expression menacing and expectant. She was not young. Drumming her long red fingernails on the table, her hand strayed back and forth to a long-bladed knife. On the table a cradle. Two other chairs in the room, one to which she was bound and another alongside. The gaffer tape still sealed her mouth. Helpless, all she could do was listen and watch.

The baby – her baby – Elena's baby cried softly. The woman's face suffused with rage as she reached into the cot and roughly pulled the baby out, set her down on the table on her back, arms flailing, legs kicking. The woman ignored her scream until she could no longer. Her hand covered the baby's face. Penny was frightened. Terrified that the woman would suffocate the baby. Penny pulled at her bondings, rocking the chair back and forth. The woman approached.

"I hate babies. I had a brother once. He cried incessantly when he was born. He cried right up until the day I put paid to it, once and for all." Reaching out, she ripped the gaffer tape from Penny's face. "Ugly, dirty, demanding…"

Recoiling, Penny steeled herself not to cry out with the pain. Her mind drifted back to a previous time when she had found herself in a not dissimilar situation. That woman had been taller and stronger than her by a mile, a psychopath, and hell-bent on killing her for no good reason other than the demons in her mind. She had survived that time by keeping her cool and conversing with the woman like one reasonable human being to another while she had waited for help to arrive, which fortunately it had in the nick of time. Burying her anger, Penny drew on her inner resources to deal with this woman in the same manner.

"I know you don't want to hurt that child," Penny said. "Take your hand from her face."

The woman laughed, withdrew her hand, and picked up the knife. "Oh, I do, and I shall, but not until the time is right."

"The child is in my care. I need to take her home."

"In your care? So, where is Elena? She and I need to have a little chat."

"I don't know. And, that's an honest answer," Penny said. "I'm Penny, and you, I assume, Miriana." The one woman named in Elena's letter. It was a wild guess.

"Correct."

"Word is that you're a very successful woman. Well respected and people look up to you," Penny said.

"Correct again. And not a woman to be crossed, as you will see."

"Why have you taken the baby?"

"All will be revealed," Miriana said, checking her watch. "Not long now."

"Curiosity," Penny said. "How did you know where to find the baby?"

"Friends in high places. A friend in the police force. So kind of your friend – Gabby, I think that's her name – to tell him where I would find her."

"The crying gets on your nerves, doesn't it? The screaming is worse. If you put her back in her cot and cover her with a blanket, she may quieten." Penny drew in her breath. The air was cold and damp. Uncovered and wearing nothing but a flimsy bodysuit, the baby would soon freeze to death. She had to buy time. "Untie my hands and I'll help you."

"One more word and I will kill her now," Miriana said.

Penny sat staring at the baby and shivered as Miriana hovered the knife above her little body. No longer crying, she lay still. It was not a good sign. If she spoke, then Miriana would kill the baby.

. . .

"We have guests," Miriana said, turning towards the steps.

A man hurtled down the steps. Winded and bruised, he lay on the concrete floor, fighting to catch his breath.

"Grab him, Marku. Codrin, tie him to that chair," Miriana said, pointing to the remaining chair before turning her attention back to the new arrival. "Thank you for dropping in, Flaviu."

Seeing the bandage on the hand, Penny flinched and turned her head away. Her eyes glazing over, what little hope she had was fast fading.

"Front row seats for the two of you." Miriana paced around behind the two of them before returning to the table. "Trussed up like pigs. So, what do you have to say for yourself, Flaviu?"

"For God's sake, Miriana, what the hell is this?" Flaviu yelled, the same moment that he caught sight of the baby on the table. It did not go unnoticed.

"Allow me to make the introductions," Miriana said, picking the baby up by her arms. "This, Flaviu, is your daughter, I do believe. Ugly little thing, isn't she? And the lady beside you is called Penny, the baby's fairy godmother."

"Whatever your problem, Miriana, we can talk it through. It's got nothing to do with the baby. This is between you and me." Flaviu kept his voice low and even.

"She's got your eyes and your nose. I don't, however, think she's got your stamina. Look, she's all floppy," Miriana said, lifting the baby up by her arms.

A weak cry escaped the baby's lips. Penny looked up; there was still hope.

"Put her down. You can call off the wolves too. I'm not going anywhere," Flaviu said. "If you want to talk, then we'll talk, just you and me."

Miriana shrugged her shoulders. "Thank you, boys. You may go now. These two will not be giving me any trouble."

"I don't understand. What's this all about?" Flaviu said.

"Justice. Revenge. Retribution for all the lies that you have told me over the years."

"I haven't lied to you."

"About Tonya? Dropping in to see her at one in the morning…"

"Our paths crossed in Bucharest. Years ago. We were friends. No more than that. It was an emergency…"

"So, you didn't sleep with her?"

"No, never."

"On your baby's life?" Miriana stroked the baby's cheek with the side of the dagger.

"You wouldn't do that," Flaviu said, a cold chill running down his spine. Miriana was capable of anything. Killing a baby would be child's play.

"I'd enjoy it immensely. I haven't felt quite so excited for over forty years. Did I ever tell you about my baby brother…I started to tell Penny before you dropped in…I was just seven at the time. He was two. My father hung on his every word, of which there were few. Anton this and Anton that. Never Miriana this and Miriana that. He had a terrible accident. Some careless person left the side of his cot unlocked. He climbed out and, you know how curious terrible twos can be, made his way out of his little bedroom and to the top of the staircase. Poor little mite bounced all the way down two flights of stairs like a rubber ball. It was me who discovered him lying there. I denied all knowledge, of course. Cried my heart out in front of my parents. Laughed like a hyena behind their backs.

"The knife is sharp. I sharpened it myself. Razor-sharp,"

Miriana said, cutting off a lock of the baby's hair before brushing it over Flaviu's face. "Does it smell sweet to you?"

"Please, Miriana, put the knife down," Flaviu said, growing increasingly anxious.

"What's to like about a baby other than that they are worth money? Childless couples will pay anything, almost anything, for a blue-eyed, Caucasian baby like this one."

"Then sell her," Flaviu suggested. "But don't waste a life."

"And what would your darling Elena say about that when she found out – and she would, I'd make sure about that."

"Miriana. Listen to me. Elena's not my darling and never has been. The baby is not mine. Tonya's not my darling and never has been. It's strong women like you that I value the most – beautiful, elegant, powerful, clever…" Flaviu listened to his own words, knowing full well that his face told an entirely different story.

"So why did you defy my orders? I couldn't have put it more plainly. Elena and the baby were to die. So, if you won't carry out my orders, then I have no choice but to do it myself. The baby first, and then, I promise, I will find Elena," Miriana said, positioning the tip of the blade close by the baby's heart. The baby kicked her legs as a trickle of blood ran sideways from her chest and down onto the table.

"I might trade the child for the mother." Miriana raised the knife away from the screaming baby. "Where is she?"

"I don't know. You've got to believe me."

Miriana shook her head. "Why should I believe you about anything?"

"For crying out loud, you're sick. Sick in the head," Penny shouted, clearly at the end of her tether, unable to watch any more. "A fool. A loser. Look in the mirror. What do you see?"

Miriana took a deep breath and smiled. "I see someone who holds all the cards. A woman totally in control of herself and one who doesn't take kindly to being insulted by an old slag. Your turn will come, Penny. I'd like you to enjoy the show first.

"So, Flaviu, where is she? Do you want to do a trade?" Miriana turned her attention back to Flaviu.

"I don't know, and I wouldn't tell you if I did..." Flaviu paused. The first slip. A fatal slip?

"Now we're getting somewhere. You do know where she is, and you won't tell me because all this time it has been exactly as I thought. You fell in love with her. Big mistake. You put her above me. Nobody does that. And this"—Miriana pointed the knife at the baby—"is the result of your seed."

"Okay. Okay, you're right. You're right. I did fall in love with Elena. She was sweet and innocent. A breath of fresh air. It wasn't her fault. It was mine. She doesn't deserve to be punished, and neither does that baby."

"They'll be here any minute," Penny shouted. "You won't get away with this. Elena told us all about you and The Ivy and where it was. The police will be on their way right now."

Miriana raised her eyebrows. "I'll be long gone by the time anybody turns up. Pastures new. But you? I don't think so. The only problem I have is to decide which out of the three of you I hate most. That will decide the order in which you all die. But what am I saying? The baby must die first. I want you both to watch as I kill her. Slowly...Such tiny fingers. Such soft bones. Eight fingers and two thumbs, one by one. And then her toes." Miriana grinned as she took the tiny hand and spread the fingers apart. The baby screamed.

The door to her office was unlocked. Putting his ear to the door, Laddie listened for movement or sound. There was none. No sound of footsteps. No sound of a phone in use. No sound of drawers being opened and closed, or papers being shuffled. Nothing. Believing it too good to be true, Laddie carefully turned the door handle and pushed the door open a couple of inches. If she were in there, he had his excuse ready, and as it happened, it was the truth. He was going to ask if he could finish early that day. If he had to.

The office was empty; now was his chance. If he could find Elena's passport then they could be on their way the following day. And if luck were on his side, he'd find a passport that would work for the baby as well. He knew that Miriana kept a good stock in case some of her babies, as she called them, were destined for foreign parts. Maybe he'd pocket Irina's passport as well, even though she was going nowhere. Once he'd found what he needed, he'd be out of there. All he needed was five minutes.

Her desk was clear of paperwork, the drawers either side locked. Congratulating himself on his foresight, Laddie drew a bunch of keys from his pocket, made from impressions that he had taken over the years. There was not one single door, cupboard, or drawer in the whole of The Ivy that he couldn't open when it suited him to do so. His collection, as he called them. In the distance, he thought he might have caught the muted sounds of a baby carrying on the wind and soon dismissed it as part of his imagination.

In one of the drawers, two bundles of passports. In the first bundle, names that he recognized. Names of the girls in The Ivy, The Beeches, and The Cedars, Elena's not far from the top of the pile. Picking one passport out of the second bundle, Laddie quickly returned it. It was for a baby boy. The next was for a girl – white, Caucasian, blue eyes, and fair hair. Perfect. A small gun nestled in the corner drawer. It was only as he closed the last of the drawers that he caught sight of a notepad on which was written an address. Magnolia Court. The very same address that Elena had given him and his next port of call.

Leaving drawers unlocked, Laddie turned on his heels. In the same moment, he heard the blood-curdling scream of a baby. It was coming from along the corridor and the open door that led down to the basement. Reopening the drawer, he picked up the gun and examined it. Loaded, it was small but lethal. He headed in the direction of the scream.

Listening at the door, he opened it slowly and made his way stealthily down the steps. No one was going to hurt his baby. No one was going to take the baby away from him and Elena. Not ever again.

Her back to the steps, Miriana didn't hear the footstep behind her, nor the gunshot. Penny closed her eyes tight and trembled as she felt Miriana's blood run down her face. And then a sharp pain before the night started closing in again. In that moment, she knew that the blood was not Miriana's but her own.

Laddie scooped the baby from the table and held her with one arm, the other held ramrod straight, and turned slowly towards Flaviu, his finger on the trigger. So long as Flaviu was alive, Elena would never be entirely his. "Elena is mine. Safe with me." The last words that Laddie ever spoke.

Back to the steps and intent on the task, Laddie did not hear the light fall of rubber-soled shoes on the steps.

45

ENGLAND
2022

Everyone was beyond shocked about what had happened. Although they had had their adventures in the past, nothing of this nature had ever happened before. None of them had ever been injured as a result, at least not physically. Magnolia Court had been violated, and it was going to take a long time before they would feel safe again.

Doors were locked and double locked even in daylight hours. Max was worried. Even in their darkest hours when the Mansion House had been uninhabitable and their cottages cold, damp, and draughty, it had never been quite like this. Somehow, they had always managed to put a brave face on things, count their blessings, and find joy where there was little.

It had not helped that they had lost Amy so recently. And now with Penny's life hanging in the balance, there was no laughter. Max took it upon himself to open the Mansion House at nine every morning, insisting that the doors be left unlocked and open until after the evening cocktail hour. And there he stayed for ten hours each day, leaving only after the last of the residents had gone home once more to lock their doors.

It was just ten days since Penny had been kidnapped but it felt more like a lifetime.

"You've been reading that same page for the past two hours, dear," Hetty said, putting her knitting down.

"I still feel responsible. I know we did it for all the right reasons, but what good has come out of it?" Max folded his paper and rubbed his eyes, gritty from a continuous lack of sleep. "I keep asking myself the same question over and over again."

"Elena is safe, and the baby is safe, and they're being well cared for in a residential family centre for the moment. That in itself is a blessing."

"I shan't rest until they're all behind bars," Max said. "And we don't even know who shot Penny or why. Surely, they could have told us something by now."

"Remember Ahmed and the silver dagger? If my memory serves me correctly, and it's not that long ago, it was at least a week before that nice Chief Constable was able to come and talk to us about what had happened. And I suspect that unravelling this mess has been a whole lot more complicated," Hetty said.

"Is that the phone?" Max said, lethargically.

"Well, I don't know what else it would be. Shall I get it?" Hetty slammed her knitting down on the floor. Really, it was time he pulled himself together.

"Hello." Hetty picked up the phone and held it to her ear. "Yes, dear…Yes, dear…Excellent…No, no further news…Tomorrow at one…Thank you, dear.

"You had better add second sight to your never-ending list of skills, Max. That was Gabby. We have visitors tomorrow. She is coming up and we are expecting Detective Superintendent Neil Rogers at one in the afternoon. He's going to explain everything.

So, make yourself useful and ring around and tell everybody twelve-thirty for one, and while you're doing so, ask Dot and Ros if they have any cake made. I will be in the kitchen – baking – if you need me."

It was a full house except for Emanuel and Dinah, and Stan who had insisted that his place was at Penny's bedside. Max counted heads one more time to check that everybody was present and correct. "No long speeches from me today. I'll skip the beaches stuff. We're all here for the same reason. So without more ado…"

"Thank you, Max, as you know my name is Detective Superintendent Neil Rogers and I have been the Senior Investigating Officer for this case. Probably one of the most complicated cases that I have ever come across involving injury to persons, multiple murders, human trafficking, and abuse. If I may say straight away, everyone on the team is rooting for Mrs Reilly.

"I think you all know that we found Elena Albescu, who had the pleasure of being your first guest in your new five-star hotel…"

Max grinned as he heard a couple of chuckles from the room.

"We've interviewed Elena, and you were right in thinking that she had left here, leaving the baby behind, to find and rescue her twin sister. Tragically, and unbeknown to Elena, Irina, her twin sister died shortly after she arrived in the UK. Her next of kin have been informed. We have yet to establish the cause of death, but foul play seems likely. With support from counsellors, Elena is slowly coming to terms with the loss of her sister.

"Some parts of this story you will find disturbing, but I have decided on balance that it would not be fair to withhold them. It will come out in the press, and I would rather you heard it from me than read it for yourselves. I quite appreciate it if some of you may wish to leave before I start down that track."

The DS paused. Nobody moved.

"The baby was found alive, but she had sustained some injuries. A minor injury to her chest and the loss of one finger, sliced off close to the knuckle. A heinous crime, a crime committed by the late Miriana Constantin and witnessed by Flaviu Dumitru, a partner in crime who is nonetheless proving very cooperative. Names that you will all recognize from the note that you found about Elena's person—"

"But the baby is alright now?" Ros interrupted.

"She is and with her mother. Both are doing well.

"The bullet that struck Mrs Reilly was fired by a Romanian by the name of Ladinas Popescu, the so-called house manager for one of Constantin's residences, as she liked to call them. Brothels by any other name. The bullet was not intended for Mrs Reilly but for Constantin. Shot at close range, it killed Constantin outright, passing through her and lodging in Mrs Reilly's head. Popescu was shot dead by armed police in the process of aiming the same gun that killed Constantin at Dumitru.

"On the morning Mrs Reilly was kidnapped, you provided us with the number plates of two vehicles, one of which we were able to locate within thirty minutes of that information. The same vehicle led us to The Ivy, a smart residential property owned by Constantin in the suburbs of Bristol. The three occupants of the car – Dumitru and two men by the name of Marku Stoica and Codrin Toma – left the vehicle and entered the premises, Stoica and Toma leaving the premises again shortly afterwards. Both were later detained and subsequently charged. An armed police force arrived shortly afterwards. Hearing a gun shot, they immediately entered the premises. Had we not had those leads from you, I fear that Mrs Reilly might not have survived.

"In order to explain more, I need first to paint the big picture for you. Romanian by birth and of a wealthy family, Constantin was the mastermind behind trafficking girls into England and imprisoning them in houses that she had bought for the purpose of selling them for sex.

"Constantin had been on the radar of the Romanian authorities for many years up until the time she left Romania and started up in the UK. With a solid network of contacts in politics, the police, and in other high places, she was untouchable. And then in 2014 Constantin moved to England, establishing three brothels in the suburbs of Bristol. As you may know, it is against the law in this country to recruit others into prostitution for gain and such crimes attract significant sentences along with the seizure of assets. This is a textbook case in which all the girls were recruited into the country on false premises, many of them, like Elena, seeking the opportunity to continue their education before going on to find professional careers. Others were offered jobs in such trades as hairdressing, waitressing, beauty salons, hotels, and health clubs. All eighteen girls that we have since released from these properties have given sworn statements that they were imprisoned – locked in their rooms – and routinely abused by clients. All of the girls are now in the care of social services, pending review.

"There is paperwork to show that Constantin had big plans for 2023 with the opening of another twenty brothels in cities across the length and breadth of the UK. With your help, we have just saved one hundred and twenty, possibly more, victims from the same fate…"

"A great deal of good has come out of this sorry episode," Hetty whispered in Max's ear, squeezing his hand in hers. "We were right."

"With her contacts in the criminal world, Constantin ruled her empire, albeit small, with a rod of iron. She succeeded in business by terrifying both those who were her paid employees and those that she forced into prostitution. Mainly threats against their families. Threats that she never hesitated to carry out, some as a warning about what might happen if they did step out of line, some as punishment when they did step out of line. Houses were burnt down, family members attacked, and children threatened. Weeks after Elena left Romania and the very day that Irina followed her to England, Alexandru, their younger brother sustained injuries that, although not life threatening, mentally scarred him for life. Elena had no choice but to comply for fear of further reprisals. The other girls tell the same stories. Dumitru claims that he too was coerced into working with Constantin. Some of his claims have already been substantiated.

"And Constantin's crimes did not end with the brothels. In 2017 she set up a subsidiary business and located it in Stroud—"

"Tonya Cosmo..." Duncan interrupted, nodding his head. "I knew it!"

"The very same. Operating out of The Towers, purporting to be a bed and breakfast establishment. Cosmo was responsible for bringing unwanted babies into the world, while Miriana sold them on the black market...It was here that Elena spent the last month of her pregnancy and gave birth to the child that, unbeknown to her, Cosmo had sold to another family. Dumitru took Elena from The Ivy. Dumitru claims that following repeated denials to Constantin that he was the father of the child, Constantin ordered him to kill both Elena and the baby. Instead, he took her to The Towers, the only place he believed to be safe, and had every intention of returning to take Elena and the baby away following the birth. Elena confirms this story. Overhearing a conversation about the imminent sale of the baby, Elena took flight before finding sanctuary here at Magnolia.

"Having heard this, you may wonder why Elena did not speak

out when she arrived at Magnolia Court. She says, and we have no reason to disbelieve her, that she was afraid for her sister's life whom she still believed to be alive.

"When she left here for the second time, she went to seek help from Dumitru. Finding him absent from home, she turned to the only other person she thought would help her find and rescue Irina. Ladinas Popescu, the house manager who had befriended her and won her trust during the period she lived at The Ivy. Unbeknown to her at the time, Popescu had his own agenda – to kidnap Elena and her baby and keep them for himself. The contents of a shrine in the flat bear witness to the fact that he had lied to Elena throughout.

"Following his death, Popescu was found to have passports for Elena and a baby about his person."

"Excuse me, DS, but is there much more of this? I, for one, need a cup of tea or preferably something a whole lot stronger," Thomas said. "Could we take a break?"

The DS nodded. "Good idea, and we'll pick up again in, shall we say, in fifteen minutes?"

Thomas made a beeline for the bar, closely followed by Gerald.

Looking at the incoming number, and anticipating the worst, Gabby took a deep breath, knowing that if it was what she expected, then it would be down to her to break the news. "Oh my God!" Gabby yelled as all heads turned her way. "She's only gone and done it. Penny's coming round. She's on her way to recovery!"

Cheering and whooping, the residents rose to their feet in unison.

. . .

With the residents resettled, DS Rogers cleared his throat.

"The best news. I'm so pleased for you all," he said. "To pick up where I left off—"

"May I ask a question before you restart, Detective?" Jennifer's hand shot up in the air. "I still don't quite understand why this Constantin woman would want to harm the baby…"

"At the moment, we have only Dumitru's word for it, but he says that Constantin looked upon him as her personal possession and was totally obsessive about him. At first, she believed he had followed her instructions to kill the girl and the baby, but she later discovered that he had not. The girl and the baby were very much alive. Dumitru recalls Constantin stating that her motive was that of justice, revenge, and retribution. Hopefully that answers your question."

"Thank you," Jennifer said. "Despicable woman."

"Turning now to Dumitru, his role in the operation was to bring the girls across from Bucharest and then prepare them for their new life, which clearly was not going to be what they hoped for. He also ran Constantin's cover company in England: Exclusivity. A recruitment company. A legitimate business as far as we can see. Dumitru, 18 years of age when he was first recruited, claims that it was only later when he was in too deep, that he realized the full nature of Constantin's business. In his statement, Dumitru claims that he then tried to distance himself from her. Coincidental with that decision, Dumitru's father was arrested in Bucharest for drug dealing. His father's case is currently being reviewed by the Romanian police.

"Dumitru by his own admission was a bit of a playboy, having had ongoing relationships with both Constantin and Tonya Cosmo. Meeting Cosmo back in 2013 in Bucharest at the age of seventeen, they formed a relationship, which they rekindled when Cosmo came to England."

"And now the sixty-four-thousand-dollar question...Is Flaviu the father of Elena's baby? A DNA test has confirmed that to be the case.

"And another question of the same ilk, of which there has been speculation. Did Elena kill Tonya when she uncovered the fact that Tonya was about to sell her baby? The answer is no, she did not. The verdict of death remains accidental, following a fall in which Cosmo struck her head on the mantelpiece."

"Dot Gardener." Dot stood up. "Surely those men who abused the girls aren't going to get away with it scot-free? You haven't mentioned any of them. It's not right."

"Constantin was right up there on security. She had cameras installed in all the bedrooms. We will be going through the CCTV footage. Those who abused the women will be prosecuted."

"Last but no means least, Mrs Reilly. We have reason to believe that Mrs Reilly put up quite a fight to prevent the abduction of the baby. The blood found on her carpet was found to match that of Marku Stoica, who also had a nasty bite to the hand. Until such time as we can interview Mrs Reilly, which hopefully will not be too long now, we'll not know the details of the actual kidnapping. It seems likely that Mrs Reilly was not an intended kidnap victim, but in putting up a fight, during which she sustained injuries herself, she was taken together with the baby. Quite a heroine.

"Elena openly admits stealing the sum of two hundred pounds and a mobile phone from Mrs Reilly but is insistent that she had every intention of repaying the money. Yesterday Stan asked me if he could organize for Elena to visit Mrs Reilly in hospital." The DS looked at his watch. "I believe that she is there as we speak... And, praise be, it seems to have done the trick.

"You may rest safe in your beds in the knowledge that the perpetrators of these crimes are either deceased or in custody.

Good job, one and all. And one of my counterparts in Bucharest has asked me to convey his thanks to you too. Constantin's businesses in Bucharest have finally been closed down and all those associated with it arrested...Is there any more of that tea in the pot?"

"No," Gerald said. "But the bar is open. On the house!"

Leaving the residents behind in the Mansion House, Gabby escorted the DS to the car park.

"And what about Handley," Gabby asked quietly. "Off the record. Was it him who told Constantin where to find the baby?"

"There's a call to her number on his phone."

"Will he go down for it?"

"Big time."

46

ENGLAND

2022

She looked so small and vulnerable. Still breathing with help from a ventilator, her chest rose and fell, rose and fell. It was nothing short of a miracle that she was alive at all. The bullet had nicked her brain. Seven hours they had waited while the surgeon operated and he had not been over optimistic about the outcome, but Penny had survived. Now she was in a coma and in the hands of Father Time.

No discernible change over the past ten days, but Stan wasn't going to give up – ever, and neither was anybody else. She was still critical, but all her vitals, as they called them, were holding up, which was the most important thing. They'd all been told not to expect miracles and that it could be anything from two to four weeks before she came out of the coma. Even in a deep sleep, they had said, she might well know that there were people around her. Remember the five senses, they had said: hearing, smell, vision, touch, and taste.

Stan had never forgotten those words.

Taking care not to disturb the cannula, Stan reached out and gently stroked her hand, and then her arm, and then her forehead.

With an almost empty tube of hand cream in the bathroom back home, his hands were as smooth as they had ever been. *Touch.*

"Morning, Pen. Looking pretty as a picture as always. Sleep well? Can't say that I did. Had something on my mind, but I'll tell you about that later. Don't you fret. It's all good." *Sound.*

"I've brought you some flowers. Fresh out of the garden at Magnolia. Dennis picked them not a couple of hours ago. Roses mostly. Reckon they've flowered early just for you. Red and yellow roses, and there's some orange ones too. According to Dennis, the red one is the most fragrant – his word, not mine. Reminds you of the smell of honey, so Dennis said to tell you." *Smell.*

Stan lifted one of the rose's stems out of the vase and held the flower close to Penny's face. "What do you reckon? Honey? Smells more like Dot's strawberry jam to me. Have a good sniff. Squeeze once for honey, squeeze twice for jam...I didn't quite catch that." *Sound, touch, and smell.*

"So, today's news, Pen. They're all up at the Mansion House right now, drinking tea and eating cake. Bet you're sorry you're missing out on that one. I tell you, Pen, if it hadn't been for me, that bedside table would be piled six feet high with cake. Hetty, Dot, and Ros haven't stopped baking since the minute you disappeared. By the time you get back we'll all look like puddings, wobbling around the place." *Sound and the redolence of smell.*

"But what I started saying before I got diverted by cake is that there's a Detective Superintendent up with them right now," Stan said, checking his watch. "And he's telling them what he can about what happened. Course he's waiting for you to fill in the gaps when you're ready. Gabby's going to tell me all about it when I get back, so tomorrow, we'll have lots to talk about." *Sound.*

"I hope you're up to it today, Pen. You've got a stream of visitors. Gary's coming down later and Gwen's driving down from Birmingham, and then there'll be some of the Magnolia gang in later."

Stan grinned to himself. He'd saved the best for last. His pièce de résistance. *Sound, touch and smell* all rolled into one. "And you've got another visitor as well. No, two visitors. Who is it, apart from me, that you'd want to see again, above all others? Shall I give you a clue? Squeeze once for yes and twice for no... I'll take that as a yes. Went to see her yesterday – me and Ros. She's not living far away, just fifteen minutes in the car. Can you guess? Alright, I'll stop teasing you. It's Elena and the baby. And by reckoning, she'll be in the visitors waiting room right now. I'll go and get her. You wait there."

His eyes lit up. She was pretty as a picture. Dressed in a short-sleeved, calf-length floral dress; her eyes sparkled, and her hair shone like gold. At her feet, the baby lay quietly sleeping in a cot, the very same cot that Andy had made for her, her little thumb nestled in her mouth.

"She's waiting for you," Stan said, wrapping his arm around Elena's shoulder. "Can I carry her?"

Elena smiled.

"She's quiet now but it won't last long. She's due a feed and a nappy change. I hope she doesn't disgrace herself in front of Penny," Elena said apologetically.

"Better and better," Stan said. *Sound and smell* and plenty of it. "Just talk to her when we go in. She's not a great conversationalist right at this moment, but she'll hear you."

. . .

"Penny. It's Elena. I wish I could have come sooner, but there were things that needed to be sorted out, but I'm here now and I've brought somebody else to see you." Elena glanced at Stan.

"Lay her on the bed," Stan whispered, "and we'll rest Penny's hand in hers." *The touch of a baby.*

"She's waking up. I knew she would. Shush, little one." Elena leant forward and put her fingers to the baby's lips.

"Let her cry if she wants to. Just for a few minutes," Stan said. *The sound of a baby crying.*

"Look at her face, Stan. You know what that means," Elena said, reaching down into her bag.

Stan grinned. Yes, he knew exactly what that expression meant. She had just filled her nappy. "Leave her for a couple of minutes," Stan said as the baby opened her mouth and let out a scream that might well have woken the whole hospital. *Touch, sound, and smell.*

"Shall I change her?"

"No wait…Call it telepathy…Call it second sight…Call it whatever you will…And say a prayer, Elena…"

Stan leapt up and threw his arms around Elena. "Alleluia. We did it. Did you see that?"

Elena shook her head.

"I didn't imagine it. I saw her hand move and there was a flicker of her eye. We've done it, Elena. You, Flossie, and me. We've done it. It's the first sign she's coming out. You feed the baby. Change the baby. I'm going to get the nurse, and if I'm right, I've got a phone call to make."

"It's the best news I have had, Stan. Now I might be able to start repaying her for all her kindness. You go and I'll stay," Elena said, picking the baby up.

"Hello, Penny. Now I can start to try and repay you for your kindness. We wouldn't be here today without you. And I'm sorry I left, taking money and without saying goodbye. It's all here in my handbag. I'll leave it on the bedside table before I go – with your phone. I've called the baby Flossie, your name for her. She'll be christened Florence, and known as Flossie, and one day when she is a bit older, I'll tell her that her name was given to her by her Auntie Penny. She's asking to be changed and fed. I'd better do that before we get told off."

Picking the baby up, Elena watched as Penny wriggled her fingers, and her eyes opened.

EPILOGUE

G reeted at the airport by the whole family – Gary, Bobby, the girls, and every single one of the grandchildren and, of course, dear Ronnie – I landed back in Sydney on Tuesday 12th July. Close-run thing but managed to persuade Gary that I didn't need an escort all the way back, was still perfectly capable of taking care of myself. Strewth, someone had been looking down on me that day. A couple of millimetres closer and I wouldn't be here today, and I recovered quicker than they reckoned.

Went to England to say goodbye to Amy and get to the bottom of that letter she sent me. Didn't bless her at the time, but I do now. Did both. Fair do's, it was genuinely at the back of my mind that I might stay in England, my birthplace, and where better to live than with such wonderful friends as I found at Magnolia Court. Not just the goodbye, or the letter, or a deep-down longing to come 'home', I felt as though I had been put out to pasture back on the ranch. Bit angry and resentful. And envious of Amy. Me, sitting in a rocking chair on the deck while she had all the fun. Guess that's why I went in feet first and said almost right away that I planned to stay at Magnolia. It wasn't a lie; it was how I felt at that time.

Didn't mean that I felt any less guilty when I told them my decision. Gary had a lot to do with it. Stayed on for two more weeks after I came out of the coma – long enough for me to have recovered my senses and hear him out. He was straight with me. Told me everything there was to know about the money situation back home and showed me the plan that he and Ronnie had worked up together to get the ranch back on the straight and narrow. It meant selling off land. There was more than enough of that. There was a buyer lined up. And fire forensics had confirmed the barn fire to be accidental. Wasn't going to be an easy ride, he told me, but I could see he was determined.

Can't say that I wasn't a bit sceptical at first. I hadn't forgotten Ronnie's last words to me before I left. '…And don't forget that this is your inheritance from your sister. Yours and yours alone.' Still wondered if it wasn't just about the money. But it wasn't. There was no mention of any windfalls in the new business plan. No golden goose.

Guess the clincher was when he said that it was time he and Bobby got their hands dirty and did some real work on the ranch, leaving the business in more capable hands. Ronnie, I assumed. But no, he asked me to take the helm. Times when you have to trust your family. I couldn't let him down, nor Bluey.

I'm writing this in my own office. 'Penny Reilly, Chief Executive Officer' it says on the door. Made me smile when I saw it.

Saying goodbye to Gwen, or *au revoir* as she phrased it, wasn't easy. We talked for hours. Told her all about Amy and my life and my family. Shame I couldn't tell her anything about her mother. Didn't know anything more about her than Gwen. She's not the resentful type. An only child, albeit adopted, she worked hard to get to where she was. First celebrity in our family for sure.

Director with the BBC, she's won plenty of awards for her productions. Clever and ambitious, the same traits that she saw in Elena not long after they met.

Gwen took a real shine to Elena. Made in the same mould as Amy. When Gwen decided to do something, she did it. Didn't mention it to anyone but just made enquiries about the possibility of getting Elena British citizenship. To cut a long story short, Elena and the baby are now lodging with Gwen. Elena's starting school again in September, the baby booked into a nursery.

Gwen said she was happy to pay for everything, but in the end, we cut a deal. Gwen would cover board and lodgings, I'd cover school fees and university fees from part of the proceeds from the sale of the cottage. Elena would pay us back over time – her decision.

And never one to miss a trick, Jennifer sweet-talked Gwen into directing the 2023 performance of the Magnolia Court Amateur Dramatic Society.

Breaking the news to Stan was tough. Hadn't really crossed my mind that I might marry again, but if I had, I would have chosen Stan, even over my lifelong friend Ronnie. There isn't a selfish bone in Stan's body. 'Whatever is best for you, Pen,' he said, 'gets my vote, and maybe one day I'll even come and visit the land of kangaroos, wallabies, and koalas.' No *maybe*s, I told him. You're coming. And he is, in three months' time, for six whole weeks. Gary was with me on that one. He and Stan may have had a bit of a rocky start when they first met, but it wasn't long before they became best pals.

Elena came to visit me every day while I was in hospital, always with little Flossie. We talked about Flaviu. Hard, I didn't want to talk about the events in that basement, but I did for her sake. Told her what she needed to know. Left the rest out. Flaviu had said he loved her. It'll be a while before she knows his fate, but one day they'll be together again. Mother, grandmother, aunt; I'm now a godmother as well.

Queues at the door, Amy's cottage sold almost overnight. The residents took their pick of the bunch.

So many wonderful things have happened over the past few months – friendships made, Gwen, Elena, and Flossie, Stan and, of course, being back in the heart of my family and reunited with Tara.

Every cloud – and there were many along the way – does have a silver lining.

And the icing on the cake. A parcel was waiting at the collection point when I arrived back home. A set of books, five of them – *The Life and Times of Magnolia Court*, all held together with a pink ribbon: *California Dreaming, The Silver Sting, The Silver Dollar, The Silver Dagger,* and the most recent, *The Silver Lining*. I shall treasure them.

ALSO BY ANGELA DANDY

The Gypsy Killer

When a fire destroys a gypsy caravan and kills LJ's wife, Jess, all eyes turn to the residents of Bartonford, a picturesque village in Warwickshire. With property prices plummeting, the villagers will stop at nothing to see the back of the gypsies. But will they resort to murder?

Student Elizabeth Goodge is no lightweight when it comes to ferreting out information. What she discovers is shocking. The life of another gypsy hangs in the balance - one more in a long line of victims.

A story of family, hope, despair and obsession - no-one is safe while the gypsy killer roams free.

ABOUT THE AUTHOR

Angela Dandy, author of thrillers, *The Silver Sting*, *The Silver Dollar*, *The Silver Dagger* and *The Gypsy Killer* also writes plays, one of which has been performed on stage in her home town of Stratford-upon-Avon.

From a corporate career to carer, from carer to being cared for - a survivor of breast cancer, Angela reinvented herself as an author and playwright in 2015. She has made it her mission through her writing to be the voice for those whose abilities are often underestimated or are excluded from society for reasons outside of their control.

Living in a warm and caring community, she is an active member of a writing group, a playwrights' group and a drama group. In her spare time, Angela enjoys theatre, spending time with her family, travelling, gardening and entertaining.

Web Address
www.angeladandy.com

facebook.com/angeladandyauthor
x.com/angela_dandy1
instagram.com/ajd.author

Milton Keynes UK
Ingram Content Group UK Ltd.
UKHW041837160824
447024UK00004B/138

9 781917 326001